# FLIGHT OF THE UBERBITES

## No Time For An Epiphany

GABRIELE MARTIN

ISBN-10: 1489514317
ISBN-13: 978-1489514318

# DEDICATION

To My Wonderful Family
'Thank You'
Each and Every one of You.

ACKNOWLEDGMENTS

Art Work by Gabriele Martin

## DISCLAIMER

The characters and events in this book are fictitious. Any similarity to real persons, living or dead is coincidental and not intended by the author.

## GLOSSARY

Some of the language used in the Novel has been deliberately changed to create a comical adaptation of the text. Please refer to the glossary at the back of the book for clarification of any words you may not understand.

# 1 THE GREAT ESCAPE

Algernon leant back in his seat ever so slightly and gave his buttocks a little wriggle as he lifted the lower regions of his great girth up towards the steering wheel. 'Ahhh that's better' he sighed, 'there was nothing worse than having a prickly piece of starched linen caught between your butt cheeks whilst you were driving.' Squirming back against the cool leather seat he reached for his handkerchief and mopped his sweaty brow as the sudden realisation of just how utterly exhausted he was hit him with a vengeance.

Stealing a quick glance across the car at his wife Cornelia, he couldn't help feeling a tiny twinge of guilt when he observed the look of contempt that had crept in beside the craggy little lines that dominated her withered pinched face. Quite unexpectedly her look gave rise to a feeling of complete helplessness as the total gravity of their current situation started to sink in. Algernon bit down hard onto his receding bottom teeth and knotted his great furry brow into one of his famous frowns.

Casting another furtive look into the rear view mirror towards the slumbering Alistair, who at first glance appeared to be unconscious, he realised he would need to start selling the location in a far more positive light if he was going to get them both onside.

"Splendid scenery I must say," he announced enthusiastically. "Horatio often bragged about how spectacular these mountains were but until now I had always felt he was exaggerating. Not to mention the outstanding accomplishment of the surrounding countryside. I must say, I have never seen so many vineyards and olive groves packed together so tightly. A marvellous feat of agricultural ingenuity if you ask me!" He nodded his head in appreciation towards Cornelia.

"Oh don't go on Algy, this is nothing like Tuscany, far from it I dare say. Furthermore, you know perfectly well how much I loathe the country side. Particularly when it comes to the type of terrain that is usually reserved for those who don't know any better." She thrust her thin elongated nose into the air.

"Cheer up old girl, it's really not as bad as all that. Look on the bright side; you can be sure the weather here will be far more pleasant than it was in Old Blighty."

"Stop it Algernon, you know bright sun and fresh air has never really agreed with me. Even more so when I have to share it with all manner of beast and man;" she waved her hand towards the flock of fat fluffy sheep, that were grazing peacefully in the field beside them.

"Yes I know dear you are right." He inched forward in his seat. "I must admit, I was a little presumptuous when I told you it would be similar to Tuscany, but putting that aside for just a minute, you must agree coming here is quite a novel thing for us to do. You have often said so yourself, how you would love to throw caution to the wind and take the road far less travelled," he pleaded. "I personally find it all rather exhilarating almost adventurous wouldn't you say, Old girl?"

Algernon clicked his tongue and winked devilishly at her. He stretched his tweed clad arm, out across the car and gave her a light little pat on the knee. Cornelia instinctively flinched back from his fat frisky fingers and shuddered.

"Adventurous Hah! When have I ever wanted adventure Algernon? The only type of adventure I could imagine having here would no doubt belong in a 'Boys Own Annual' or possibly resemble some foolish folly written on the pages of Rudyard Kipling's, Kim." She folded her arms tightly across her flat, bobble of a chest and turned her body away from his wounded gaze.

"Oh do give it a break will you? I am practically comatose back here. All the while you two go on fighting like a pair of rabid dogs, literally tearing each other to pieces." Alistair leant forward and poked his pointy head through the space between the front and back seats. "How about sparing a thought for me and providing a bit of cool air? You can start by switching on the bloody air con," he snapped as he collapsed back into his seat.

Grateful for a chance to clear the air, Algernon jumped to his attention. "Oh terribly sorry Alistair, did we wake you? Yes it is a little warm, but I really can't switch on the cooling device in here. You see I am using it all for the lads in the back. Never mind, it won't be too much longer before we get there," he chuckled, as he tapped his fingers along the edge of the leather encased steering wheel.

"But of course Alistair how foolish of you to expect anything more. Let's not forget the precious lads and how important their needs are compared to ours." Cornelia sifted through her handbag for her sunglasses.

"Come now don't be like that dear." He reached across and placed his broad hand on top of her sharp shoulder. Suddenly losing control of the car, for just a moment, he wheezed in and out heavily like an old 'Squeeze Box' as he attempted to correct the shaky, wonky steering. "You know full well they are both getting on in years and without a doubt this drive has been a bit of a challenge for them to say the least. Especially for poor Churchill, he never really recovered from that shooting incident a few years ago." Algernon shot another concerned look into the rear view mirror towards the caravan on the back.

"Oh how could I ever forget Algernon? You practically slept with him for the next twelve months; meanwhile the two of us had to suffer your relentless guilt about shooting him in the first place." She turned back halfway and raised her eyebrows at Alistair, who had collapsed into a pitiful heap across his seat, with a monogrammed handkerchief placed over his bloodshot eyes. Obviously this little piece of linen was intended to act as a temporary; 'Do not Disturb' sign.

Turning back, slightly deflated, she added, "Honestly Algernon the ridiculous way you go on about those dogs truly makes me wonder whether or not you would prefer them as your family rather than us. I can't believe even 'You' would be so insensitive. The fact that you have provided them with a state of the art van for travelling in whilst Alistair and I have to sit and swelter in this wretched hot box, speaks volumes." She pushed her bag back down onto the floor of the car.

"Now Now Cornelia; there's no need to be like that. Why don't I open the window for you? I am sure a bit of fresh air is all that's needed to help clear out those cobwebs." He tapped the electronic window button on the driver control unit.

Cornelia turned away haughtily, closed both her eyes and pressed her face as close as she could into the bracing fresh air. For a few short glorious moments she took in the cool breeze as the car whooshed past the open green pastures that were generously decorated with majestic old trees and pretty white daisies. However, when she opened them again, she immediately shrank back in horror, when she spotted an ugly black crow, pecking the carcass of a putrid dead dog that had been callously mowed down by the roadside.

Algernon squirmed around in his seat as he made another awkward attempt to shift the sticky clingy underwear that barely covered his bulbous buttocks. For the next few minutes a rare stifled silence reigned supreme over this disgruntled little group. In fact, it almost seemed as though a perverted brand of justice had been served upon them, as each of them attempted to endure their own private hell, as best they could.

Finally rousing himself back to consciousness, Alistair sat up and looked out with red bleary eyes onto the seemingly endless hills and dales that spread on and on for kilometres. Flopping back onto his seat, he undid the top button of his shirt, loosened his cotton singlet and fanned himself with his hanky.

"Are we there yet?" He picked pitifully at the piece of stale bread that had wedged itself in the crack between the back seats. "What I really mean to say is where the hell are we? I don't think I can take much more of this."

Algernon sprang into action and looked hard at the Tom Tom that was perched ceremoniously on the dashboard of the Silver Ghost. "Yes Quite, Alistair, Hmmm Let me see." He squinted his eyes together and leant in towards the super shiny gadget. "Right, according to the Tom Tom we should be approaching the town of Pastacula within the next twenty miles or so," he stated. He leant back into his seat, with a satisfied look.

"Well Father, now might be a good time to explain what exactly we are meant to be doing here. I mean correct me if I am wrong but I don't believe we have heard very much from good old Horatio for the past ten years." Alistair smoothed his lanky locks back off his large protruding forehead and looked miserably out onto the collection of little farmhouses and out-houses that occasionally broke the hypnotic monotony of paddock after paddock after paddock.

"Now Now Alistair, I think you could be exaggerating there. Actually Horatio and I have kept in touch on a fairly regular basis. "In fact he called me seven years ago to pass on his congratulations to you when you finally graduated from University."

"Besides that, as you may well understand, there are quite a few things from the past that he and I would like the opportunity to catch up on. As I explained to you before we left, it was quite important for us to firm up our friendship again. Especially in regard to the situation we currently find ourselves in."

Algernon shot a stern look through the rear view mirror whilst nodding his head towards Cornelia, who was now lightly dozing in the afternoon sun. In fact she was slumped half way down her seat with her head rolled to one side. However, quite unintentionally and without meaning to appear uncouth, she literally looked as though she was giving the impersonation of a sick goldfish as the pale thin skin of her sallow saggy cheeks, puffed in and out rhythmically.

"Me exaggerating? Don't you think you may be the one who is Exaggerating Father? I mean I got the distinct impression from the little discussion we had yesterday, that we were merely facing a slight cash flow problem."

"Yes quite right Ali, but there are a few other considerations we may need to take into account before we are totally free of this Situation." He leant forward and casually checked the Tom Tom.

"What situation are you referring to now Algernon?" Cornelia growled in a gravelly sleep affected voice. She snapped open the thick lid of her left eye, the one that was strategically angled in his direction and gave him a deadly one eyed stare, providing her face with a far more sinister appeal than usual.

"Oh dear, I am sorry, did we wake you? Never mind, why don't you just rest up a little bit more until we get there? It has been an awfully long drive for you my Dear." Algernon wheezed pitifully, the purple patches under his eyes were rapidly expanding.

"Answer the question Algernon," Cornelia barked. She sat up and bristled. "I can assure you, I am not going back to sleep any time soon. In fact I am wide awake now and looking forward to hearing what you have to say to our Alistair."

Algernon wheezed again and cleared his throat. "Errr Yes dear, of course and I am more than happy to share it with you," he said, casting a warning look through the rear view mirror. "As I was saying earlier to Ali, Horatio, as you know is an old friend of mine. Actually we were in Prep school together before his family moved him up North in the final year to Glasgow, 'Ghastly' place. Fortunately we were able to rekindle our friendship again when we were both in University in London," he wheezed.

"Yes I know all this but what has that got to do with us now?" She stubbornly insisted.

"Well yes, as you know he has always been very fond of our Ali and was quite upset when he couldn't be his God-father due to his," Algernon paused for a moment. "How can I put it? His ….. his ……alternate lifestyle." He raised his eyebrows and nodded his head sagely as if he were imparting some sort of secret knowledge.

"Yes father do get on with it," Alistair quipped. "We all know Uncle Horatio bats for the other side that's nothing new."

"Well yes as I was saying, Horatio, never had any children of his own due to … You know …. and he always considered our Ali as the son he never had. Well as you know, he recently contacted me and reminded me that we hadn't seen each other for quite a few years. Not to mention the fact we are not getting any younger either."

"Oh for heaven's sake Algernon stop beating around the bush and get on with it will you?" Cornelia cast a long suffering look over her shoulder towards Alistair.

"Hmmm yes" …..Clearing his throat once again, he rigidly clasped the steering wheel, let out a long sigh and continued. "So to cut a very long story short, as I was saying he invited us all, to come over here and spend some time with him in his Villa. I suppose he was hoping to become reacquainted with us again and …." He paused for a moment. "Please pay attention, this is the important part." Algernon looked intensely into the rear view mirror.

Taking a deep breath, he raised both his mammoth eyebrows until they almost touched his hair and announced in a steady voice, "Horatio has indicated to me that he intends to bequeath most of his worldly goods to our Alistair."

"What did you say?" Alistair blurted, he instantly sat forward. "Did you say he plans to leave all his worldly goods to me? I mean why didn't you say something earlier Father? What sort of value are we looking at? Has he been ill recently?"

"Steady on Old boy," Algernon blustered back, shooting another stern look towards the mirror. "I didn't say all his worldly goods I said some! But judging by the situation and this sudden invitation, I'd hazard a guess, he has quite a sum in mind .... However gauging exactly when, is indeed another matter." He knitted his massive eyebrows together again.

# 2 DEBRIEF AT INSTAPOL HEADQUARTERS IN ROME

*A few Hours Earlier on the Same Day*

A very serious meeting was taking place involving no less than five senior Agents from four different nations.

Senior Agent Andrew Brown from England had been assigned the task of chairing the meeting which was attended by four other International Instapol agents.

- Mitchell Smith from America.
- Pierre Thierre from France.
- Guido Ventosi and Riccardo Martinelli from Italy.

After making sure all the Agents in the room had received an individual copy of the Investigative dossier, Andrew Brown, a moral man of medium height and a fair complexion stood sideways in front of the small group. With his face half turned towards the Power Point presentation that was projected onto the far wall of the office, he pointed the electronic pointer towards the screen and commenced the discussion.

"As you can see gentleman, the primary Suspect

Algernon Oswald Uberbite is most certainly a person of interest to Instapol and more specifically in regard to the International Money Laundering scam we believe his bank is linked to. According to our latest intelligence reports the money laundering operations are not entirely independent. Recent data received from our men on the ground indicate quite conclusively that these international transactions originated from a well-known foreign bank that is suspected of sharing links with the activities of an International Criminal group involved in the Illicit Traffic of Works of Art. Please refer to page two of the Personal Dossier and in particular Table four outlining specific information regarding the relationship between these two banks, also including the data detailing the suspect's more recent activities."

Senior Agent Brown turned back to face the small group of men and continued the presentation that he had hurriedly put together, late last night.

"Therefore, coupled with our most recent reports it is apparent that the international surveillance team that had been collecting data and documenting the activities between Britain and other suspect countries over the past twelve months has unfortunately become severely compromised. Furthermore the primary suspect Algernon Oswald Uberbite has refused to cooperate with Instapol, who have been appointed as the international police body and he has fled to mainland Europe with his wife Cornelia Hyacinth Uberbite and their adult son Alistair Ignatius Uberbite."

Agent Brown paused for a moment and took a generous swig from the water bottle placed on the desk in front of him. Putting it down again he adjusted the glasses that were precariously perched, at the end of his long freckled nose and continued.

"Our most recent reports have indicated that the entire Uberbite family was able to escape due to the inability of the National Police force, who were previously working on this case to secure an arrest warrant.

The same Police force were also unable to secure the relevant search warrant to conduct a search on either the home or the office of the suspects. Other Sources linked closely with the National Police force in Britain and acting on behalf of the independent inquiry body for Instapol have reported that the suspect Algernon Uberbite was previously offered Police protection."

Agent Brown shifted his body weight from one foot to the other and twirled his pen in his hand. He then briefly surveyed his audience for any possible signs of confusion before continuing.

"According to the information provided by these same sources, an agreement had been made between them regarding the possibility of complete immunity. The agreement stipulated that the suspect, Algernon Uberbite would only receive a suspended sentence for his part in the International Money Laundering activities." He paused again briefly. "This agreement was undertaken on the understanding it would be exchanged for his evidence in regard to the relationship his bank had forged with the foreign bank in question. As a result, he and his family were not brought into custody at police headquarters."

Agent Brown discreetly cleared his throat and drew a deep breath before he continued. Looking back intently at his colleagues he added, "Further investigations regarding the activities of the bank have revealed an income tax audit has not been lodged for the past three years and we believe this may be the reason why the owner, Algernon Uberbite has decided to reject our offer of immunity."

"This is a vital investigation and one that we have been working hard on for the past year and until now were very close to exposing. Therefore for the benefit of the more recent members who have joined this investigation, Agent Ventosi and Agent Martinelli from our Italian office, I will now present you with the most current up to date fact file referring to this case, which has been filed under the name of "Operation Clean Dough." Please direct your attention, towards the whiteboard and take a few minutes to note the personal characteristics of each family member. You will also find a copy of this fact file on page six of your dossier. I will allow a five minute perusal period of the file before I begin to take questions."

Agent Brown checked his Blackberry for the next few minutes whilst the other agents jotted down their notes. He welcomed the respite from this sudden responsibility.

<table>
<tr><th colspan="2">OPERATION CLEAN DOUGH<br>CRIMINAL PROFILING OF PERSONS OF INTEREST</th></tr>
<tr><td>Algernon Oswald Uberbite.<br>Sex Male<br>Age (years) 70<br>Nationality English<br>Current Residential Address No fixed address<br>Physical Description.<br>1. Very stocky with a large pot belly paunch.<br>2. Handle bar moustache, with protruding nostril hair.<br>3. Thick, gray, wavy hair.<br>4. Bulging blue eyes.<br>5. A very Ruddy complexion.</td><td></td></tr>
<tr><td colspan="2">General Attributes and Features<br>1. Carries a fob watch with him everywhere, from the circa of the early twenties.<br>2. Dressed in a tweed checked jacket with dull beige linen trousers.<br>3. He suffers from profuse sweating episodes when he is nervous.<br>4. He suffers from high blood pressure and has a significant wheeze, especially when stressed or doing any physical exercise.<br>5. Owns a bank in England.<br>6. Takes his two hunting dogs with him wherever he goes.</td></tr>
</table>

<table>
<tr><th colspan="2">OPERATION CLEAN DOUGH<br>CRIMINAL PROFILING OF PERSONS OF INTEREST</th></tr>
<tr><td>Cornelia Hyacinth Uberbite.<br>Sex Female<br>Age (years) 65<br>Nationality English<br>Current Residential Address No fixed address<br>Physical Description<br>1. Slim build.<br>2. Tall in stature.<br>3. Short Dark Straight hair.<br>4. Large facial features with a long elongated nose.<br>5. A Withered complexion.<br>6. Piercing Blue eyes.</td><td></td></tr>
<tr><td colspan="2">General Attributes and Features.<br>1. Has a dominating personality.<br>2. Known for her scathing, sarcastic remarks and dry wit.<br>3. Has never worked.<br>4. Carries with her at all times a black cigarette case stocked with slim line designer cigarettes.<br>5. Has an addiction to any alcoholic beverage.<br>6. Is the daughter of a deceased Billionaire from the Banking and Financial World.</td></tr>
</table>

**OPERATION CLEAN DOUGH**
**CRIMINAL PROFILING OF PERSONS OF INTEREST**

**Alistair Ignatius Uberbite.**

**Sex** Male

**Age** (years) 36

**Nationality** English

**Current Residential Address**

No fixed address

**Physical Description.**

1. Tall over 190 cm.
2. Slender build with long arms and legs.
3. Large pointy head, lanky dark brown hair.
4. Hazel green eyes, ski jump nose and large ears.
5. Big chalky teeth.
6. Pasty complexion.

**General Attributes and Features.**

1. Insensitive, obnoxious and deceitful.
2. Incompetent when socialising amongst his own peer group.
3. Employed as the CEO of the bank that his father owns.
4. Considers himself to be quite a player with the opposite sex.
5. Usually spends his annual holidays in Majorca, Spain.

Finally finished with all his checking, Agent Brown turned his body back around to face the audience and announced, "Thank you for your attention gentlemen, we have now concluded the Presentation segment of the Fact Files associated with 'Operation Clean Dough'. Again for the benefit of the new members of this team I would like to use this opportunity to take some questions from the audience."

His mobile phone suddenly began to vibrate lively on the boardroom table.

"Excuse me I think it is essential to the investigation for me to take this call." He made a hasty snatch and picked up the phone. Agent Brown took a few moments to listen intently to the caller. After delivering a few well-paced, Hmmm's, followed by a couple of, I see's he officiously thanked the caller and hung up.

"Gentleman," he began seriously, "That was the latest report from our twenty four hour tracking services on the Italian road network surveillance system. According to recent data that has just arrived the vehicle in question displaying the license plate Doggie 555 UK has been photographed approaching the Rome to Pastacula expressway SP 202 and is heading towards the Gran Sapaa Mountain Range, please refer to page three of the dossier if you are not familiar with the vehicle in question. After confirming the owner of this vehicle is indeed our prime suspect Algernon Oswald Uberbite, we have made a decision to dispatch a vehicle immediately and also to assign an 'Interim' agent to carry out surveillance duties on the suspect and any other suspects accompanying him. The assigned agent will be responsible for gathering further evidence regarding the activities of the suspect and his accomplices and will be reporting back directly to a senior agent from the Rome office."

There were a few murmurings from the audience as they digested this latest intriguing morsel of information. Agent Brown made one final announcement.

"May I request the presence of Agent Ventosi and Agent Martinelli, from our Rome office to meet with me in the adjoining board room to discuss this matter further?" He picked up the water bottle sitting on top of the desk and took a long swig.

## 3 GUIDO'S MISSION

Guido Ventosi was in the middle of attempting to text back a very important message for the tenth time, when out of the corner of his eye he spotted the Silver Ghost, sailing towards the battered old signpost that marked the beginning of the town of Pastacula. Guido rapidly slammed his phone shut and grabbed the digital camera that had been lying idly on the car's dashboard for most of the morning. Sitting as close as he could to the windscreen, he snapped a series of long range shots in the direction of the vehicle before it completely disappeared from view as it navigated itself around a particularly twisty bend.

He thrust his keys deep into the ignition and hastily sped off, spinning out dangerously along the edge of the dusty road before sighting the Ghost again. Easing his foot back lightly off the accelerator, he slowed down to a crawl and quietly skulked along the narrow country road. He made it a point to carefully hug the side of the road at all times. He certainly didn't want to be spotted by any of the inhabitants in the other car.

Once he realised the vehicle in question had suddenly started turning into a nearby car park, he swung his car off the road and parked it in a position that not only afforded him an uninhibited view but one that also kept him at a safe and discreet distance. Sitting back into the deep leather bucket seats of the Black Citroen Sedan he urgently surveyed the photos, before picking up the phone and making a call.

"Pronto," he said officially into the tiny end of his mobile phone.

"Dimme," (tell me) said the crisp voice of his colleague, Agent Riccardo Martinelli, "And please can you make sure you speak English? It is important that you remember these conversations may be used for further investigations by our international colleagues."

"Si Si …… I mean Yes, Yes, of course. I was a little excited and so I didn't remember to follow all the rules. All right I want to report to you, that I am sure I have seen the Persons of Interest just now."

"You mean the family in question the Uberbites?" Riccardo asked. "Please in the future can you make sure you use the correct names for all the suspects? You must understand these conversations may end up as transcripts and we must be sure they are totally correct," he issued sternly.

"Si ….. I mean Yes. Of course I am sure it was them the Uberbites. Actually I have taken a series of photos and I am certain it is the same car we were informed about with the British Number plates."

"Bravo well done Agent Ventosi. It seems as though all your quick thinking and hard work has started to pay off at last."

"Well to tell you the truth, it wasn't really that hard. You see, I know this area very well, actually my first girlfriend from Roma, her family owned a very old farmhouse in the countryside not far from here. During the summer break, we spent many a romantic night there, just the two of us," a tiny trace of nostalgia lingered in his voice.

"Oh that is very interesting …….Dimme ……. Oh scusa, I mean ….. Tell me, have you documented it all and sent it by email, including the photos, so I can make a note of it, before we send it off to Head Quarters?"

"No, not yet. But of course I will do that once I am back in Rome. You should expect to see the report in your system first thing tomorrow morning," Guido replied efficiently.

"What is that noise?" Martinelli asked suspiciously, "I have heard it a number of times while we have been speaking. Are you sure you are not tapped? Have you made sure to check the Car carefully for a wire?"

"No, no, I am sure it is nothing," Guido responded. He urgently flicked his other phone into silent mode before it beeped again. The words, 'can't wait to hold my Italian Stallion', blinked back at him.

"I think this is just the sound of the countryside," he laughed uneasily. "It is very rural here and I theenk you are not too familiar with theese noises. But I am sure you will learn to know them, very quickly, once you have been here for a while."

"Yes of course that could explain it, but as I told you before it is very important to check the car for any kind of interference. This is a High Priority Operation and we cannot afford to take any risks."

"Of course, I agree with you, more than one hundred percent. If you like I will drop the car at the garage of the Head Quarters before going home tonight and Marco, I am sure will go over it with a fine toothed comb before giving it back to you tomorrow."

"No, no, that won't be necessary; I won't be using that car tomorrow. Tell me, can you still see the suspects? What are they doing now?"

Guido craned his neat neck out as far as it would go and peered through the wide windscreen in front of him.

"Yes I can see them. I theenk the car is moving very slowly down the street. The father seems to be looking out the window for something. But I am not sure what. Maybe he needs to use the Bagno (bathroom). So about the car? Guido asked hesitantly, "You said you don't theenk you will need it tomorrow morning tell me, Why? Do you have a better one that you can drive down here?"

"So are they still sitting in the car?" Riccardo asked. "Perhaps they have lost their way, please make sure you always keep within a hundred metres of them. It is very important that we don't lose sight of them. Riccardo paused for a few seconds before he continued. "You ask me again about the car? No, this is a very good car, which is why we assigned it to you. It is one of the best."

"Yes Grazie, I mean thank you, I appreciate that. But of course I won't need it once I return back to Rome this evening."

Another pregnant pause played innocently between them before Martinelli responded again.

"So you haven't read any of your emails today?" Martinelli asked, hesitantly.

"Actually no, until now, I haven't had the chance. As you know most of my time has been completely taken up by this sudden surveillance assignment," Guido sighed back into the phone.

"In that case then I should let you know there has been a slight change of plans." Agent Martinelli paused for a moment. "You should know that you won't be returning to Rome this evening. To tell the truth you have been assigned to this case and you will remain with it until it is all over."

Guido gasped loudly, this was followed by a quick succession of raspy little breaths as the colour from his normally well-tanned face drained all the way down to his neatly trimmed toenails leaving him with a panic stricken look of despair.

Not only that. When he saw the latest text message flashing boldly back at him. *'What's up babes? Why haven't you txt me? I got the night off from the Casino!'* He immediately broke into little beads of sweat that sunk deeply into the tiny springy curls around the edge of his forehead. The full weight of the impending tragedy suddenly dawned upon him as he stared down at the message. Not unlike a man, who had been cast adrift, after the cruellest of shipwrecks, Guido reluctantly dragged his shattered psyche back to the conversation with Martinelli.

"But I don't understand, I thought You," he emphasized the word 'You', "Were taking over thissa very important case, after I return back to the Headquarters tomorrow. This was the decision we agreed to take at the meeting this morning."

He looked gloomily out the window and back at the dark plastic phone now lying lifeless between them.

"Actually, I am afraid things have changed since then. I have been called away to Monaco. The truth is they need my expertise about a certain case they have been working on in a Casino. I will leave first thing in the morning."

Guido sat speechless for a few moments before breaking into a desperate plea. "But how can this all change in just one day?" he squeaked. Everybody knows I am the expert when it comes to Casinos. Besides this I have already made all the necessary arrangements with my contacts in Monaco," he cast another hopeful glance at the mute phone.

"Yes of course no one is questioning you Guido, but you must understand theees particular case is …. How can I say, very, very complicated and Headquarters thinks it requires somebody new." Riccardo paused briefly again before continuing in a stern voice, "Somebody who doesn't know anything, about anybody there, you understand whatta I mean? Somebody who has, No contacts," he emphasised the word, No.

Guido's heart skipped a beat when he noticed the latest text message angrily blinking back at him, *OK SCREW U JERK* it stated in bold Capital letters before eventually receding back into darkened silence. "Does this mean I am no longer needed on the Monaco case?" He asked, gazing sorrowfully out the window.

"Yes, yes, that will be the situation for the time being or until things change," Martinelli replied.

"So you don't want me to return to Rome this evening?" He hissed.

"No, you will remain in the countryside and continue your surveillance duties around the family in Question. I have sent you a complete dossier regarding this case including your accommodation and expected rendezvous co-ordinates within the region."

"How long do you expect me to stay here?" He demanded bitterly, through a tight throat. "I only packed enough clothes for one or two nights," he ran his hand down the lower side of his face and deftly felt the fuzzy stubble of regrowth that had already started to appear.

"Don't worry, for this situation, you have an expense account. You can use it to buy anything you need. Within reason of course."

"But… but ….. I need to know how long you expect me to stay here?" Guido pressured.

"At this moment we can't be too sure but I think you will be there for at least one week. In the meantime, I will expect you to send daily reports starting from tomorrow. In any case, don't worry it will be alright. Things as you know in this part of Italy have improved a lot over the past few years. The little Pensione we have organised for you actually has the internet connection so you will be able to keep up with all your emails whilst you are there."

"Reports! You are just keeping me here so I can send daily reports?" Guido hit his closed fist hard against the steering wheel and shook his head before continuing. "Alright, I will give you the reports. But I think this decision to keep me here is completely wrong. As soon as I get back to headquarters I will file a complaint to the upper management," he threatened. He nodded his head up and down vigorously.

"Yes and of course that is your choice. But I must advise you to think twice before you make such a hasty decision," Martinelli responded.

Guido deliberately chose to ignore this little piece of advice. Leaning forward again in his seat he strained his neck out and peered out intently. Staring as hard as he could through tear soaked eyes, he tried to determine what the Man in Question, in the Car in Question, was actually doing.

"Agent Martinelli, I will of course need to finish this conversation right now. I am sure I have located the suspect and he looks to me that he is about to leave his car. I can see from the data provided by the GPS that the building he is next to is the same building that is corresponding to a local bank in Pastacula. I would like to drive a little closer now so I hope I can discover some more information. Because, I theenk the sooner I finish this investigation the better," he said, as he grappled around on the floor of the car for the binoculars he had left there when he stopped at the beach earlier that morning.

"Of course Agent Ventosi, in any case I have finished giving you all my instructions now and am available to assist you today in any way I can, with this investigation. But please be aware, after tomorrow morning I will no longer be contactable because of my new urgent assignment in Monaco but I am sure somebody else from the head office will be assigned to this case and so you should be able to forward all your reports to him."

Agent Ventosi bid Agent Martinelli a hasty goodbye. He then snapped down the cover of his mobile phone, snatched up his other mobile, which was lying dormant on the seat and scowled at it.

After determining that the battery was indeed well and truly dead, he flung it with all his might towards the back seat of the car. The impotent phone hit the rear view window with a loud crack; it then bounced back at him and landed on the floor before breaking up into a random group of brittle plastic pieces. Struggling hard to keep his composure, Guido wiped erratically at his eyes. He thrust his keys roughly into the ignition and skid out across the road in a reckless manner as he reluctantly made his way towards the parked car in the distance.

# 4 PIDGIN ENGLISH

As the Silver Ghost approached the tree lined streets of Pastacula it was clear from the onset that the pretty little town, although quite clean and tidy had nothing really special to write home about. True, it had a charm about it in a rustic sort of way but the tired old park, haphazardly sprawling off the main drive with its broken gate and rusted carousel conjured up images of a splendour that was long past its use by date.

Algernon tired and harried by now, but in need of desperate funds, slowed the car down almost to a halt and gazed intently into the bright sunshine. Sitting forward in his seat he quickly scoured the street hoping to spot an ATM that carried the international symbol of monetary exchange.

Braking awkwardly, he swerved the Ghost onto the left hand side of the street causing both Cornelia and Alistair to jerk forward violently.

"Father, have you gone completely mad? What the hell are you doing now?" Alistair shouted as he fell back with a whoosh against his seat.

"There's the bank, I am sure it was the one Horatio told

me about," Algernon blurted. He sidled the car into a parking spot adjacent to a stately old building.

"That's no excuse for almost killing the two of us," retorted Cornelia. "I am quite sure you have caused me a severe case of whiplash." She rubbed the back of her thin neck with her long spindly fingers.

"Oh dear, I am so sorry. I hadn't realised you had dozed off again. Perhaps you could rest up for a bit whilst we wait here. I won't be a minute," he said. Opening the door he moved his large bulky body out of the car. "You do understand don't you? I really must get some money I mean we just can't turn up empty handed can we?" Slamming the door shut, he walked away.

Algernon hastily surveyed the large concrete square in front of the bank and was delighted when he spotted an ATM situated on the front side of the building. He was feeling quite warm by now and so he loosened the flowery cravat tied tightly around his throat. He shrugged his shoulders in a vain attempt to move the heavy tweed jacket that had been doggedly sitting on his body for the last eight hours. Then he lumbered as fast as he could towards the ATM ever mindful with every step that he really should have done something earlier, about his gammy arthritic knee.

Sighing loudly, he placed the card he had retrieved from his leather wallet, into the mouth of the machine and tapped his pudgy fingers impatiently against the metal plate as he waited for the instructions to appear. Squinting back, he tried in vain to understand the barely visible foreign language that had presented itself on the touch screen.

'That's not English. This place is just as backward as France', he muttered as he pinned his four digit secret code into the spaces he imagined it should go.

Immediately and without the slightest hint of a warning his card was rapidly engulfed into the hungry jaws of the ATM. This was followed by a loud slamming noise as the machine maliciously closed itself off for any further use. Algernon, instinctively alarmed, thumped the metal barrier with his open palm as he attempted to reopen the all-important orifice, which was now firmly closed.

He was just in the process of giving it another hefty thump when a young woman who was coming out of the bank, looked over at him and wisely quickened her step to a semi trot.

After turning his gaze to where she had come from Algernon realised that he had been in full view of not only her but of all the other people in the bank, who had been watching intently through the big glass windows. Upon realising he had a captive audience, he threw his hands up, high above his head and then back over towards the machine.

"Blasted machine has swallowed my card," he proclaimed. He anxiously glanced back and forth at the audience that had gathered at the window and then across to the exiting woman who had now stopped, to stare.

"Non capisco,"(I don't understand) the woman answered fearfully as she started to walk away again.

"No wait on a minute," Algernon called out. He turned and followed her. "Do you know how to operate this wretched thing, I mean; surely you can read Italian can't you?" He pleaded, puffing heavily beside her.

"Scusa non capisco,"(I am sorry I don't understand) the woman replied as she opened the door of her car and quickly jumped in.

"Look I don't think you understand," he insisted, "The machine has swallowed my card and I need to get my money out," Algernon shouted at the closed car window now only inches away from his ruddy face.

Starting her engine rapidly the young woman, drove off as fast as she could, completely ignoring the wild gesticulations of Algernon, as he stood there all flushed and sweating in the boiling sun.

Turning back to face the bank, he looked again at the large glass windows and noticed that the stylishly dressed armed guard, was walking quite briskly towards the exit of the building.

Panicking by now, Algernon decided to cut his losses and make a bee line back to the parked car, where Alistair and Cornelia, were both peering back at him with a pair of identical scowls stretched across their pasty faces.

Dreading the unavoidable backlash, Algernon raised his

large flushed face towards the sky and threw his arms high above his head. Closing his heavy eyes for just a few seconds he allowed himself a moment's rest, whilst he reassessed his, "Lot in Life."

However this respite was only ever short lived. As soon as he felt the generous dollop of warm slime that landed in the middle of his broad forehead he quickly opened them up again.

Rapidly blinking against the sudden glare he could feel the unknown slime traverse its way in a slip sliding motion down between his humongous eyebrows. Wasting no time the slimy fluid boldly charged on and within seconds it had slid halfway down his purplish lumpy nose.

Reaching for the linen handkerchief that was stuffed in the top left hand pocket of his tweed jacket he yanked it out roughly and began to swipe at the offending substance, that was threatening to take up lodging in his thick untidy moustache.

He then dashed back to the car and swung open the door with his other free hand. He maneuvered his large body into the seat with surprising agility and shoved his keys into the ignition.

Pushing his foot flat against the accelerator, he hurriedly drove off, causing the car to perform a series of convoluted kangaroo hops all the way down the road. As the car recklessly wobbled from side to side, Algernon, despite his best efforts to wipe the remains of the filthy fluid away, found himself making a series of frenetic swipes at the back of the seat instead.

Finally, after taking control of the situation, he eventually eased the car back towards the middle of the road and breathed out a heavy sigh of relief. Turning awkwardly, in his seat, he swiveled his head around towards, a rather startled Alistair and said in a less than polite tone, "Blasted Italians .... I thought they had eaten all their Bloody pigeon's by now."

<table>
<tr><th colspan="3">INSTAPOL POLICE REPORT</th></tr>
<tr><td>Agent Guido Ventosi</td><td>Day: One/ Afternoon</td><td>File Number 1200/12/20098</td></tr>
<tr><td>CASE</td><td>LOCATION</td><td>Report No</td></tr>
<tr><td>Uberbite Surveillance</td><td>Buona Fortuna Bank Pastacula</td><td>1</td></tr>
<tr><td colspan="3">Persons of Interest<br>Algernon Uberbite, Cornelia Uberbite, Alistair Uberbite.</td></tr>
<tr><td colspan="3">ACTIVITIES</td></tr>
<tr><td colspan="3">13.05 Suspect walked over to the ATM Bancamat.<br>13.10 Suspect hit the Bancamat Machine.<br>13.12 Suspect shout words to the bank window.<br>1315 Suspect followed a woman in the car park.<br>13.18 Suspect shout loudly at the woman.<br>13.20 Suspect runs to his car away from the bank guard.<br>13.22 Suspect drives away in a big rush.<br>Important Warning: This man he seems to be agitated and dangerous and should be approached all the time with cautions.<br>Expenses:<br>One new Apple iPhone, I drop my blackberry in the gutter when I try to run away from a horrible dog.<br><br>Don't spit in the wind – it might land on your head. – Non sputare in aria – che ti ricade in testa</td></tr>
</table>

<table>
<tr><th colspan="3">INSTAPOL POLICE REPORT</th></tr>
<tr><td>Agent Guido Ventosi</td><td>Day: One/ Afternoon</td><td>File Number 1200/12/20098</td></tr>
<tr><td>CASE</td><td>LOCATION</td><td>Report No</td></tr>
<tr><td>Uberbite Surveillance.</td><td>Buona Fortuna Bank Pastacula</td><td>1</td></tr>
<tr><td colspan="3">Persons of Interest<br>Algernon Uberbite, Cornelia Uberbite, Alistair Uberbite.</td></tr>
<tr><td colspan="3">COMMENTS</td></tr>
<tr><td colspan="3">The suspect Algernon Uberbite walked over to the ATM Bancamat. It is the one on the side of the wall of the building of the bank it is near to the car park of the Buona Fortuna Bank. I theenk he wanted to take some of his money.<br>He hit the machine, very very hard, many times with his big fist. He also shouted very loudly at the glass window. I theenk he theenks there is someone behind theese glass. Not so intelligent.<br>He followed a beautiful young Italian woman. She was coming out of the bank; she just wanted to go to her car. The suspect shouted very loud things to her through the closed windows of the car. This poor girl was very afraid. I theenk he doesn't understand Italian language.<br>He looked up to the sky and he shouts very loud again. I see something, I am not so sure, but I think it is the pigeon poop it has fallen on his head. He tried very hard to wipe away from his face the pigeon drops, with a large piece of cloth he had kept there in his very ugly jacket.<br>He rushed back to his car, but he could not go too fast, he is very fat. He speed off down the street in his car towards the lovely little town of Pastacula.</td></tr>
</table>

## 5 FRIENDLY FAUX PAS

After ringing the bell for the third time, Alistair no doubt exasperated by now, grabbed the large heavy brass ring situated firmly in the centre of the door and banged it furiously, causing a loud echoing noise to resonate all around them as the sturdy ring of burnished metal collided against the old wooden door.

"Steady on Lad," Algernon warned, "you don't want to upset him before we even step foot into his house. After all he is doing us all a big favour." He nodded his head and raised his eyebrows, wisely.

"A favour I hardly call this a favour," Cornelia hissed through clenched teeth. "We have been standing here hungry and tired for the past ten minutes and he hasn't even had the decency to acknowledge us."

"Don't be so hasty to make a judgment dear. Remember Horatio is no spring chicken, it's quite possible he may not even have heard the bell at all."

"Hah don't talk nonsense, Algernon! Surely he was expecting us. I mean you have made some arrangements with him haven't you? And even if he didn't hear us what about his staff? Surely they're not all deaf as well."

"Shhhh … Be quiet will you. I think I can hear something," Alistair whispered loudly. He thrust his long angular body closer towards the door.

Just then, the large heavy door swung open and revealed a short round woman. She was dressed in black nylon from head to toe, except for the colourful broad apron she was wearing, which incidentally, was lavishly adorned with an assortment of dried out clumps of egg and flour.

Cornelia shuddered to herself when she noticed that as well as sporting the unsightly clumps of uncooked produce, the woman also appeared to be housing a generous sprinkling of bread crumbs, which looked as though they were 'Clinging for Dear Life,' throughout her greying unkempt hair.

"Buongiorno Signore anda Signora Ooopabyta, please step thissa way. Signore Horeatzio has been inspecting you's," she waved a floury hand towards the open door and waggled her head back and forth.

"Oh Grazie madam," Algernon said gratefully. He stepped forward enthusiastically. "May I introduce you to my wife Cornelia and my son Alistair?"

"Si, I am very happy to be intermixed with you," she beamed as she held out her other floury hand. "Signore Horeatzio has told me too much, how he is looking very happy to see you go to here. Please can you walk like me to this room? I am sure you are very much waiting to have your intercourse with Signore Horeatzio."

Before they had even had the chance to react accordingly, to this clearly outrageous 'Faux Pas', the two large doors to the atrium courtyard flew open and revealed an elderly man with silvery grey, shoulder length curly hair, dressed in a white extravagant silken suit, with black satin ruffles down the front and a pair of pink and purple, polka dotted, leather shoes.

"Algernonnnnnn my dear old chum, its Sooooo good to see you again," said Horatio as he glided towards him, both arms outstretched. Then without the slightest jot of a warning, he melodramatically lunged forward in a passionate gesture of embrace and flung his thin, liver spotted arms around Algernon. Finally, after a few awkward moments, that also included the untangling of limbs from around Algernon's rather large girth, Horatio with a tear in his eye turned his attention towards Alistair, who had been watching in stunned silence from the sidelines.

"And this must be little Ali," he said. Stepping forward he grasped Alistair's hands in his own withered pair and swung them from side to side. "My Word how you have grown. You were just a lad the last time I saw you, where does the time go?" Looking back at them curiously he, continued to clamp Alistair's hands in a vice like grip as he rapidly blinked his watery eyes "Open and Shut," "Open and Shut," over and over again.

It was safe to assume by the shocked expression on Alistair's face that he wasn't really comfortable with the entire situation, and it would be fair to suggest he didn't really relish the idea of being gushed over either. However bearing in mind the fortune that was up for grabs and his current need for immediate sustenance, he decided it would be better to bear it all, and humour the silly 'Old Queen.'

"Yes Uncle Horatio it has been a very long time hasn't it?" He replied with as much sincerity as he could muster. "But that doesn't mean you haven't been on our minds," he stated, as he looked wistfully at his parents. Feeling more confident by the second with his ability to deceive, he added, "The truth is Uncle Horatio, we have often thought of you with great fondness over the last few years. As a matter of fact when Father told me exactly where we were going and whom we were going to see I was so excited I even cancelled my annual holiday to the south of Spain, just so I could be a part of this trip."

"How charming," Horatio enthused as he primped and preened the long silver locks of his thin wavy hair. "My goodness me, I must say what a delightful young man you have turned out to be." He turned back to face Cornelia and Algernon and with a wave, worthy only of a famous Maestro, said "Please come in and make yourself at home."

Cornelia, who miraculously hadn't spoken a word until now, suddenly broke her unusual silence. Taking a haughty step towards Horatio she stood directly between him and the doorway and in a deliberately sarcastic tone introduced herself. "If you don't mind, may I introduce myself before we go in? I am quite sure you wouldn't want a perfect stranger to enter your humble abode," she chided. "I am Cornelia," she said with feigned politeness. "Algernon's devoted wife and of course that would also make ME our dearest little Ali's dedicated Mother. I know we haven't seen each other for many years," she added sternly, "But that is no excuse for what could only be perceived as sloppy manners. But then again you are getting on in years and perhaps your memory is starting to fail you." She peered intently into Horatio's startled face.

"Oh .... Oh..... Do forgive me dear," Horatio stammered as the dark pupils of his luminous eyes dilated. "I am so very sorry, of course I remember you fondly. For heaven's sake how could I or anyone ever forget your wedding day? You were such a ravishing bride," he replied with lightning speed and an automatic smile. He held out his soft manicured hand.

"Well, shall we go on then?" Algernon asked, bobbing up and down on the spot. "After all it is getting late and I am sure we could all do with a good strong drink," he advised with an amicable nod towards his wife.

"Oh, yes yes, Of course please follow me," Horatio issued. Stepping towards the door, he ushered them in, only this time, with a less enthusiastic wave of his arm.

They followed him through the open doors into the dark wood panelled hall and walked on until they were met with another set of heavy wooden doors.

These opened up into a grandiose room full of bookcases and classic paintings that were surrounded by an eclectic mix of Victorian furniture and cheap economical substitutes that looked as though they had recently been assembled from a Swedish flat pack.

They were just about to sit down on the Victorian chaise lounge when a dreadful high pitched screeching sound, similar to the noise made by a fingernail being scratched across a balloon, dominated the air and drew their startled attention to a darkened corner of the room. Cornelia, fell back awkwardly onto the lounge and instantly lapsed into a heavy sneezing fit.

"Ohh dear, I am terribly sorry, It is only Sebastion, has he frightened you? He does so love company and we don't get too many visitors to the house these days," Horatio apologised. He watched as she sneezed over and over again into her thin, lacy, handkerchief.

Just like a precocious child who knew when they had snared your attention the hideous screeching sound radiated towards them again, only this time it was accompanied by a frantic series of flapping actions.

"Calm down Sebastion," yelled Horatio, clasping the end of the heavy metal Celtic cross that hung perversely around his wrinkly old neck. "These are our friends and they've come all the way from England to look after you whilst Daddy goes to Paris! We don't want to scare them away now, do we?"

Cornelia, who had only just stopped sneezing suddenly gasped and immediately, fell into a relapse. However, this time, she was coughing as well as violently sneezing.

Algernon, Alistair, and Horatio, exchanged quiet looks of consternation.

Cornelia, in the meantime continued to Cough, Cough, Cough, in a staccato style stutter in spits and spats, actually it sounded very similar to a car that had a problem with its starter motor. Eventually she ran out of breath and, Stopped!

She fixed her eyes in a hateful glare towards Algernon, and declared from an oxygen deprived voice box. "Don't just stand around gawking at me like I am some relic in a museum you pack of blithering fools. Surely one of you could have thought to bring me a drink?" She spluttered and choked, her eyes bulged as she started to cough again.

"Oh, dear how rude of me you must all be terribly thirsty. After all you have been travelling the entire day haven't you? Please sit down and make yourselves comfortable," Horatio waved his arm towards the lounge.

Looking apologetically towards Algernon and Alistair he added. "Let me go and see what Magdalena is up to, shall I? I have a funny feeling she should be serving afternoon tea very soon," he stated with a haughty sniff, as he looked over at Cornelia's pinched face. Without waiting for a response he dramatically spun around on his pointy toed shoes, gracefully glided, across the room and exited through the door, in one 'Ephemeral Puff'.

"Aaawwwrrreeeeeechhh,"a terribly loud screech followed by a series of frenetic 'flap, flap, flapping' noises suddenly filled the air. The startled little group automatically turned their heads in unison in the direction of the cage and gawked back in sheer disbelief at the great ugly bird, now munching ferociously on what appeared to be a large chunk of Blue Vein Cheese.

Cornelia shuddered from head to toe as she watched the bird, viciously bite into the crumbling mound of stinky substance. Having regained her composure by now she wasted no time unleashing her hot stinging anger on Algernon.

"What exactly did he mean we have come all the way from England to look after that hideous thing over there?" She sniped. "You know full well I am terribly allergic to birds. If I didn't know any better Algernon I would say you were trying to KILL me," she hissed in a low voice as she dabbed her hanky under her red dribbling nose.

"Yes Father please explain, I thought we were here to collect a bundle, how can we expect to do that whilst HE is in Paris?" Alistair demanded. He sat down on the end of the lounge. "God I am famished! When is he coming back with the food?" He jiggled his long gangly legs up and down. "Not to mention I am in desperate need of a bathroom," he whined. He looked around the room for any signs that may possibly lead to a toilet.

"Well, yes, yes, there are a few details I have been meaning to explain" …. Algernon started. However before he could say another word, Magdalena reappeared wheeling in a cheerfully decorated Victorian, two tiered "Tea Cart," that was stacked to the brim with an assortment of delicate cakes, cucumber sandwiches, a silver tea service and a large bottle of Prosecco.

Horatio followed closely behind, holding out two fragile fluted glasses in each hand.

"Please don't be shy, help yourselves you must be absolutely famished by now," he instructed in a jovial mood. He delicately handed them all a fluted glass and opened the bottle of Prosecco. He then proceeded to fill each glass almost to the top, making sure the bubbles didn't overflow, leaving just enough in the bottle for another toast before placing it back on the far side of the Cart.

"Oh, I am so glad to see you all again," he gushed in an effervescent tone as he raised his glass towards the little family group. 'Cin Cin' to the beginning of your new adventures here in Bella Italia."

Algernon looked over at Cornelia and Alistair. He dipped his bushy eyebrows discreetly and goggled both his eyes, indicating that they too should return the gesture. Then like the true friend he was, he raised his glass high into the air and thrust it into the circle surrounding them, and declared, "Cin Cin."

After taking a long and thirsty gulp, Cornelia immediately broke into a fresh new bout of coughing and sneezing. Teetering dangerously for a moment, on her unfashionably high heels she conveniently used the stiff edge of the Victorian lounge, behind her, to steady herself.

"Are you all right Mumsy," Alistair inquired. He stared back in horror at her thin, convulsing statue.

"Oh dearie me, I had forgotten that you are not used to such exotic beverages. I suppose you don't really drink this type of thing back in Old Blighty do you? More than likely you are used to a tepid Pimms on a balmy afternoon," Horatio declared. He timidly plucked at the ruffles of his shiny silk shirt before taking another modest sip from his glass.

Algernon, sensing that his wife was not amused and quite possibly terrified that she might say something incredibly caustic, jumped into damage control mode before Cornelia could possibly have a chance to respond.

"Oh quite right Horatio, although I must say Cornelia is rather well rehearsed with 'French' sparkling wine. "However this is the first time we have ever tried the Italian equivalent and what a fine drop it is too," he said. Raising his glass into the circle again he took another big sip and almost emptied it down to the last little bit.

"Yes, yes, it is a terrifically good buy," Horatio quipped, smacking his rubbery lips together. "The Italians call it Prosecco; I usually purchase it by the box from the German supermarket down the road. I find they stock everything including Sebastion's favourite cheese all the way from France. Unbelievable really, considering they are German," he smiled back smugly.

At the sound of his name, Sebastion let out an earth shattering screech causing Cornelia to lapse into yet another coughing fit, which rendered her temporarily speechless for the next little while, much to the relief of Algernon.

"SEBASTION where are your manners?" Horatio demanded in a stern voice. "I am warning you for the last time if you don't pipe down immediately I will be forced to cover your cage with the BLANKET."

Looking back at his guests he added, "I really do apologise he is not always like this. It's just that he gets over excited when new people arrive," he finished, with a nervous twitch of his eye.

Cornelia was looking far worse for wear by now. She sat down on the lounge and opened her mouth to its fullest extent. Given the current set of circumstances and the fact she was hardly in the mood to make chit chat one could safely assume she was only milliseconds away from delivering one of her famous vile tongue lashings.

Alistair had been busy gorging himself on all the tasty little tidbits on the Tea Cart and just happened to catch Cornelia's thunderous look as he bent across to pick up another sandwich. Knowing his mother only too well and remembering past bitter episodes of her inability to 'suffer fools' at the best of times, he realised something needed to be done. So, without asking, he reached out across the trolley and quickly grabbed one of the neatly cut triangles of cucumber sandwich. Turning back towards his mother he pushed it insistently against her rather taut lips. "Try one of these Mummy they really are quite delicious," he declared. He shoved the sandwich in as far as it would go.

Cornelia more than likely surprised to find herself about to engulf a sandwich had no choice other than to change her mood. With that in mind she vindictively bit into the crumpled sandwich.

"Well, well, it seems as though everybody is more than content now," said Horatio beaming. "I dare say judging by the way you wolfed down those cucumber sandwiches you must have been simply starving. Mind you it's just as well; I wouldn't like to think of letting them go to waste. Real English cucumbers are awfully expensive in this part of the world," he said, holding a crooked curly finger out before them.

"Talking about expense Uncle Horatio, just for interest sake, how much would anyone expect to pay for a bird like Sebastion? I mean he is not your everyday run of the mill bird is he?" Alistair picked up a delicate little cake and cautiously sniffed it around the edges before taking a bite.

"Alistair mind your manners. I am sure Horatio would prefer to keep the running costs of his peculiar lifestyle quite private," Cornelia chastised. She popped the last little piece of cucumber sandwich into her mouth.

"Oh no not at all, it's a jolly good question actually," said Horatio. "No need to worry about me Cornelia. I certainly don't mind divulging how much I am prepared to pay for the finer things in life. Especially when it comes to those things that bring me great pleasure and Sebastion without a doubt is one of them."

Upon hearing his name, Sebastion let out a loud ear splitting shriek yet again. Only this time it was followed by a long series of whistling. It almost sounded pleasant, except for the fact it was accompanied by manic gusts of wind, as he wildly beat his large wings against the cage.

Cornelia and Alistair exchanged secret looks of disgust as the mixture of mouldy old seed husks and bird droppings that had been propelled out of the cage, suddenly became airborne. They continued to look on in horror as the putrid mixture floated through the air and eventually found its final resting place amongst the left over cucumber sandwiches.

"You see what I mean? He is truly an extraordinary bird," Horatio added, beaming at the bird cage. "Actually, he comes from a long line of champions. In fact his family belongs to a very exclusive lineage. Have you ever heard of the Blue Mutation Yellow Naped Amazon Parrot?" He paused momentarily and looked into their stunned faces before going on. "Well just in case you didn't know, they are far more intelligent and larger than other Yellow Napes. In fact they can actually teach themselves to talk. Sebastion for example can talk fluently in both Italian and English, not that you would know it now, but give him half a chance to warm up and he will talk the hind leg off a donkey," he gazed proudly at the Bird.

"Well I must say I find that remarkable. I had no idea a bird such as Sebastion could have such hidden talents," Algernon declared. He quaffed down the remaining sip of his Prosecco.

Feeling much more relaxed by now he checked his fob watch and was genuinely surprised to discover how late it was. Turning towards Horatio he said, "Well Old Chap this has all been very pleasant hasn't it? But as you yourself have already said it has been an awfully long day. So If you don't mind, I think now, might be as good a time as any to show Cornelia and Alistair to their rooms," he suggested. He nodded his head in a knowing way towards his wife. "After all they will need time to settle in and freshen up before going out for dinner this evening," he advised.

"Oh yes, yes, of course you must be exhausted, after all you are not used to all this lovely sunshine are you?" Horatio said, smiling back smugly. "Why don't you both come away with me now and we can pop upstairs and see what Magdalena is up to. I think she may have prepared something lovely for both of you." This was followed by another sardonic smirk.

Looking back over at Algernon he said. "Just make yourself comfy Old Chap; I will be back in a Jiffy. I am so looking forward to having a little chat," he gushed as he sailed over towards the door. "It will be just like old times he beamed," as he disappeared with Alistair and Cornelia in tow.

# 6 FORTUNATE FRIENDSHIPS

"Awfully good of you to come over at such short notice Old Boy," Horatio crooned. No doubt eternally grateful to finally have Algernon all to himself. "I was really at my wits end trying to find someone to look after the Villa whilst I am away and more importantly, Sebastion," he nudged himself a little bit closer to Algernon. "These ecclesiastical conferences don't come up very often and when they do, I do like to accept them. After all they do pay rather well and one can't be too proud these days can one?"

"Well yes, Indeed, I agree money is money isn't it? And if somebody literally wants to give you some for practically doing nothing then why not?" Algernon stared back at his friend. "But I mean you are managing quite well Old Chap aren't you? What I mean to say, this Paris trip, it's just a bit of a junket isn't it? I mean you don't really need the money do you?" He chuckled uneasily as he reached across the Cart and refilled his glass.

"Oh no Quite," replied Horatio. "I for one am a lot better off than many of my contemporaries. At least I can keep all my art collection together in the one place at the same time without having to run off to an art dealer every second week."

"What do you mean?" Algernon asked, genuinely surprised. He took a hurried sip from his glass.

"Oh I do apologise, I keep forgetting we don't mix in the same circles do we?" He patted Algernon on the shoulder. "Let me try to explain, Old Boy," Horatio took another modest sip from his glass. "It's like this, If somebody owns a valuable art collection and they are unfortunate enough to run into, what can only be best described as a bit of a "Cash Flow" problem. Then they can simply take one, or all of their artworks, depending on the severity of course," he chuckled. He nudged Algernon again, with his elbow and continued,"To a reputable art dealer and ask to have it valued. Then they can present the evaluation certificate to the bank as a means of obtaining security."

"Yes of course, being in the financial business myself I understand your point entirely but the truth is I am not too sure exactly, what you are getting at? What I mean to say is, how does presenting a painting change anything? Surely that alone wouldn't be enough to solve the cash flow problem," Algernon asked irritably. It appeared as though the long day was finally catching up with him.

"Well yes quite, you are right and I can fully understand your confusion. Of course the painting alone wouldn't be enough to get you completely out of trouble. Obviously you would need something more behind it, something more valuable to hold on to. But of course someone in your position would never have had to consider doing such a thing would they?" Horatio laughed lightly again, "And bear in mind my friend things are done a little differently around here compared to how they are done back in Old Blighty." Still not completely convinced that Algernon had fully grasped his little analogy he patiently ploughed on.

"Let me make it a little simpler for you shall I? Let's imagine an art dealer here in Italy is a bit like a bank, someone like you perhaps," he laughed again as he patted Algernon on the back. This was followed by a satisfied sniff. "When somebody brings him an art piece and asks to have it valued he usually has to send it away for a couple of days for testing, before he can give a definitive answer."

"But I still don't understand how that can change the cash flow problem," Algernon replied impatiently. "As far as I am concerned only the bank can do that," he flicked off a few pieces of floating chaff, from the top layer of his cucumber sandwich before taking another generous bite.

"Yes, I was just coming to that point," Horatio pointed out. "As I mentioned before, things are done a little differently over here. So let's just say in this situation, before the art dealer can send the artwork away he needs to give the owner a monetary deposit either cash or cheque as a means of guaranteeing the safety and the ownership of the artwork and then, Wallah instant cash." Horatio comically rolled his eyes and snapped his fingers together. "It is one of the oldest tricks in the book for getting one out of a very tight spot." His eyes glittered brightly.

"Oh I see," Algernon nodded, "the Art dealer like the bank, forwards on the money as a security measure towards the piece of art. How very interesting, I had no idea. Hmmmm just for interest sake Old Boy, exactly how much money would the owner expect to receive in such a situation?" This question was followed by the last chomp of his sandwich.

"Well I can't really say from personal experience but I do believe the rate is around ten to fifteen percent of the value of the original artwork," Horatio offered. He tapped the side of his glass with the end of his Celtic cross. "Anyhow old chap that's something we really don't need to concern ourselves with, is it?" He gave Algernon a final, reassuring pat on the arm. "We're one of the few lucky surviving ones aren't we? As I said before, it's simply not enough to own a valuable painting. Obviously one has to have a more substantial means of income besides it. Now that's the key to a good life," he stated. He cast an affectionate glance across the room towards his impressive art collection.

"Well yes Quite! One couldn't base ones entire fortune, simply on one painting alone could one?" Algernon exclaimed. "As you said earlier, there needs to be something a lot more substantial going on behind the scenes." Nodding his head towards Horatio he anxiously gulped down the last of his drink.

"Anyway old Boy, as I said before it is awfully good of

you to come over at such short notice," Horatio gazed wistfully at Algernon, who was over at the Cart refilling his glass again.

"Not at all," boomed Algernon. "After all we go back a long way and that sort of thing can't be discounted these days," he added as he reached for another cucumber sandwich.

"My word I can't believe how much Alistair has grown up," Horatio said. He rolled his eyes up towards the ceiling and back again, as he shook his head.

"I mean he was no more than a boy when I last saw him and look at him now. All grown up and such a handsome looking lad too. Cornelia and you must be so proud? "

"Oh yes, Quite, old boy, Quite. Cornelia and I have invested an awful lot of time and energy into Alistair's upbringing and I dare say it is moments like these that make it all seem very worthwhile," Algernon replied smugly. He tweaked the end of his moustache with his sandwich clutching hand.

Feeling rather pleased now with the way things were turning out he took a very large bite of the sandwich. Munching it down voraciously he was just in the process of taking another generous sip of his Prosecco when a sharp squealing sound, similar to the sound a microphone, makes when it receives too much feedback, filled his ears.

At first he couldn't make out where on earth the awful din was coming from. After straining his hearing and concentrating a little bit harder, he discovered it was resonating from a small black box sitting on top of the dark mahogany cabinet on the other side of the room. He couldn't be sure but from where he was standing it looked like one of those 'Baby Intercom Devices' that new parents often use.

Algernon, shuddered and literally shrank back in horror when he recognised the nasally high pitched whine of Alistair's voice. To make matters worse, he almost choked on the cheap acidic liquid, merrily cascading its way down his tight throat, when he actually realised what was being said.

"If Father thinks for one minute that I am going to stay in this flea bitten one horse town, then he has another thought coming. I can't believe I was stupid enough to give up my precious holiday in Majorca to join him in this Fund Raising, Arse Sucking, Junket," Alistair protested loudly.

"Believe me Alistair, you will have to stand in line and wait your turn. I am definitely going to have first dibbs at him and if there is anything left, after I have torn him to shreds, then you are most certainly welcome to it," sniped Cornelia.

"I mean what was he thinking?" He shrieked even louder. "It's bleeding obvious that his so called, childhood chum is as Mad as a Hatter, not to mention as Gay as a Picnic basket! I can't possibly Imagine what he actually thinks we are here for," Alistair screamed.

"The nerve of that pompous little git to insinuate that I wouldn't know what a good champagne tasted like, who does he think he is? And just look at the state of this room it hasn't been decorated in years. If your father thinks that I intend to take this whole situation lying down then he certainly has got another thought coming indeed."

Even though Horatio was known to have a significant hearing problem and could often miss spoken details, after taking just one hurried look at the horrified expression plastered all over his friend's stricken face, Algernon had no doubt whatsoever, that Horatio had heard and understood every single word that had been said.

Heavily wheezing in and out, he clamped his sweaty palms together in a gesture of goodwill and was about to launch into some sort of halfway credible explanation, when mercifully, any further conversation was drowned out by a series of blood curdling howls, compliments of Winston and Churchill. Within a minute, none other than Magdalena came bursting through the closed doors, all pale and breathless, erratically flailing her arms around her bobbing head.

"Scusa Signore Horeatzio come quickly." She waved her flabby skinned arms towards the outside wall. "Come, now, I theenk, the Carne, they is a having the very, very, big problem," she spouted, eyes wide open and hair all a tremble. "I see one is having his head stuck in the back van window."

Algernon, genuinely concerned for his beloved pets and

no doubt desperately relieved to escape from the awkward situation, bolted as fast as his extended waistline, would allow him, towards the open doors. Unfortunately in his haste to escape, he accidentally tripped up on the fraying edges of the faded carpet and staggered around awkwardly for a few dazed seconds. To add insult to injury, the back of his heavy tweed jacket, caught the edge of the Victorian tea trolley,  and caused it to topple over and spill the remaining cucumber sandwiches all over the dark wooden floor as he hurriedly made his way out, into the descending sun.

# 7 SMOKE AND MIRRORS

The handsome group of four, elaborately dressed by anyone's standards but far more, compared to the locals, did certainly raise a few eyebrows and render looks of genuine curiosity, as they arrived at the entrance of 'Casa Di Loanda,' Pastacula's most prestigious restaurant.

It wasn't as if the locals were not already accustomed to seeing Horatio parade about in all his fabulous finery, it was more a case of being surprised by the sheer volume of flamboyance that was presented to them, that evening.

Cornelia, for example had especially gone to great lengths to impress and definitely drew a few second looks. In fact she almost looked attractive, all decked out in her shiny sequined gown and silvery grey gloves. However the real scene stealer was her bell shaped, Cloche Hat that actually looked as though it may have once been used as a prop, from the film set of "The Great Gatsby."

Alfonso, an affable, albeit, a bland Italian man, had been eagerly awaiting their arrival ever since he had taken the telephone booking late that afternoon and as soon as he saw them arrive, he rushed over from the bar, where he had purposely positioned himself, to greet them. The restaurant itself was charming in the usual kind of way even though it looked very similar to most of the other restaurants, found in most of the other rustic Italian towns.

Overall the presentation was nothing short of pleasant, with its neatly laid wooden tables, topped off with the obligatory red and white checked tablecloths and gaudy hand painted ceramic accessories. As well as that, it also housed an overabundance of tacky "knicky knacks" and "treasured regional trinkets" that dutifully hung from wooden hooks on the traditional faded, white washed walls.

"Buona sera Signore Horatio it is so good to see you again and theesa persons must be your dear friends all the way from England. I am so pleased to meet you," Alfonso gushed He held his hand out enthusiastically towards Algernon.

"Yes, yes, indeed," Horatio replied stiffly, followed by a watery smile. "This is Algernon Uberbite an old school friend of mine from my childhood days and his delightful wife Cornelia and their charming son Alistair," he added rather mechanically, with a lacklustre wave of his hand. As soon as he had finished speaking, his big "inky pot" blue eyes suddenly began to blink, in a peculiar, uncontrollable manner giving the impression that he was going to have some sort of strange epileptic fit.

They all stared back, for the next few seconds, no doubt alarmed by this sudden strange spasm and more than likely wondering what could possibly happen next. After a little while the incessant blinking finally stopped and Horatio, clearly embarrassed, dabbed deftly at the corner of his eye with his Italian Lace hanky.

"Oh dear," he said looking up with swimming pool eyes. "I am afraid some of the chaff from the outer fields must have blown into the town this afternoon. It seems as though a couple of sharp pieces have made themselves at home in my eye," he declared, as he continued to dab away.

Greatly relieved, that there was nothing seriously wrong, Alfonso stepped forward and with added gusto, resumed the all-important introductory segment for the evening.

"Signore Algernon it is a pleasure to meet you at last and this must be your lovely wife Signora Alistair? May I say how beautiful you are looking this evening? Just like, how you say in your most famous of novels, You look like an 'English Rose,' he gushed effortlessly. Stretching his tuxedo clad arm out towards Cornelia he gently took her hand, drew it up to his lips and gave it a passionate kiss. "You know it has always been my lifelong dream to kiss the hand of a real English thoroughbred," he crooned. He flashed them all a cheesy smile that bore the uncanny likeness of a piano keyboard.

Cornelia, was absolutely speechless and instantly shot a tight lipped narrow eyed look across to Algernon. Silently standing for a few more moments they secretly exchanged a series of indignant glances, inclusive of a sufficient level of raised eyebrows. It was so quiet you could have heard a pin drop except for the loud shameless growling coming from Algernon's stomach. Then almost telepathically, they all seemed to agree, that it would probably be best to avoid any more unpleasantries for the evening. Bearing that in mind, the four of them smiled back and nodded their heads in unison.

Innocently unaware, of any blunder, he may have made, Alfonso proudly sailed across the room as he led them to an elaborately set table that was neatly tucked away in a private alcove, far from the prying eyes of the other patrons. Who, coincidentally, had all miraculously finished their conversation, at the same time and were now twisting themselves into a series of contorted shapes and sizes, hoping to gain a better view of the unusual little group as they sedately walked by.

As they were being seated, Algernon couldn't help noticing a very well dressed young man, dining alone at a table on the other side of the room. Turning his face towards him in order to gain a better view, he couldn't be sure but from where he was sitting, it looked as though the young man was staring back at them through an old fashioned Monocle. Similar to the one his grandfather had always used whenever he read the newspaper. 'That's odd' he thought, frowning back at the man 'mind you, we are in Italy and the Italians are quite well known for their eccentric sense of dress,' he consoled himself.

"Please would you be so kind as to take your seats," Alfonso offered, as he pulled out a chair for Cornelia. "And please, make yourselves, how do you say in English,

Comftey," he smiled back blandly, flashing the keyboard again. "I will return most shortly with the Wine list and water."

Feeling much better now that she knew that a glass of wine was definitely not too far away, Cornelia deemed it was high time to be a little more civil and generously made a mental note to overlook "everything," including the name blunder. So perking up as best she could and attempting a semi genuine expression, she looked directly at her sulking host and declared, "Well this certainly is a quirky little establishment you have here Horatio. I can see why you chose such an intriguing place for us to dine. I mean it is so very provincial isn't it? Yet at the same time it seems to have an allure about it that even the most hearty of sophisticates' could not overlook." Despite her good intentions, she couldn't help finishing her little speech with a slight snigger and snort.

"Yes, yes, dear, that is quite, correct, however one cannot discount the rustic authentic appeal an establishment such as this holds. Just look at the menu for example where on earth have you seen anything like it?" Algernon boomed across the table. Picking up the menu, he gave it a cursory glance.

Convinced now, that everyone was doing their utmost to set things right again, Horatio softened his stance and with the grace of a martyr he picked up the menu lying on the table next to him. Waving it around in front of them he said, "Yes of course you are quite right Algernon, the food here is indeed something to write home about." He nodded sagely. "What I really mean to say is, anything beats English food, especially the type we used to eat at boarding school," he added. He looked over at Algernon with just a trace of affection.

"Oh yes! Wasn't it horrid?" Algernon blustered, his big cheeks all ruddy. "How could we ever forget Toad in a Hole and Brown Betty? Although I do recall you had quite a fondness for good old 'Spotted Dick' didn't you?" He laughed heartily and then stopped sharply, when he realised the connotations of what he had actually just said.

Alfonso had now re-joined them. This time he was accompanied by a large chunky wooden trolley that was laden with glasses, bottles of wine and water, some decanters with olive oil and balsamic vinegar and two generous baskets of freshly baked crusty bread. Without saying a word he very eloquently started setting out the glasses. After he had finished this task, he stealthily walked from one side of the table to the other and reverently placed a bottle of Red wine on either end.

Looking blissfully content with the result of his efforts, he reached behind him and picked up the remaining bottle of red wine from the trolley and carefully wrapped it in a linen napkin before raising it upwards in a gesture of offering. Cornelia eager for an alcoholic beverage picked up the glass directly in front of her and thrust it out towards him, hoping he would respond quickly.

"Yes I do believe the wines here are quite remarkable," piped up Alistair. "Well at least that's what I have been told. However I can't say I have ever tried any of this local Vino, it never quite made it to Highgate," he laughed. He picked up his generously filled glass and gave it a haughty sniff before taking a sip. "What do you think Mummy?" Alistair asked, suddenly aware that Cornelia was already helping herself to the second glass.

"Well I must say, I am pleasantly surprised it is far better than what I was expecting. Actually, I really think we should order another bottle, clearly one red is never enough," she smiled; displaying a mouthful of crimson, wine stained, teeth.

Alfonso, finished now, with all his decorative duties stood benevolently in front of them with a notepad in one hand and a gold plated pen, poised above it, in the other.

"So what are you feeling like to eat this evening," he asked glancing from one to the other. "Tonight on the menu we have available a very delicious Polenta, with a homemade Ragu sauce and of course our very famous Tiramisu."

"If you don't mind, I should like to take a look at the menu," Alistair interjected. "I mean I am not too sure about this type of food so I would like to stick to something I am slightly more familiar with, like Pasta you know, "Spaghetti." Do you have any Pasta?" He laughed loudly, winking at the others comically.

"Scusa Signore," Alfonso replied fretfully, rubbing his hand up and down on his chest, "I am very sorry but this evening is the day when we have a set menu only. You see today is the day the cook goes to visit her brother in Roma and so she doesn't have the time to prepare too much," he confessed, staring back at them with a pair of pale, dead fish, eyes.

"Oh, Oh, I see, Well in that case I suppose it will be Polenta all around followed by your Famouzzzzzz Tiramisu," Alistair replied, sarcastically, with a wry smile.

"Yes, Yes, thank you Alfonso, I had forgotten that little detail," Horatio said, nodding his head apologetically. "Well never mind, I am sure we will enjoy the Polenta Ragu and of course as Cornelia suggested earlier another bottle of the red will most definitely jolly us along," he added, with a nervous little titter.

As if on cue, Cornelia flung out her glass for another refill. Alfonso, ever obliging, sprang into action and promptly refilled everyone's glass. By making sure he completely emptied the bottle, he cleverly justified the need to purchase another one.

"Bottoms Up," Horatio beamed, as he took a long deserved sip. With just the slightest hint of a quiver to his voice he declared, "I must say how delighted I am to see you all again, after all this time. Believe me it is an absolute thrill." He dabbed at the corner of his eye with his napkin. "You know I am not getting any younger and these days I find good friends are frightfully few and far between," he said, with a faraway look.

"Come, come, old chap, don't be like that," Algernon soothed. "You know how much it means to all of us to be here with you now." Casting a quick glance around the table he continued. "Only last week Alistair reminded me of that wonderful holiday we all had together in Somerset and what a terrific time we had in the Roman baths together, isn't that right Ali?"

"Sorry father, what did you say? I didn't quite catch you," Alistair replied in a bored tone He took a break from his relentless texting, for just a moment.

Algernon, was slightly annoyed, but nonetheless, he was determined to make a point. He spoke sternly to his son. "I was just saying to Horatio, how only last week you asked after him and wondered how he was getting on in Italy!"

"Oh yes, quite right," he said snapping to attention, "Uncle Horatio, as you well know, has never been far from my thoughts. Ever since we had that wonderful holiday in London together, I can still remember it so clearly it was just like yesterday."

"Bath Ali, it was in Bath," Cornelia hissed as the effects of the alcohol started to kick in.

"Oh yes, how silly of me, Bath Hmmm but I am sure we would have had a wonderful time in London together too," he offered. A foolish grin dominated his face.

"Oh please don't apologise, none of us are getting any younger are we? And we all have our little quirks to deal with. That's why it is so good to be able to count on good friends like you, especially when I need them," Horatio said. He turned the large chunky ring that was perched vulgarly on his index finger, around and around again.

Just then, Alfonso arrived back with another bottle of red wine and a platter of aperitifs. "Signore Horatio," he said rather urgently, bending down closely to Horatio's ear whilst he placed the food and the wine on the table. "I have been asked to tell you, that all your food and wine this evening will be taken care of by one of the patrons eating here at the restaurant tonight."

"Oh really Alfonso that is extremely generous may I ask who it is? Do I know them?" Horatio enquired. He automatically looked around the room.

"Signore Horatio, I don't know if you have ever met this gentleman before but if you look closely over in the corner at the table across the room you will see there is somebody sitting there and that is the man who has paid for your meal tonight."

Algernon had been 'listening in' on this little conversation and so he instantly looked over at the table he had noticed earlier. He scrunched his eyes up together into a hard stare as he tried to get a better look at the man that he had seen sitting there before. After double checking, one more time just to make sure he wasn't imagining things, he turned back and exclaimed to the table, "But there is no one there, the table is empty!" His eyes bulged.

Alfonso, also turned and double checked before turning back again to answer. "Si, I see you are right, Signore

Algernon. The gentleman, it now seems that he is gone. But, please don't let that stop you from enjoying very much the wonderful food and wine he has provided for you," he said looking from one to the other. "Now if you will please excuse me. I will like to check on how your meal is coming along in the oven." Bowing stiffly, he turned away and headed back towards the kitchen.

"My word that is most peculiar, I must say," commented Horatio. "I mean it just goes to show, doesn't it? That there are still quite a few kind souls left in this world. Well, well, what a wonderful way to start our time together," he said as he raised his glass for another toast, "Cin Cin."

"I'll drink to that," said Cornelia in a louder than normal voice, vigorously throwing out her hand for a refill.

Starting to feel much more relaxed now after a few glasses of wine, Alistair decided, that this would be the perfect time to bring up the conversation that he'd had, in the car, earlier that day, with Algernon. The one all about the bequeathing of worldly goods. Deep down, he secretly hoped that this little intimate discussion would set the scene for the far more important discussion about Horatio's benevolent intentions and of course that discussion would then, no doubt, take precedence for the rest of the evening.

"Oh yes indeed, Uncle Horatio, I couldn't agree more. Isn't it wonderful to know there are still some good souls left in this world. Speaking of which, I can't begin to tell you how grateful I was when father told me about your extremely generous offer to bequeath me most of your worldly goods."

Horatio, who only seconds before, had been, gloriously basking in the warmth of the heartfelt praise of friendship and kin, suddenly spluttered his wine up into the air like a spouting whale and virulently coughed it out all over the table. "Oh dear, oh dear, please excuse me, it must have gone down the wrong way." He swung his head from side to side as he coughed again. "I am sorry Alistair, I am not quite sure I heard you correctly, did you say something about giving away all your worldly goods. I must say that is very generous of you. But if you don't mind me asking, aren't you a bit too young to be doing something like that?"

Alistair was absolutely 'gob smacked' by Horatio's rather strange question. No doubt, the confused expression plastered across his pale face, clearly indicated he was not exactly sure what Horatio had meant. Nevertheless he decided to ignore the old fool's inane twittering for the time being and focus his energies on bringing the conversation back around to where he needed it to go.

Mustering up as much sincerity as he could, he opened his mouth wide, in readiness to deliver his golden speech once again, but was unfortunately prevented from doing so, due to a sudden ear splitting, 'Boom!' Actually it sounded awfully like a cannon shot. It rang horribly in their ears and bounced across from wall to wall as it resonated its way around the large cavernous room.

This horrid noise was quickly followed by an insidious blackout where they were obliged to sit in complete darkness for the next few seconds before the lights returned. This impromptu little diversion was finally topped off by an awful Whirr, whirr, whirring sound, similar in a surreal kind of way, to the noise made by the dying blades of a lawn mower.

The next minute, the kitchen door flung open and the entire staff came bursting out, screaming theatrically as they waved their hands high into the air, this was followed by great gusts of dirty black smoke that billowed ominously behind them.

Alfonso, who had been the first to emerge, rapidly made his way across the room towards them. "Signore Horatio please get up and go. It is not too safe for you here. Please you must understand, at this moment we have in the kitchen a little fire and we must a wait now for the Vigili Del Fuoco, (Fire brigade) to come," he yelled in an agitated tone, glancing around at the rest of the customers who had haphazardly left their tables and were making their way towards the door.

In light of the current situation, it seemed as though everyone at the table had unanimously agreed, that any further conversation about worldly goods and other associated matters, should be put back neatly on a shelf and tackled at a more appropriate time. Clearly the most sensible thing for them to do was to get up and leave.

So with that in mind, they all headed silently towards the

door. Cornelia however made it a point, to heroically grab the unopened bottle of wine that was in danger of being left behind.

Once outside, they aimlessly stood around, in the cool fresh air and waited for further instructions. Most of the other evacuated customers were Italians and didn't seem in the least bit deterred about the dangerous situation. Loud shrieks of laughter and continuous chatter filled the air as they exchanged animated conversations with one another.

After waiting around for a few more minutes in what could only be described as a rather subdued mood, Horatio flashing a genuinely apologetic smile decided he really ought to do something.

"Well I must say, this has certainly turned out to be an eventful evening hasn't it?" He laughed light heartedly. "I mean here we are, standing in the street with no idea when we can go back in. Meanwhile there is a perfectly good Villa just down the road full of good food and wine simply waiting for us. Mind you, I hope it isn't blacked out too," he added almost to himself. "I mean it wouldn't be the first time. Trust me this sort of thing happens regularly in this part of the world," he said, with a double blink of his eyes.

"Hmmmm, yes I see what you mean," said Algernon, frowning quite hard by now. "I must say I am feeling more than a bit peckish and it has been an awfully long day."

"Yes and we are almost out of wine," Cornelia warned. She held up the rescued bottle, "Not to mention my feet are absolutely murdering me." She jiggled up and down on her throbbing toes.

"It's settled then," Horatio declared with a clap. "Let's all go back to the Villa then shall we?" Briefly turning his attention back towards Alistair he added, "And of course, after we have all had something tasty to eat and drink, I think we may be able to discuss the wonderful surprise I told your father all about, Alistair."

Alistair, overjoyed that the conversation had so effortlessly found its way back to where they had left it, immediately leapt to attention. "That would be simply splendid Uncle Horatio. I am so looking forward to it. Father and I have discussed it briefly but I am really keen to hear what you have to say about the matter."

So without any further ado and hopefully before anything else untoward could happen the resolute little group, strolled off together across the dimly gas lit Piazza and out onto the tree lined viale.

<table>
<tr><th colspan="3">INSTAPOL POLICE REPORT</th></tr>
<tr><td>Agent Guido Ventosi</td><td>Day: One/<br>Evening</td><td>File Number<br>1200/12/20098</td></tr>
<tr><td>CASE</td><td>LOCATION</td><td>Report No</td></tr>
<tr><td>Uberbite Surveillance</td><td>Casa<br>Di Loanda<br>Restaurant</td><td>2</td></tr>
<tr><td colspan="3">Persons of Interest<br>Algernon Uberbite, Cornelia Uberbite, Alistair Uberbite</td></tr>
<tr><td colspan="3">ACTIVITIES</td></tr>
<tr><td colspan="3">18.45 Suspect went to the very nice restaurant.<br>19.00 Suspect stared rudely at me.<br>19.30 Suspect spoke loudly to the waiter.<br>19.45 Suspect drank too much wine<br>20.00 Suspect ran out of the restaurant.<br>20.15 Suspect left to go to another place.<br><br>Expenses: One new Gucci suit for me to wear to the dinner and a new pair of Italian Leather shoes. The complete cost of the meal for the Group of Suspects. This way I am sure they would relax and enjoy the hospitality of the people who live in the countryside. It will be easier for me to follow their movements.</td></tr>
<tr><td colspan="3">COMMENTS</td></tr>
<tr><td colspan="3">The primary suspect and his two family members and another very strange looking old man entered the Casa Di Loanda restaurant at Pastacula at 6.45.pm.<br>Also when I was inside the restaurant, I see they spoke rudely and loudly to the wait staff and also to each other. They drank more than one bottle of wine in this very</td></tr>
</table>

| INSTAPOL POLICE REPORT | | |
|---|---|---|
| **Agent** Guido Ventosi | Day: One/ Evening | File Number 1200/12/20098 |
| **CASE** | **LOCATION** | **Report No** |
| Uberbite Surveillance | Casa Di Loanda Restaurant | 2 |
| **Persons of Interest** Algernon Uberbite, Cornelia Uberbite, Alistair Uberbite | | |

short time. I didn't see any good Italian Prosecco on the table. The suspect Algernon Uberbite was staring very rudely at me and at the other peoples in the restaurant. When I was waiting outside I see they left the restaurant very quickly after a suspicious smoke came into the air.

**Important Comments:**

There are some very important reasons that made me theenk this was not really a proper dinner appointment. For example I was a leetle suspicion because :

1.The dinner reservation was made far too early for eating the dinner, the other customers were only enjoying a very nice aperitivo, before their dinner.

2. The Primary Suspect Algernon Uberbite had not changed his clothes and was still wearing the same Horrible jacket he was wearing earlier at the Bank. I am sure it still has the pigeon poop all over it. Nobody would ever come to dinner dressed like this.

A woman who cries, a man who swears, a horse that sweats; are all imposters.

## 8 THE MORNING AFTER

"I still can't believe the Barmy old Git would have the nerve to just go sailing off to Paris as if nothing had ever happened. I mean who the hell does he think he is? What sort of planet does he live on anyway?" Alistair bitterly complained to his mother as he sat at the dining room table rocking backwards and forwards on the back legs of his chair.

"Alistair would you please keep your voice down? I have a splitting headache and your hysterics are not doing me any good," Cornelia snapped. She reached out and poured herself another cup of tea from the elaborate silver teapot sitting on the table in front of her.

Clearly the night had not been kind to her. Both her eyes were almost hidden by the great puffy bags of skin that shamelessly hung down to her cheeks. Not to mention her hair, which was usually her saving grace, looked as though it had been replaced by a well-used scouring pad.

"Yes, well no doubt that appalling Limoncello we were forced to drink, before we witnessed the inaugural 'Unveiling' last night would have caused that," he moaned, his beady eyes popping out comically from his brightly flushed face.

"I still can't believe what actually happened," he said shaking his head woefully. "A portrait Mother can you believe it? A portrait!" He repeated, popping his eyes again. "Why the Hell would anyone think, that I, You or even Father for that matter, would want to inherit a portrait?" He insisted with a squeak. "It's just totally unbelievable." Alistair slumped forward onto the stately old dining table and cradled his head in his hands.

"Alistair pleeeease," Cornelia pleaded, as she fished around in the contents of her handbag. "I won't ask you again, can you just keep your voice down to a minimum? I can't find my lighter and your outbursts are only making it worse."

"Keep my voice down, what about you?" he said. Lifting his head slightly he turned his motley face towards his mother. "You're a great one to talk; perhaps we should call you 'Madam Foghorn,' in the future, especially after witnessing your continual bouts of hyena like laughter last night. Not to mention your selfish relentless smoking. Have you ever spared a thought for all those poor souls that have to put up with the smell? Isn't it about time you kicked that filthy dirty habit?" He sneered, before he buried his face again.

"Oh here it is," she sighed. Looking very pleased with herself she lit the end of her slim line cigarette and inhaled deeply before replying. "Don't be like that Ali, you know smoking is one of the few pleasures I have left in this life," she blew great puffs of smoke into the air.

"There is no doubt about it, the man is a lunatic," Alistair sat up and banged his fist down on the table. "I mean, can you believe the way he carried on before he unveiled the portrait? It was ludicrous, nothing short of disgusting if you ask me. He practically looked as though he was having an orgasm. Flailing his arms around his head and rolling the whites of his eyes around like a shark." Alistair mimicked the actions as best he could before looking back over towards his mother. "He reminded me of a demented version of Picasso, that's what he bloody well reminded me of."

"Yes I must agree the whole thing was completely unorthodox," Cornelia said. "Not to mention those disgusting Cuban cigars he and your father were smoking. I can understand NOW, why the Americans have banned them," she declared as she exhaled profusely, blowing even more smoke over Alistair's bowed head. "Really, what I mean to ask is, What on Earth was your father thinking? Making us all gather together like a herd of silly sheep in that stifling stuffy room. Not to mention the fact, we had to share it with that ghastly, squawking, creature." She quickly puffed in and out and poured herself some more tea.

"Arrrrgggghhhh …… I just can't believe I was stupid enough to give up my holiday in Spain for Nothing, Zilch, Sqiddley Dot," Alistair shrieked. He collapsed his head onto the table again.

Just then Algernon appeared, from the outside courtyard, looking all ruddy and hot.

"Well that's it then he's off," he announced in a matter of fact way. "Let's hope he has a safe trip then shall we?" Strolling over amicably to the table, he pulled out a chair and sat down. "And you will be pleased to know all is well with the lads too. They've just eaten the huge bowl of porridge I made for them earlier," he said, reaching for a piece of cold dry toast that had been left on the plate in front of him.

"Well thank goodness for that," Cornelia said sarcastically. "I have been up all night worrying about their dietary needs. Never mind the fact that I can't get a decent pot of tea and the bread here is as hard as a rock," she snapped.

"Oh come dear, it's not all that bad the bread here is typical for this part of Italy, you will just have to get used to it," he took another large bite of the toast.

"Frankly, I think it is a disgrace and I can't imagine for one moment what these people see in it," she scoffed. She picked up the piece of toast in front of her and bounced it across the table.

"Well I for one, have no intention of getting used to such peasant food. I plan to leave here as soon as possible," Alistair announced. He suddenly seemed highly energised. "By this time tomorrow, I shall be stretched out in a deck chair and indulging myself with a very tasty Empanada and washing it all down with a nice long glass of ice cold Sangria," he said. He looked longingly towards the window on the other side of the room.

Algernon shuffled uneasily in his chair as he wolfed down the last few bites of his toast. Clearing his throat loudly he announced to nobody in particular but to everyone in general, "I am afraid to say that may not be possible, well at least not in the immediate, in fact it may be quite difficult for some time."

"What do you mean difficult father? I mean I know we are out in the sticks and all, but surely we are within fifty miles of a decent international airport?"

Algernon had slowly edged his way, to a standing position at the side of the table. He swayed restlessly from side to side before giving a definitive answer. "It is not really a question of how close we are to the Airport Alistair. It is rather more to do with the current set of circumstances that we find ourselves in," he cautioned in a grave voice.

"Oh for goodness sake Algernon what on earth are you prattling on about now," demanded Cornelia as she poured herself yet another cup of tea. "Surely you can see the poor lad has had enough and I for one don't blame him. After all he was promised a small fortune and all he has ended up with is a rather appalling portrait of himself dressed up as an 'Easter Bunny', when he was four years old."

"Yes dear, Quite, and that is why I feel in order to avoid any more disappointment, it is of the utmost importance, that he fully understands, the reality of our current situation," Algernon warned.

"Oh for crying out loud father, would you just stop talking about me as though I wasn't here and just come out and say what you mean?" Alistair demanded. He got up from his chair and walked stiffly across the room.

Feeling cornered now and with nowhere to run, Algernon steadied himself on the side of the chair and puffed out his chest. "Well you see Alistair, as I told you before, it is not really a question of geography but rather more a question of finance," he stated gingerly.

Alistair was standing very close to Algernon by now and he was seething red with anger. He looked his father fairly in the eye and poked his pointy finger into his face. "Yes father I am very aware of that. It's not exactly rocket science, to work out that things have gone horribly pear shaped since we arrived," he shrieked. He flicked back a chunk of lanky hair that had escaped from his frazzled fringe and breathed in and out heavily, as he shook his lily white finger up and down.

"Well yes quite, but it's not really that simple, there is a bit more to it I am afraid," Algernon replied stepping back slightly. "The thing is Ali, and I don't mean to alarm you but I think it is important for you to understand," he said shuffling his feet around awkwardly. "You see the truth of the matter is," Algernon paused for a moment and clasped his pudgy fingers together before continuing.

"The reason you can't go to Spain, is not because the airport is too far away, Ali. It's because ….. because, we don't have the means to pay for it!" He disclosed, looking at a spot on the wall somewhere above Alistair's head. He swayed back and forth on his heels.

Alistair stopped dead in his tracks and turned a deathly shade of pale and back to grey again. "What do you mean father?" He shrieked in a high pitched voice. "But I saw you only yesterday, go to the ATM and take some cash out. Mother, you were there, you saw him too didn't you?" He urgently swung his head around to the side.

"Algernon have you got heat stroke or something, what mad ravings are you entertaining now?" Cornelia bullied, she was standing completely out of her chair.

"Yes Of course I went to the ATM yesterday but the point is I didn't receive any money did I? And to make matters worse my card was swallowed, so I don't have access to any other funds do I?" Algernon confessed.

"Father, listen to me carefully," Alistair pleaded. He spoke in a slow steady voice. "Just because we are in a foreign country it doesn't mean they won't have English speaking representatives at their respective branches. I mean, all you have to do, is give them a call and simply mention WHO you are and I am sure somebody in customer services will be able to help you out." He looked at Cornelia for support.

"Alistair is quite right Algernon. Have you lost your senses? We are not back in the dark ages, I mean these kinds of problems are easily resolved nowadays," she said reaching for another cigarette.

"If only that were the case," Algernon sighed loudly. "I have already rung the bank this morning and it seems that they have frozen our account. Unfortunately at this point I cannot withdraw one single penny. However let's not overly panic. I have a few ideas in the pipeline and I am sure by tomorrow I will be able to come up with a solution," he added stoically.

Deathly silence reigned down upon them for a few moments more, whilst they each digested what had just been said. Then, just as all hell threatened to break loose, the calm before the storm was broken by a sudden loud barking from Winston and Churchill followed by an even louder knocking at the door.

Algernon eternally grateful for the reprieve, quickly made his way out to the atrium and after opening the door, was quite surprised to discover Magdalena standing there.

"Buongiorno, Signore Ooopabyta it is again me Magdalena, today is the day I will come to the Ousa to clean out the shits," she declared cheerfully.

Algernon gave her a puzzled look, "I am sorry, I am not quite sure I understood you correctly. Did you say you were coming here to do some cleaning of a rather delicate nature?" He proposed.

"Ohhhh scusa, I theenk you no understanda my Inglish. OK now I tell to you, at theesa moment, today is the day I come to yourra Ousa and I take all the shits from the beds. Every time I do this job for Signore Horeatzio he notta like to keep the dirty shits in his bed."

Algernon broke out into a big, booming, laugh that literally came from the soles of his feet, when he realized Magdalena had actually been talking about, changing the bed linen.

"Oh I see, you mean the Sheets, you have come to change the sheets," he said deliberately emphasising the *"ee"* sound in Sheets.

"Si Signore Ooopabyta, I have come to cleanna the Sheeeits."

Eager to avoid any further confrontations with Alistair and Cornelia, he invited her into the house and quickly busied himself with tidying up the few dishes that had been left on the table. Magdalena bright as a button, greeted them both with the usual congenial greetings, which were met with a very cool, "Good Morning," from Cornelia and a grunt from Alistair.

"As I already told to Signore Ooopabyta. I am coming to the Ousa this day to take the sheets from the beds," she announced beaming proudly at Algernon.

Before either of them could respond, with what was bound to be a ruthless onslaught of linguistic corrections, the conversation was interrupted yet again by a bout of hysterical barking from the dogs in the back.

"Signora Ooopabyta, I theenk the doggies is a very ungry," Magdalena puffed as she looked anxiously towards the window. "I see they are a crying, very much to me when I come just now to yourra Ousa."

"Oh I see," replied Algernon. "I do apologise if they frightened you. They didn't mean to of course. It's just that they are in a strange place and it will take some time to get used to it all."

"Si Si Signore Ooopabyta but eef you like I weeel make to them some of my famous polenta. This will help them very much not to be very angry."

"Hmmm," Algernon looked at her with a puzzled expression and scratched his head. "Well that is quite kind of you but they have already eaten a large bowl of Porridge this morning." Looking over towards the other two in the enemy camp, he added, "I think what they really need now is a bit of a walk. Perhaps you could take them for some fresh air sometime this morning Alistair?"

"Oh of course Father, obviously it won't involve any money and clearly by what you have just told me earlier I have nothing else better to do with my time now. Lucky for me that I managed to salvage a few hundred pounds before we left England isn't it, but of course I better hang on to it just in case it is needed for the "Uberbite Charity foundation," he replied sarcastically, as he pulled his wallet into his chest and hugged it.

Cornelia sat back down at the table and poured herself another cup of tea. It wouldn't be too far wrong to suggest she was starting to feel quite shattered by the recent turn of events, not to mention being horribly confused.

As far as she could make out, she had been bundled into a car on the promise of a Tuscan holiday only to find herself stranded in the middle of nowhere. On top of all that she had no idea how long she would be there. To make matters worse, she was supposed to be genuinely grateful for the privilege of staying in a rundown hovel with a bird from the cast of "Jurassic Park" for company.

Finding the whole ordeal slightly overwhelming, she decided to turn her attention towards Magdalena's hair. Scrutinising it carefully, she peered long and hard at the wiry locks for any signs of the bread crumbs she had seen the day before. To her utmost surprise she found it to be reasonably stylish. Not only that, from where she was sitting it appeared as though Magdalena's freshly washed hair was also sporting a glossy new colour.

Cornelia had always firmly believed, that the only real cure for stress and trauma was to immediately indulge yourself with a little pampering and with that in mind; she decided to quiz Magdalena about her hair.

"Magdalena, may I call you Maggie?" she began. "I must say your hair is looking awfully stylish today, compared to how it looked yesterday," she sniped, as she watched Magdalena's waggling head.

"The thing is, Magdalena, I am not feeling terribly well today and so I think a nice little visit to the hairdresser would do me the world of good. Do you understand what I am saying, Cut,Cut,Cut." Cornelia made cutting motions with her fingers as she emphasised the word cut. "Actually, I just need a little trim not too much," she explained. "Is there any hairdresser nearby that you could recommend to me?"

"Una momento Signora Ooopabyta," Magdalena replied. She narrowed her eyes and pursed her mouth into a little round circle, she touched her own hair and continued, "Scusa I wanna cheeck to you, Wotta you say. Allora you Aska to me, Eef I can tell to you, somebody who will fix uppa yourra hair today?"

"Well yes, I should like to have my hair trimmed today and I asked you if you knew anybody who could do it for me?" Cornelia replied, taking a sip of her tea.

"OK, Eeef You want, I canna take you to my Cousin's shop, she is a verry verry nice how you say, 'Hair Dryer' and I am sure at theese moment she can fix uppa your hair whichever way you like it."

"Do you mean a Hair Dresser? Is your cousin a Hair Dresser?" Cornelia asked, with just a hint of a smile.

"Si, she is the Parrucchiere, her job is to make the Old hair to look verry pretty again. Like you say Cut,Cut,Cut."

"The shop, is it far from here? I mean how would we get there?" Suddenly distracted by Alistair's squeaky voice, Cornelia instinctively looked across the room and discovered Algernon and Alistair were having a very private conversation, over by the window. Continuing to watch, as best as she could, she noticed this little 'Tete a Tete' also included the exchange of money, wallets and fingers on lips.

"Signora," Magdalena insisted loudly, "It is a very close by to here and I have with me today my son's auto. Eeef you like, after I clean the she-its I can take you to her."

"Good," Cornelia said, bringing her attention back to Magdalena. "Can you also bring me back? I am afraid I don't have a license to drive in Italy. I would need someone to drive me there as well as bring me back again."

"Si Signora," Magdalena waggled her head earnestly. "I see it is a very important for you to change your hair today, so for me it will be a very big pleasure to take you there. But Signora I amma very sorry today is the day I will go to see my Mother. It is so very important that I go to her today. She is now a very old woman and she doesn't like to be alone. But I theenk after my cousin try everything to fix Uppa your hair she can bring you back to the ouse", she smiled brightly.

"Oh, I am not terribly keen on the idea of asking somebody I hardly know to ferry me about the town. Perhaps if you give Alistair your cousin's address he can pick me up after a couple of hours. Is that all right with you Alistair?" She called out, clearly hoping to derail any suspicious alliances.

"What? Are you insane Mother?" Alistair snapped. He started to walk back over to her. "Do you really think that I could walk into the town and back again with the dogs and then take Horatio's bomb of a car and pick you up, all in the space of two hours?" He sneered at her.

"Ohh Signora, I am very sure my cousin doesn't mind too much, Eeef you have to stay a little longer with her in the shop. She loves to talk Hinglish with so many people from London, it would be for her a very big pleasure. Then when it is the *Siesta* she can take you in her car into the town and your Alistair, he can meet you there O Kay?"

Cornelia, was feeling slightly confused but she was also quite keen to get her hair done. So, without thinking about it too much, she nodded her head in agreement.

"Very well then it is settled. I shall go with Magdalena to her cousin's shop to have my hair done. Alistair, you will take the dogs  for a much needed walk and then pick me up later in Horatio's car. So then, that only leaves you Algernon," she stated as she fixed him with her famous icy stare. "What may I ask are your plans for the rest of the day?"

"Oh I think I shall just potter around here for a little while dear. Horatio did ask me to attend to a few things for him whilst we are staying in the Villa. I should imagine that will keep me busy for the rest of the day, My Dear."

Just when it finally seemed as though things were starting to settle down and a sense of calm had been bestowed upon them again, an incredibly loud screeching sound, travelled in from the smoking room next door and completely shattered this fragile semblance of peace.

"Mama Mia," cried out Magdalena. "I theenk Sebastionne is a very ungry. Signore Horeatzio he always tells to me. That this is the time, Sebastionne he can eat the hind leg from the doggie." Magdalena stood there wringing her hands in despair, whilst they all gawked back at her, completely aghast.

"Yes well, I shall go in and attend to him then shall I." Algernon offered, eventually breaking the ice. "Let me go and see what the fuss is all about."

## 9. SWINGS AND ROUNDABOUTS

Strike whilst the iron is hot. *Batti il ferro quando è caldo.*

Once he was inside the heavily draped, musty room, Algernon breathed out a much needed sigh of relief, as he considered how narrowly he had escaped the wrath of not only Cornelia, but Alistair as well.

As he cautiously approached the oversized bird cage, he noticed the outline of Sebastion's large wide wings, flapping backwards and forwards under the malevolent black cover that Horatio had placed there the night before. As it moved up and down it seemed to generate a sinister kind of energy that increased significantly with every spasmodic move of the bird. Algernon shuddered deeply, as bright vivid visions of the Klu Klux Klan and International Debt Collectors surged in and assaulted his tired old mind.

Reaching his arm out, as far as he could go, without getting too close to the cage, he whipped the cover off quickly and was quite startled when he discovered two dark beady eyes staring directly back at him.

Sebastion standing on one leg and as close to the bars as possible, was busily chewing on the last remnants of a chunk of blue vein cheese. He looked even more bizarre than he usually did, as he held the cheese in his other claw and bobbed up and down, to some strange rhythm that nobody else could hear.

Algernon surveyed the situation cautiously and noticed that the container holding the bird seed was almost empty.

"So this is what all the Squawking is about old chap?" He asked as he reached in and grabbed it quickly, making sure he didn't accidentally come into contact with any other part of Sebastion's bloated, feathery, body.

Carefully locking the cage door again, he felt genuinely relieved that nothing was seriously wrong with the bird. After all, according to Horatio this type of bird was quite rare and was worth well over twenty thousand pounds and therefore would be nigh on impossible to replace.

Algernon felt a deep pang of anxiety strike him to the core when he heard the sound of angry voices coming from the room next door. Standing all alone in the darkened room, he instantly bit down hard on his quivering bottom lip when he realised, it was only a matter of time before he would have to go back into the lion's den.

As he reluctantly turned to leave, a strange light headed sensation washed all over him and for a minute or two the room turned completely black as he stood there teetering and tottering from side to side, trying hard not to lose his balance. He finally opened his eyes again just as the room had almost stopped spinning. Looking out into the semi darkness, his eyes were instinctively drawn to a colourful painting hanging on the wall on the opposite side of the room.

From where he was standing it appeared to have a brilliant kind of glow around it. In the first instance, it seemed as though this may have been caused, by the single shard of sunlight that was bouncing from the slit in the drapes and back onto the edges of its gilded frame. Now, however, when he looked at it again, the bright multi coloured lights, dancing around the edges, like a mural in a kaleidoscope, seemed to hold more of a magnetic kind of quality that almost bordered on the mystical.

Algernon, completely bedazzled by this pleasant sensation, dropped the bird feeder to the ground and stood mesmerised, as the bright light bursting from the edge of the painting captivated his senses and beckoned him over.

Like a man possessed, Algernon walked across the room, desperate now to get a closer look at exactly what it was that was drawing him in so powerfully. As he moved closer and closer towards the painting, he started to feel his weary soul soar.

Finally standing in front of the glowing artwork, he gasped loudly and trembled from head to toe when he realised exactly what it was about the precious artwork that had touched him so profoundly.

The heartwarming image, which was so brilliantly painted on the ancient canvas, depicted the simple scene of a

'Kind and Loving family,' that were sitting together at a crude earthy table, as they shared the festive food and drink of a special celebration.

Feeling deeply touched, by such genuinely innocent images, Algernon couldn't stop himself from reaching out and embracing the painting. As he laid his face against the age old canvas he was overwhelmed by a deep warm glow and an enormous sense of peace flowed through him. Sad to say, this surreal sense of harmony was only ever short lived and unfortunately came to a very abrupt end when the painting fell off the wall and came crashing down to the ground.

Reaching out with both hands he grabbed it up again and still feeling slightly dazed, he held it out before him, desperately longing to rekindle the wondrous feelings he had enjoyed ever so briefly. Algernon couldn't really tell how long he remained standing there. Strangely, time seemed to stand still. It may have only been for a few minutes but then again it really felt like a lifetime. But there was one thing he knew for certain. After this wonderfully unique experience, he no longer felt afraid. Actually, he finally knew, what it was, that he needed to do and how he was going to do it.

So, just like a blighted old soul, who had finally seen the light, he put the painting back on the wall, checked the time on his faithful old fob watch and peacefully walked out of the room, feeling like a brand new man.

"Diamonds are a girl's best friend," squawked Sebastion,

before he went back to chewing the remains of his blue vein cheese.

# 10 ALL A MAN CAN WANT

Alistair sneered in disgust when Winston stopped rudely to cock his hind leg up against the wheels of the shiny new BMW parked defiantly in the Piazza beside the Café. He discreetly looked around the square hoping nobody else especially the owner had seen this tawdry display of carnal needs. Pulling hard on the metal chain he jerked the dog back into line again and continued to walk up the stairs into the lively open air café.

Sitting down at the nearest available table he picked up the menu and made a snap decision to have a coffee and a bite to eat before going back to the house. "After all," he reasoned he had been walking with the blasted dogs for at least half an hour and at this point he was starting to feel quite hungry. He had barely had a chance to investigate the menu when a young athletic looking waitress approached the table and greeted him with the standard, "Buongiorno."

Looking up from the menu, he quickly discovered that she was wearing a rather unorthodox ensemble for a waitress. Scrutinising her a little more closely he noticed her outfit consisted of a pair of black leather hot pants, an orange Lycra body suit and a pair of heavy steel capped work boots. These were topped off with a pair of thick black woollen socks that sported a pair of colourful bird feathers on either side.

"Good Afternoon," Alistair responded after checking his watch to confirm it was indeed after midday. "I would like a cappuccino, mild not too strong, a slice of ham and cheese pizza, not too spicy and some water in a bowl for the dogs," he said looking her up and down. "By the way, it is all right isn't it if I have the dogs in here with me? I mean we are in Europe after all and that's what you people do here isn't it. You don't mind if you eat with your animals, do you?" He finished with a smirk.

"Scusa Signore, I am afraid we don't have available any of the ham and cheese Pizza, but we do have a Prosciutto and Formaggio Pizza and about the doggies, yes they can stay here and eat with you, but I cannot serve them any water."

"I am sorry did you say you had no Ham and Cheese Pizza? My GOD I find that unbelievable. I mean Italy is known all over the world for its ham and cheese and the idea of not having a pizza of that type is simply Ludicrous. Even my local take away, back home in Highgate, serves Ham and Cheese pizzas. This is just outrageous;" he snorted. He pulled back hard on the lead when he noticed Churchill was just about to perform what could only be described as an obscene gesture, involving one of the young ladies feathered legs.

"Si Signore," she replied after stepping back cautiously. "I do know Italy is famous for the Cheeses and the Ham and that is why I try to tell you we have the Prosciutto and Formaggio Pizza. You must understand this is the same words in Italian for the Ham and Cheese," she advised. She stared back at him with steady eyes.

Before he had a chance to even consider an apology the conversation was brought to an abrupt end by the sudden onset of loud barking. Alistair had momentarily let their lead go slack in his hand and he jerked forward violently as both dogs rushed out excitedly from beneath the table, to confront the tiny manicured toy poodle that was now yipping and yapping as it boldly approached them. The waitress, wisely wanting to avoid any more confrontations quickly sidestepped the oncoming pooch as she made her way back through the open doors.

Not content to simply bark at this new arrival, both Winston and Churchill preceded to run up to the dog's owner, who just so happened to be a very attractive young woman and wedge their way between her shapely legs, inadvertently tangling their lead with the long leather straps that were flowing from her expensive French handbag.

Trying hard to pull away as best she could, the young woman let out a shriek of horror as the contents of her bag spilled all over the floor of the café. Revealing no less than six lipsticks, three mobile phones and four packets of cigarettes.

Feeling panic rise up in the back of his throat, Alistair who at this stage was standing up on his feet, instinctively began to pull back hard on the lead hoping to curtail any more manic activity. Unfortunately in his haste he had failed to notice the lead had accidentally wrapped its way around the woman's very stylish stiletto heel, causing her to lose her balance and fall forward into thin air as he jerked hard at it again.

Visions of horror momentarily flitted through his mind as the sound of her high pitched wail filled his ears. However just when he thought an unstoppable disaster was imminent, the falling woman as if in slow motion, gently dropped down like a floating feather into his outstretched arms and by some bizarre stroke of luck, he found her two ample breasts had come to rest neatly into the palms of his pale trembling hands.

Alistair stood there completely flabbergasted for just a moment as he battled hard to digest the notion "that none other than the Universe," via a divine twist of fate, had granted him absolute permission to hang onto the breasts of an extraordinarily beautiful young woman, In Public!

Not wishing to ruin what could only be described as a truly "Ecstatic" moment, he slowly pushed upwards with his strong agile hands. All the while savouring every fragment of a millisecond until the woman was finally standing upright in front of him.

As he stood there panting, Alistair felt as though time had ultimately stood still as he looked directly into the face of the most beautiful woman he had ever seen. Looking more intensely into her large blue eyes, he also got the feeling that she too was aware of the sudden connection that had miraculously blossomed between them.

"This is incredible", he marvelled. "Who would've thought such a thing was possible. Now I know WHY I had to come here today. I can't fight fate. Not when it has given me such a golden opportunity. This is definitely meant to be! Otherwise why would I have ever had the chance to hold onto her amazing Tits?'

Realising by her completely blank expression, that she was still slightly dazed and possibly disoriented, Alistair heroically held her tightly across the shoulders whilst she managed to steady herself and regain her composure.

Eventually after what had seemed like a lifetime, this rare and beautiful moment, finally started to recede and was broken by a fresh new bout of barking as the dogs renewed their hyper active advances towards her.

The patrons in the café quite convinced by now that the show was over, slowly turned back to their tables and resumed their eating and drinking, amidst a constant flow of loud Italian chatter.

"I am terribly sorry," he offered in a trembling voice. "Are you all right?" And then almost to himself, "Oh you probably can't understand English."

"Yes I am OK," she replied curtly. "But where is my dog?" "Fifi," she cried out tearfully. "Fifi where are you Darlink? Come to Mumma."

Turning her back on him as if to walk away she almost

stumbled again as the lead pulled tighter at her ankle. Alistair, aware by now that she was referring to the little dog that had started all the commotion in the first place, looked around wildly, hoping against all hope that nothing would possibly ruin this magical opportunity. He pulled back hard on the lead and in the nicest possible tone he could muster; he ordered both Winston and Churchill to SIT.

"Please take a seat, you must be shaken," he said returning his attention back to her as he swiftly pulled out one of the chairs. "Why don't you sit down here and let me look for your dog." He asked patting the table with his hand. "I am sure Fifi, that is your little dog's name isn't it? Couldn't be too far away," he consoled her with a cheesy smile.

Just then the waitress, who had taken his order earlier, reappeared holding a pot of coffee and two large slices of Pizza. Alistair whipped the pizza off the plate as fast as he could and forcefully threw it under the table for the dogs.

"Here stick this down your trap and don't move," he hissed quietly through his clenched teeth. "Any more trouble out of either of you it will be the dog's house for the rest of the year," he threatened.

Returning back to a sitting position again, he couldn't help noticing the confused expression flitting across the face of his accidental guest. "Amazing isn't it," he stated. "How much they love the food here. Pizza has always been one of their favourites."

"Excuse me, but I must look for my dog," the woman said. She began to untangle herself from the lead.

"I am afraid that won't be necessary," Alistair chimed. "Here she is," he announced cheerfully, holding out his upturned palms.

Looking behind her, the woman was overwhelmed with gratitude, when she saw her cute little pooch, none the worse for wear, staring back at her from the arms of the waitress who had delivered the coffee and pizza.

"Fifi" She squealed, as she reached out and grabbed her.

"And do these belong to you also Signora?" The waitress said handing over the large Louis Vuitton bag, the spilt contents now, all neatly restored.

"Yes, yes, Grazie," she replied tenderly hugging the dog to her heaving breasts.

Alistair, definitely not wanting to let this chance for true love, slip away from his grasp, quickly leapt into action. "Oh thank God," he exclaimed feigning concern. "I was worried sick. Please let me make it up to you. Can I order you something a cup of coffee, a glass of water perhaps?"

"Yes thank you," she replied in a heavy eastern European accent, "And maybe a Puppacino for Fifi."

"Yes certainly," as he turned back to the waitress. "Make that two Cappuccinos, two more slices of that delicious pizza and one Puppacino for our dearest little Fifi". He gave the dogs a slight kick, when he felt them strain against the lead in their latest attempt to escape.

Not wishing to be embroiled in any more drama the waitress sensibly scurried back towards the kitchen, leaving them to sort out their imminent introductions.

Sitting alone for a few long moments Alistair wracked his brains for something meaningful to say. After all he didn't even know the woman's name.

"So do you come from here?" He asked, casually. He was trying hard to disguise the edge in his voice.

"No," she replied. "I come from Estonia but I have been living in Pastacula for the past year. I am learning Italian."

"Oh Estonia, what a beautiful country. I have heard so much about it from all my friends who have been there. They said it was like the Paris of the East." He smiled wistfully, giving Winston and Churchill another firm nudge under the table with his foot.

"Really what part of Estonia did they visit?" She asked as she gently stroked Fifi, who had fallen asleep in her lap.

"Oh Aahh let me think now. Hmm let me see ….. I think it was ….. Hmm ….it's on the tip of my tongue …… I think it may have been the capital, yes, yes it was the capital."

"Tallinn, they must have been to Tallinn that is the name of the capital of Estonia. Yes it is a beautiful city. What about you? Where do you come from? I think you are not Italian. Are you studying here too? "

"Oh you could say that. Actually it's a bit of a long story nothing to bother your pretty little head about now," he laughed lightly.

"So you are Italian?" She asked.

"Oh Good heavens no. How terribly rude of me. I forgot to introduce myself. I think it must have been your dazzling beauty that distracted me. Do you have a map, I keep getting lost in your eyes," he said as he looked her up and down with a sleazy leer.

"Sorry, I do not understand, why do you want to know if I have a Map? She fluttered her long black eyelashes at him.

Alistair burned with embarrassment, when he realized how badly he had handled that last attempt to chat her up. Deciding to push on rather than explain he wasted no time and introduced himself. 'After all', he contemplated; a bird in the hand is worth two in the bush.

"Alistair," he said holding out his hand. "And you are?"

"Sophia but my friends call me Sophie," she said, taking his hand for a moment before going back to patting the dog.

"Oh Sophia such a beautiful name for such a beautiful woman, may I call you Sophie?"

"Yes, if you like. Do you mind if I smoke?" she asked. Reaching into her bag she pulled out a cigarette and lighter."

"Certainly not, I sometimes indulge in a cigarette myself."

"Thank you, not many people agree with smoking in public places," she said poking the cigarette into her puckered up mouth.

"I know and to tell the truth, I think it is absolutely shocking the way smokers are treated these days as if they were some sort of social leper. For goodness sake, a little bit of indulgence here and there never hurt anyone," he said. He was trying hard not to stare at her breasts.

"Everybody smokes in Estonia," she admitted as she inhaled deeply on the cigarette. "We have a joke back home in my country that says. If the baby is born without the cigarette in its mouth then you should send it back." She laughed loudly, blowing great gusts of smoke into his face.

"Oh yes," Alistair laughed, "I have heard that one before, very funny," he said. He shook his head up and down.

"So why are you here in Pastacula?" She eyed him off suspiciously.

"Oh yes I didn't quite get around to telling you did I? Well as I said before it is a long story, but to cut a very long story short, you could say I have come here to learn," he declared earnestly.

"Learn? Do you mean a language?" She tilted her pretty head to one side.

"Well yes, that is part of it. You see, I normally live in England on a huge estate in the Countryside and as well as that I have a lovely little apartment in Highgate for when I feel like a bit of fun." He leered at her bountiful breasts in a lopsided sort of way.

"So as you could imagine, I have a very nice little life and to top it all off, I speak English too," he explained in a patronizing tone. He sat up as straight as he could in the cheap wicker chair. "But the truth is Sophie," Alistair looked at her intensely as he drew both his fists up to his chest. "Deep down I have always wanted to live abroad in another foreign country and I have always wanted to help other people less fortunate than myself. You see, I have always wanted to go someplace where I would be forced to learn another language. My ultimate goal really, is to become a global citizen and learn as many languages as I can," he confessed, flashing a warm benevolent smile that even the Dalai Lama could not compete with.

Sophia was stubbing out the remains of her cigarette just as the waitress delivered the pizzas and coffee to the table. Rearranging Fifi on her lap, she reached across and picked up a cup of coffee and as she did so, she touched Alistair, ever so lightly on the hand.

"I think you must be a very kind man," she said in a silken voice. Gazing at him, from beneath her eyelashes she took a long sip from her cup.

"Oh not really, it's nothing," Alistair replied bashfully. Looking away quickly, he tried hard to disguise the surge of excitement that caused his body to throb and his pupils to dilate.

Grabbing at his plate for the food, he threw another piece of Pizza, under the table. "The thing is Sophie," he replied looking up at her again. "At the end of the day I get back so much more than I ever give. For example, I get to see all these wonderful old buildings and I get to go to all the Museums and on top of all that I get to have coffee with a gorgeous woman like you," he smiled, his hand shook up and down as he reached for his cup of coffee.

"Oh you love history too? Such a surprise, so do I," Sophia beamed back.

"Well yes, I was only saying this morning to Magdalena, one of the locals, I am helping here. That if I managed to find some time, after completing all my important duties. I would love to visit a good museum."

"Oh that is very interesting, did you know there is a very famous Museum here in Pastacula?"

"Really? What a surprise, I had no idea! I should take a look when I get a chance. Is it close by?"

"Yes, it is very close. Actually it is, how do you say in English, Just a Skip and a hop and a Jump away from here," she smiled back sweetly.

"So you have been there already?" Alistair asked with a disappointed look.

"Yes, I went some time ago with one of my Italian friends. But I was thinking to go again tomorrow because at this time, they have the special Exhibition on Roman Empire in Pastacula and it will be finished after this week."

"Well yes, that would be very interesting. I had absolutely no idea the Romans actually lived in Pastacula; that's amazing. You see Sophie, that's what I mean about learning. Since I have been here I have found I learn something new every day". He smiled smugly and took another long sip of his coffee.

"I know the museum opens around ten tomorrow morning. If you like, you could go there with me. Are you free in the morning?" She asked politely, as she lovingly stroked Fifi's head.

"What a coincidence!" Alistair exclaimed shaking his head in disbelief. "I had only just written Sightseeing in my diary, for tomorrow morning's activities, just before you arrived."

"So you will come?" She asked coyly as she reached into her bag.

Alistair could barely disguise his glee as he watched her pull out a petite hot pink, diamante studded, designer telephone. 'Practically eating from the palm of my hand,' he calculated. He felt dizzy beyond belief with excitement.

However, despite his roller coaster feelings, he still managed to sit there coolly. He casually flipped the lid of the sugar container up and down, up and down, trying very hard not to appear too eager. 'Any minute now she's going to give me her telephone number,' he thought smugly.

Then, without any warning, a loud sound similar to somebody playing a trumpet underwater erupted from under the table. Prrrrrrruppppp it resonated proudly. This was followed immediately by a foul smelling stench that rapidly rose up around them and without wasting a second, engulfed the heavy sticky air that lay between them.

Sophia couldn't hide the shocked expression of disgust that was written all over her face as she looked across at Alistair, with a curled lip and startled eyes.

You could have heard a pin drop as they sat there in the uncomfortable silence, punctuated only by the steady sound of a dog snoring.

Alistair felt the blood run cold in his veins as he fished about in his numb mind for something sensible to say. "Looks as though I will have to cut back on the amount of Pizza I give them," he remarked light heartedly. Realising she was still staring back at him, he added. "I must say they are not normally like this; I think it's all the travel they have done over the last couple of days."

"Travel? I thought you said you had been here for a few months now," Sophia stated as she energetically waved a napkin back and forth in front of her.

"Yes, yes, I have," Alistair back pedaled quickly. "When I say travel, I don't mean travel as in Travel to faraway places. I just mean Travel as in around here. You know from the house and back," he explained waving his arm across the room to indicate a sense of distance.

"Oh dear look at the time," Sophia finally exclaimed. Glancing down at her phone she started to gather up her personal belongings, including Fifi and placed them all into her oversized bag. "It has been a pleasure to meet you, but now I am sorry I really must get going. The post office will soon be closed and I must send a very important letter today," she announced as she arose from the table.

All the colour completely drained away from Alistair's previously flushed face as he sat watching her in a stunned silence. Suddenly realising what was at stake he managed to regain some of his composure and like a man fighting for his life he sprang into action. Jumping up from the table he pulled her elbow slightly back towards him, as she turned to leave.

"But you just can't leave. What about tomorrow? What about the museum? The Roman exhibition?" He pleaded. "We haven't made any arrangements"; he declared in a high pitched squeak.

"Yes of course, you are right I forgot." She turned back around to face him. "OK, If you like we can meet here again tomorrow morning at ten. Then after that we can walk to the museum. As I told you before, it is not very far from here," she said, her lip still curling.

"Oh, so we should just meet here then?" He asked. "You don't want to exchange phone numbers in case anything changes?"

"Nothing will change," she smiled, as she started to walk off. "I will be sure to be there. As I told you it is the last day of the Exhibition and I don't want to miss it," she said over her shoulder. She walked away from the table and out onto the square.

Not quite sure whether he should cheer or curse, Alistair stood at the table and watched her intently as she strutted confidently towards the badly parked BMW and got in. She started the engine and elegantly drove off, slowing down for just a moment to give him a tiny wave of her hand as she passed by the café.

He watched until she had completely vanished from sight before he turned his attention back to the sleeping dogs. He didn't know whether he wanted to hug them or kick them or both. After all, if it wasn't for them he would never have met Sophie in the first place but then again if they hadn't farted so offensively she may still be here talking to him. 'Oh well' he mused. 'There was nothing he could do about it now, he would just have to let sleeping dogs lie,' he consoled himself as he tugged at the lead to wake them.

## 11 PAINTING AND PAPERWORK

Algernon entered the elegant baroque building through a dark metallic door that had a gold plated plaque, with the word Entrata written in bold black letters above it.

Bearing in mind his limited grasp of the Italian language and his lack of familiarity with the area it was amazing that he had found it so quickly. However also bearing in mind he was a '*Man on a Mission*', it really wasn't that surprising at all.

After being asked to wait in the reception area by a tall, blonde attractive woman, Algernon had hardly had time to consider his good luck before being ushered into the small poky office of Antonio Pomponio, the 'lacklustre' Proprietor of the business.

"Buongiorno Signore how can I help you today?" He asked tiredly, through a pair of taut lips a perfect complement to his fixed, impassive, expression.

"Oh you speak English, old chap?" Algernon boomed gratefully. Squishing himself carefully into the small antique arm chair, he gingerly tried to manoeuvre the painting he had wedged under his armpit, towards the front of the desk.

"Yes I lived in London for many years whilst I was studying at University. I also attended the British Institute here," he replied mechanically with a wry smile. "May I introduce myself, my name is Antonio Pomponio, how may I help you this morning Signore?" His steel grey eyes looked Algernon over, with just a hint of disdain.

"Oh yes, quite right, we haven't been introduced yet have we? The name is Uberbite, Algernon Oswald Uberbite the Third" he announced stretching his tweed clad arm out across the desk.

"Well I must say this is a very pleasant office you have here," Algernon began to blather. "And the Dame at the desk is not too bad on the old eye either," he laughed as he waggled his hand.

Antonio gazed back at him in stony faced silence. He shook Algernon's hand weakly for just a moment, before pulling away again.

"Yes, that Dame at the desk, is my sister, she has been working here with me for many years. Actually she recently became a Nonna. Do you understand? In Italian this means a grandmother," he said through semi clenched teeth. "Once again how can I help you Mr Uberbite?" he asked irritably.

Algernon had gathered by now that Signore Pomponio was not in the least bit amused. Acutely aware that he may have caused offense he was genuinely eager to avoid any more awkward situations. With that in mind he decided to launch into his little spiel before anything else untoward could happen.

Putting on a brave front he smiled as broadly as he could, both of his cheeks were extended to their fullest capacity and his moustache was raised at least one inch above his lips. Lifting his mammoth eyebrows innocently, he opened his eyes wide hoping to exude as much warmth as possible and began.

"Well as you can see I have brought this marvellous work of art with me today and I would very much appreciate it if you could give me an estimated figure regarding its true value and worth," he announced, with a confident nod of his head.

Antonio leaned forward and stared intensely at the large painting held out before him. After a few terse moments of head nodding scrutiny, he straightened up. He looked Algernon in the eye and asked cautuiously, "Signore Uberbite, can you tell me please where exactly did you get this painting from?"

Algernon, not quite anticipating that kind of response, hesitated for a moment before replying. "Oh it was given to me some years ago by an old friend as a birthday gift," he said, as he tugged at the tight loop of his necktie. He always developed an itchy patch around his neck whenever he was stressed.

Antonio sat bolt upright in his chair, causing his body to take on a rather rigid appearance and clasped his two hands together tightly. He made sure both elbows were neatly resting on top of the desk before responding.

"Signore Uberbite, the reason I ask you theeese question is because theeese painting looks very much like a valuable painting by the famous French artist Jean Baptiste Greuze called the Epiphany. He was one of Europe's first well known celebrity artists."

"Hmmmm how interesting it just goes to show, doesn't it? You learn something new every day," he laughed. He shook his head. "By the way, what exactly do you mean when you say Celebrity artist? The only celebrity artist I have ever heard of is Andy Warhol. Do you mean to say this Baptiste chap and Andy were one of a kind? Frankly, I find that astounding," Algernon clicked his tongue loudly.

"Signore Uberbite, I can assure you Jean Baptiste Greuze was nothing like your 'Andy Warhol'. Actually he was, how can I say it nicely, the complete opposite. For example theees painting you have bought here was made for the purpose of praising and encouraging the virtue and goodness of a simple family life. It was made like this on purpose as a message for the everyday people. You understand what I mean? It was like a contrast if you like. Signore Uberbite, Greuze's painting makes it very clear that the simple pleasures of the honest, peasant family should never be corrupted by the temptations of how you say, 'a modern, bourgeois life. Usually the owner of such a famous artwork would know about the story it holds." Pomponio folded his arms across his chest and glared back at him with flint like narrowed eyes.

"Oh yes…. Yes you are quite right, it is indeed a ….. Errrr …… very fine and virtuous painting." Algernon loosened his thick necktie just a little more. "And as you have already mentioned very valuable indeed and it is for precisely that reason that I wish to have it valued. Purely for the purpose of insurance you understand?" He nodded his head sagely, shaking his wide girth from side to side like a big giant jelly as he tried to sit further back into the chair.

"In that case Signore Uberbite, I would need to see the documents of Authenticity as well as the certificate of ownership before we could proceed any further," Pomponio replied stiffly, his arms still folded.

Algernon squirmed around for a few moments and gently lowered the painting onto the floor, making sure it was completely out of view before he began his response. "Of course and again quite right," he exclaimed. "One just can't expect you to pull out a value from thin air. I entirely agree it is completely reasonable to ask for the supporting documents. However given the fact, we are both very busy people, would it be possible to give me in your opinion perhaps, just a rough estimate, a sort of ball-park figure if you like of exactly how much this painting is worth?" He smiled thinly.

"Signore Uberbite, theesa business has been in my family for generations. Actually we were the very first Art dealers to set up and work in this city. It is because of this that we take a great pride in our reputation and are not accustomed to giving anybody," he paused for a moment, "How do you say, a Balls Park figure or otherwise, without first receiving the required certificates and documentation."

It was clear by the exasperated expression plastered all

over Algernon's face and the blotchy red patches that were rapidly spreading across his cheeks that he felt completely astounded by this last little snippet of news.

Signore Pomponio, tap, tap, tapped his pen on the antique wooden table for a few more moments before deciding to break the silence that had hijacked the discussion.

"Of course," Pomponio began again, "You may like to conseeder another kind of establishment in theesa town but Eeef you go ahead and do that Signore I must a warn you to be very very careful. Let me tell you Signore Uberbite, just because somebody tells you they are an art dealer it doesn't mean they are. Unfortunately some people have had to learn theees lesson the harda way."

"I am not exactly too sure what you are getting at old chap," Algernon blustered.

"Signore Uberbite, I know of some cases where good people like you have taken their Precious Artworks to so called Art Dealers. Only to find much later that the originals have been replaced with a worthless counterfeit painting. This, I tell you is truly tragic," he shook his head, the stiff wide collar of his impeccable shirt, never moved once.

"Yes, Yes, I see and rightly so, one can't be too casual about these things can one? Especially in this part of the world," he laughed. "You know, What with the mafia lurking about and all that. I suppose you would need to keep your nose clean," Algernon laughed again as he started to manoeuvre himself out of the chair.

"Signore Uberbite, I can assure you I have absolutely no knowledge whatsoever of the mafia and any criminal activities they may be involved in. We are a reputable business and as such require certain procedures are followed before we can give out any advice." He stood up and held out his hand.

"Oh of course certainly, that goes without saying," Algernon said as he moved away from the desk. "One can't be too careful these days can one?" He made a hasty retreat across the room, the painting firmly wedged under his armpit again. "Especially when you consider all those dreadful horror stories one hears about in those Holly wood movies," he wheezed loudly as he reached the door. "Well thank you for your time Signore Pomponio, I shall go home immediately and collect the necessary required documents and return as soon as possible. We wouldn't want to run into any Monkey Business now would we?" He added, in a contrite tone as he winked at Antonio.

"Signore Uberbite, I am afraid that will not be possible, we are closed this afternoon and quite possibly for the rest of the week," Antonio announced as he joined him at the open door. "I am afraid we have some very important family matters to attend to," he nodded his head over towards the reception desk.

"Oh, oh, I see," exclaimed Algernon, slightly dejected. "Well it shall have to wait until next week then," he boomed, as he headed towards the exit door. He then bid an obligatory "Good day" to the other people sitting patiently in the reception room and hurriedly left the building.

Algernon hadn't really noticed the short swarthy man when he was inside Signore Pomponio's office, but he did notice the man exiting the building, when he stood outside on the pavement and  wiped away at the torrents of sweat that were cascading from his furry brow.

He was just about to head off down the street and back into his car when he noticed the man was approaching him.

"Scusa are you English?" He asked, holding a card out towards Algernon.

"I am sorry old chap," I don't speak Italian. Now if you will excuse me I really need to go somewhere."

"It's a OK, I speak a little English. Please I think you needa my help," he said thrusting the card into Algernon's hand.

Algernon reluctantly took the card from the stranger and stared down at the foreign language long and hard. He was obviously looking for any clues that might shed some light on what this little man might want from him.

"I am sorry, but frankly I don't know what this has got to do with me. Now if you will excuse me I really must go." He handed back the card.

"No wait please, I canna explain," the stranger offered.

"OK, before, when I was sitting in the waiting room of Signore Pomponio I heard him tell to you it was not possible to take your painting without all the Documenta Si?"

"Yes that is correct but what has that got to do with you?" Algernon asked. He jostled the heavy painting over to his other arm.

"Signore I also am an art dealer and I have a good friend who is the same as me," he said pointing to his card. "Theesa friend will accept, theesa very nice painting without any problemo, you understand what I try to say to you?"

"Si, I mean Yes, I think I do. You said you are an art dealer too and you have a friend who is also an art dealer and this friend would be willing to accept this painting without any documents," Algernon looked at him suspiciously.

"Bravo Signore you speaka very nice Italian. Please, if you want I can take you to join him tomorrow morning. It is not too far from here."

Algernon looked at the stranger and then at the card and then back at the stranger again. "So correct me if I am wrong. According to this card your name is Donato and you have a friend who lives not too far from here, who would be interested in this painting."

"Si Correct, Signore, Signore …. Oh Scusa I haven't introduced my name to you. My Name it is Donato

Moroni and please can you give me your good name?"

"Algernon, Algernon Uberbite," he countered holding out his hand.

"Very pleased to meet you," Donato pulled Algernon's large girth towards him victoriously and placed a hurried kiss on both sides of his sweaty face.

"So, when can I meet this friend of yours?" Algernon inquired, swiftly pulling himself away.

"Tomorrow morning would be perfecto. I can wait here again and meet you, and then you can follow me in my car. It is not too far from here, maybe five or ten minutes."

"And this friend of yours does he understand English?"

"Yes Signore, hizza English is much better than mine, he went to the school to learn. Do you know the English school here?"

"Hmm, I see, and your friend will he understand that I don't want to sell the painting? I simply want an evaluation."

"Signore my friend he can do for you whatever you like. Just you come back to here tomorrow morning at 10 am and afterwards we can go together to discuss everything with him," he offered with a broad smile.

"All right then," granted Algernon. "I shall see you here tomorrow morning at ten and then we shall go to your friend's house together. But please be aware, this is a very "Private Matter" and I don't want anyone else involved, let's just keep it between ourselves," Algernon tapped the side of his nose with his index finger.

"Si Signore, I understand everything must be just like in 'James Bond', how you say 'Top Secret'," he replied tapping Algernon lightly on the shoulder.

"Very well then. Good heavens look at the time!" Algernon stared at his fob watch. "I am afraid I really must go. Needless to say I have things to do, people to see." Standing a safe distance away, he held out his hand.

"Si Signore Oooperbyta I know for the Americano's the time it is so important, it is just like the money. It is been very much a pleasure to meet you today and until tomorrow, I say to you goodbye and good day," he proclaimed proudly as he held out his hand.

"Yes, yes, likewise," blurted Algernon, eager now to get out of the sun. "Arrivederci," he said taking his hand and shaking it vigourously. "See you tomorrow."

Algernon plodded painfully along the pavement as he lugged the heavy canvas back again towards the car. With his heart pounding and his head spinning he wasn't quite sure what to make of the whole situation.However, despite all his worries and confusion there was one thing he was definitely sure of. 'Hell could freeze over a dozen times and more, before he would be foolish enough to wear his jacket again, during the height of the midday sun.'

<table>
<tr><th colspan="3">INSTAPOL POLICE REPORT</th></tr>
<tr><td>Agent Guido Ventosi</td><td>Day: Two/ Midday</td><td>File Number 1200/12/20098</td></tr>
<tr><td>CASE</td><td>LOCATION</td><td>Report No</td></tr>
<tr><td>Uberbite Surveillance</td><td>Car Park Pastacula</td><td>3</td></tr>
<tr><td colspan="3">Persons of Interest<br>Algernon Uberbite, Cornelia Uberbite, Alistair Uberbite</td></tr>
<tr><td colspan="3">ACTIVITIES</td></tr>
<tr><td colspan="3">11.15 Algernon Uberbite visited Pomponio Art Dealers with a large painting under his arm.<br>11.40 Algernon Uberbite exited Pomponio Art dealer's with a large painting under his arm.<br>11.41 Algernon Uberbite was followed outside by a male Caucasian.<br>11.42 Algernon Uberbite was approached by the same male Caucasian who followed him outside.<br>11.44 Algernon Uberbite spoke outside on the pavement to the male Caucasian.<br>11.53 Algernon Uberbite walked to his parked car with a painting under his arm and drove away.</td></tr>
<tr><td colspan="3">COMMENTS</td></tr>
<tr><td colspan="3">Warning: The suspect Algernon Uberbite is continuing to demonstrate hostile anti-social behaviour towards the members of the public. For example he refuses to politely greet the other male Caucasian properly. I theenk this other man was a very nice Italian man. He also seems to be desperate to sell a lovely painting. Theese means he has a great disrespect for Italian art and culture. Of course he</td></tr>
</table>

| INSTAPOL POLICE REPORT | | |
|---|---|---|
| **Agent** Guido Ventosi | Day: Two/ Midday | File Number 1200/12/20098 |
| **CASE** | **LOCATION** | **Report No** |
| Uberbite Surveillance | Car Park Pastacula | 3 |
| **Persons of Interest** Algernon Uberbite, Cornelia Uberbite, Alistair Uberbite | | |

again wore the same terrible clothing that was of course unsuitable for the wonderful Italian weather. From this type of behaviour I am sure theese means he has a lack of knowledge of the country he is visiting. For this situation I can only consider it to rude and ignorant. I am sure this man is becoming more dangerous with every passing day.

**Expenses:** A complete all over body massage in the Olympic Health club at the Hilton Hotel. The small bed in the Pensione is very very hard and I cannot sleep too well.
A new pair of Dior Sunglasses, the sun in this part of Italy is very strong; I must protect my eyes and skin. I am getting older now.
A new electronic English dictionary so I can improve theese reports. You complained about theeese problem in your email.

"He that goes to Rome by Foot returns a fool"

# 12 THE HAIR DO

Algernon whistled a gay little tune as he strolled through the sturdy old doors of the Villa's smoking room. With a spring in his step and a glint in his eye he headed directly to the bar, picked up an elegant crystal tumbler and poured himself a well-deserved double malted scotch. Gulping the first sip down long and deep he nodded his head in appreciation and promised himself another one before dinner.

Feeling much more relaxed now he walked over towards the heavily brocaded Victorian lounge to sit for a while because this was without a doubt, his favourite time of day. Algernon believed this was the perfect time to ponder, whilst he quietly mulled over all the up's and downs of the day. It was the best time to gather up all of his thoughts and empty his busy cluttered mind.

However, today was not going to be that kind of day, where that kind of indulgent pleasure was going to take place. In fact judging by the sight that met his old tired eyes, it would be far from it.

Algernon was genuinely shocked when he discovered Cornelia, fast asleep and sporting a heavily gelled, pink coloured, 'crew cut'. She was slumped over the end of the lounge with her long spindly arm hovering only centimetres above a fallen empty glass. He quickly stole another reassuring gulp from his glass before he tentatively approached her crumpled, dishevelled form.

Kneeling down beside the lounge, he gingerly reached for her lower arm and placed his fleshy thumb over her lily white, blue veined wrist.

"What in God's name are you doing Algernon?" Cornelia suddenly slurred. Stirring herself awake, she snapped open one red rimmed eye and glared directly into his startled face.

"Oh nothing dear." Algernon jumped back onto his haunches. "I was simply trying to make you a little more comfortable."

"Since when did you have a vested interest in whether or not I was comfortable?" She asked wryly. She began to pull herself up into a sitting position.

Algernon struggled back onto his feet; unfortunately he spilt some of the prized scotch all over the front of his shirt, as he wobbled to and fro in front of her. Taking one last gulp before he answered her question, he fished around in his befuddled mind for something complimentary to say.

"Well dear, that's a very interesting colour you are wearing, I must say. Actually I think it makes you look ten years younger."

"Surely you are not referring to my hair," she retorted. She looked away dolefully. "I can't believe even you could be that insincere." She instinctively made a blind attempt to smooth down the short feathery tufts that appeared to have taken on a 'life of their own', during her little nap. Turning her head from side to side, she looked around for her fallen glass. After spotting it laying there by the side of the lounge, she swooped down upon it with the precision of an eagle and victoriously snatched it up. "Frankly it is nothing short of ghastly. Trust me, I am in two minds as to whether or not I should take legal action."

"Well yes I must agree it is not your usual type of hairstyle Dear, but none the less I do think with a little bit of tweaking here and there it could look quite becoming." Algernon started to make his way back towards the bar, deciding now, would be the perfect time for that promised extra drink.

"Stop right there Algernon," Cornelia commanded. "Surely you would agree that I most certainly could do with a drink," she thrust her glass out in front of her. "Unfortunately I will have to settle for that perfectly horrid 'Lolly Water' masquerading as champagne, not much chance of getting anything else around here. Do these people know anything about the finer points of life?" She sniped, as she handed over her glass.

Algernon reluctantly took her glass and proceeded to make his way over to the bar. Just as he was pouring himself another stiff Whiskey, Sebastion let out a death defying squawk. Walking back over with the drinks he stole a fleeting glance towards the cage and realised in his haste to find the art dealer that morning he had forgotten to replenish the feeder.

"Good grief," declared Cornelia. "As if things were not miserable enough! Not only are we staying in a backwater haven for Barbarians we also have to share it with a Demon Possessed version of Tweety-Pie." She grabbed the glass from Algernon and threw the liquid back with a vigour that could only be matched by the speed of light.

"It's all right dear, he probably just wants some food, I think Horatio keeps it out in the pantry. I shall go and attend to it now." He picked up the feeder and headed out briskly through the door.

Algernon breathed a heavy sigh of relief as he made his way to the entrance of the kitchen. Stretching out his arm to pull back the swinging door, his relief was unfortunately replaced by feelings of fear and trepidation, once he realised he had become accidentally locked into a collision course that featured his pot-bellied paunch and the large protruding buttocks of Magdalena.

"Aye-Carrrramba," she screamed loudly as she skillfully spun around. She raised her arms high into the air, ever mindful of the delicate array of aperitifs' and tasty morsels that were teetering dangerously along the edge of the tray. Surprisingly, despite the fact she was no Ballerina, for one split second she defied the laws of gravity and was able to save the day with her astonishing balancing act, as she gracefully tottered on the tips of her toes, unwittingly revealing to all and sundry, the badly frayed edges of her black lacy petticoat.

Algernon was astounded by this sudden display of athleticism and 'quantum physics' and for a moment he wasn't exactly sure, where to look. He did notice however, during the brief period of time that Magdalena took to regain her composure and turn around and face him again, that she actually appeared to possess a rather shapely pair of legs.

"Terribly sorry ….. Err err ….. Magdalena." Algernon patted himself down in the delicate area of his lower regions, just to make sure nothing vital had been injured. "Are you all right?" He asked, as he looked into her bewildered face.

"Si Signore," she squeaked breathlessly. She straightened up the frilly maid's cap that had fallen sideways across her fluttering eye. "I no a see you comin tru the door," she puffed back at him, her breasts still heaving up and down with the sheer exertion of it all.

"Well yes, I gathered that," he concurred, standing back a little, just in case any sudden movement should trigger the whole thing off again.

"I have a here in my hands a very nice food that Signore Horeatzio ask a me to bring to you today," she said waving the tray in front of his face. "Eeef you like I will take thissa food and put it inside the table on the dining room."

"Yes, yes of course that would be splendid, please continue on," he said as he waved his arm over towards the adjacent room.

Suddenly, a loud frantic banging echoed towards them from the front entrance. Algernon glad to escape from yet another awkward situation, hastily made his way to the door and opened it up onto a rather pale looking Alistair.

"Father, I am so glad you are home. Have you seen mother?" He blurted. "I've been back and forth through the town twice and I can't find her anywhere."

"Yes, yes, come inside lad." Algernon ushered him through the door. "Your mother, I am pleased to report, despite having a disastrous day, is still none the less safe and sound and currently enjoying her second bottle of Prosecco in the smoking room."

"Oh thank God for that, I must say after making several inquiries around the town, I started to get worried when it appeared nobody had ever recalled seeing an elderly English woman."

"Ha, Ha, Ha," Algernon laughed cruelly. "There would certainly be no worries about losing her now. Not after today's fiasco at least," he laughed again, before continuing. "Taking into account the luminous colour of her hair, I am quite sure she could easily be spotted from a space station now."

"What did you say about my hair Algernon?" Cornelia slurred as she staggered her way towards them, clasping her empty glass.

"Mother!" Alistair gasped as he clamped his eyes upon her. "What on earth has happened to your hair? I thought Magdalena was taking you to a hairdresser, not the butcher. You look as though you have gone ten rounds with a meat cleaver."

"How dare you make such a horrid remark Alistair, particularly when it was your father and you that convinced me to go to the hairdresser with that imbecile of a woman in the first place. I knew I should never have listened to either of you," she retorted bitterly.

"Oh come on Mother, don't be so melodramatic, he quipped as he flicked back his lanky fringe. "

Actually after closer inspection, I must say it is not that bad after all, in fact it is quite stylish. By the way how did you manage to get home? I was looking for you everywhere in the town. As I recall you were supposed to meet me in the square."

"Home! I hardly refer to this hovel as a home, but if you must know I was taken or should I say kidnapped by that woman's cousin. That's all I needed, after my unfortunate episode at their primitive establishment marauding as a respectable Coiffeur."

"Kidnapped? What do you mean Kidnapped? Surely you can't be serious mother?" Alistair asked irritably.

"I am most definitely serious Alistair and what's more I

shall never allow myself to be driven around by any of these halfwits again. God only knows how many times I feared for my life this afternoon. I am amazed my hair did not become as white as snow after the ordeal I have had to endure. There were moments of sheer terror when my entire life flashed before me and I feared I wouldn't live to see the light of another day," she rolled her eyes up to the ceiling and back. "In the end I insisted that she  bring me back here. I mean how much going around and around in circles can a person endure?"

"Yes yes, I can fully appreciate how that must have felt dear," Algernon commented wryly. "Still, look on the bright side. It isn't every day that one gets the chance to reassess their life is it? I think we could almost consider it to be inspirational in a roundabout kind of way," he clicked his tongue loudly.

"Yes Mother, Father is quite right. They really have done you a service, far more than you will ever know I should suspect. In any case we can be almost certain we would never lose you in a crowd now," he snickered.

Cornelia instantly screwed her eyes up tightly and opened her mean little mouth as wide as it would go. Giving her face just the right amount of demonic qualities needed, to convey her contorted and painful version of the day's difficult events.

However before she had had the pleasure of uttering one single syllable, Magdalena innocently sailed back into the hallway and with both eyes gleaming and her large face beaming she announced in a confident voice.

"Allora Signora and Signore the food is all a ready for you now," she said in her best possible English. "I ope you will enjoy it and not be too ungry. Tomoorow, I come back to here and I help you again with all your personality neeeeds. And I a theenk Signore," she shot a cheeky little look at Algernon and then back again to Cornelia. "Tonight you will ave a very special night with your new Bella Donna," she added as she pointed her wriggling finger at Cornelia's hair. She then warmly bid them all a good night, picked up her jacket and made her way to the front entrance. "Buon Appetito," she called out cheerily as she slammed the door behind her.

The bedraggled little group, stood there for a few more shell shocked seconds. Until Alistair, definitely feeling ravenous by now and also quite relieved to find his mother was perfectly safe, despite her unfortunate grooming experience, decided it was high time to take matters into his own hands.

"Come along then, I don't know about you two but I could certainly do with some food. I am simply famished," he said as he waved them into the dining room. "Mother why don't you come over and sit on this side of the table at least that way father and I will be spared from the nuclear glow that seems to be pulsating from the middle of your head," he laughed. Obviously he was trying to lighten the mood. Feeling quite pleased with his efforts he reached across the broad table and snatched up a handful of black olives and greedily stuffed them into his mouth.

"Now, now, Alistair there is no need for that kind of talk. Your mother looks perfectly presentable. Actually I think she looks ten years younger," Algernon chastised, giving Cornelia a furtive sideways glance before he reached across the newly laid table and grabbed a large slice of freshly made pizza.

"How dare You," Cornelia bellowed. She slammed her fist down hard upon the table, causing the assortment of incorrectly placed cutlery to jump up and clink together in a terrified huddle before descending back onto the wooden surface again. "I have just about had enough of you both for one day. Furthermore I am warning you now. If either of you make one more snide comment about my hair or any other aspect of my appearance for that matter. I can assure you I will not hesitate to make the rest of your stay here a living hell. Do I make myself clear?" She screeched, baring her teeth in a shrill crescendo of ugly emotion.

Before either of them had had the chance to respond, a loud ominous crack heralded by an even louder thunderous rumble caused the stately old villa to shake and shudder all around them. Within seconds a rip roaring wind had whipped up the heavily brocaded dark curtains that framed the open dining room window.

The sudden force of this unusual gust pushed the dusty curtains up and out and converted them into a shape that looked similar to a hot air balloon. They hovered around in the air, billowing this way and that, before they finally dropped gracefully on top of Cornelia's pink shaven head, instantly giving her a strange Shakespearian appearance, not unlike one of the witches in Macbeth.

Alistair and Algernon stood there astonished and gawked back at her, their mouths gaping wide open, as they watched her ghoulish grimace twist and turn.

Then just as suddenly, all the lights went out and they were left standing there in the pitch black darkness, as the thunder continued to roll out its dramatic effects, complimented by the occasional flash of lightning that sent an eerie pulsating light flitting around the room.

Just like an Alfred Hitchcock thriller, Sebastion let out an earth shattering screech that conjured up images normally reserved for the most fearful scenes from Daphne Du Maurier's novel, "The Birds."

"Mother, are you all right?" Alistair finally asked. His voice sounding all frail and forlorn in the pitch black darkness that was only momentarily relieved by the glow of lightening that continued to circulate menacingly around the room.

"Ali?" Cornelia called out in a feeble voice. "Can you make your way over here as soon as possible and make sure you do it quietly?" She hissed. "I think there is something crawling on me," she finished faintly, her voice verging towards a stifled bout of hysteria.

"Stay Calm, Cornelia and try to keep perfectly still. You don't want to agitate the vermin." Algernon's voice boomed out into the darkness. "If I recall correctly,

Horatio did warn me about the Scorpions that live here. He said they can be quite dangerous. Fatal, in fact." This statement was followed by a long Wheeeeeeeze.

The muffled sound of high pitched sobbing was heard coming from the other side of the room. Alistair, determined to save the day, stealthily dropped down on all fours like an SAS squadron leader and aided by the occasional lightning strike carefully felt his way around the corners of the bulky Victorian table.

"Don't worry Mumsy, I think I can see your outline," he whispered loudly, as he made his way towards her. Hold out your arm so I can reach you but don't make any sudden movements," he insisted. "We don't want to alarm the evil fiend."

"Yes Dear, do pay attention to Ali and try not to move," Algernon issued, he wheezed again. "God only knows where the nearest hospital is around here," he lamented, as he gazed out into the darkness.

"Arrrrrrrrrrrrrrrrhhh, Hurry Ali I think it is crawling on my face," screamed Cornelia. She broke into a fresh new round of sobs.

"Arrrrrrrrrghhhhhhh ," Screamed Alistair as he grabbed hold of the spindly arm devoid of flesh maliciously outstretched in front of him.

Then quite miraculously, the lights innocently blinked back on. And within a few short seconds they comically revealed, the collapsed whimpering form of Alistair in the far corner of the room, with a plastic medical skeleton ghoulishly draped over the top of him.

Algernon bolted as fast as he could towards Cornelia who was still wailing and demanded to know where the insidious creature was.

"It's on my left cheek Algernon, can't you see it?" She demanded. My face Algernon, It's on my Face," she screeched. "Quickly, get it off me."

Algernon peered intently into her, tear drenched, face and finally spotted what must have been the alleged scorpion. Plucking it quickly from the hollow of her cheek, he held it up before him to examine its form more closely. "Is this what you were referring to dear?" He asked wryly, as he held it out towards her.

Cornelia, no longer sobbing opened up her swollen eyes and looked curiously at the twig of lavender that Algernon held up before her.

"But I could have sworn it was a spider," she insisted weakly. She looked over at Alistair who had finally untangled himself from the skeleton's bony limbs.

"And I could have sworn this was you," Alistair complained, pulling himself up irritably.

"And I could have sworn it was a scorpion not just another storm in a tea cup," Algernon grumbled as the thunder rumbled and then ...... just as quickly, in fact quite abruptly, the lights were extinguished again.

## 13 THE LOVE NEST

*Three things are beautiful in this world, a priest in his vestments, a knight in armour and a woman in her ornaments.*

Alistair made sure he had flossed his teeth as well as plucked out any unwanted nasal hair that morning before he made his way to the café. Something he always made a point of doing before a momentous occasion such as this. Not only that, he had also taken the time to painstakingly pick off any unwanted pieces of fluff from his favourite Country Road cardigan in an effort to present himself in the most impressive light possible.

Waiting under the awning of the Café he couldn't help feeling both nervous and excited at the same time. His 'butterfly wings tummy' and 'sweaty palms' were both competing vehemently for his full attention. After all, it wasn't every day he got to spend time alone with a beautiful woman such as Sophia. Although given the fact he hadn't slept very well the night before due to the hardness of the dining room floor, he was a little bit concerned about his ability to perform.

Anxiously, looking up and down the road, he tried hard to resist the urge to check his watch over and over again.

He told himself that it was only natural for her to arrive half an hour late, bearing in mind she was a woman and of course considering she was a European woman, it was highly likely that the notion of time for her could take on a whole new meaning.

However he was starting to feel more than a tad bit concerned after he noticed the bouquet of flowers he had picked from Horatio's 'quaint' cottage garden were already starting to droop under the morning sun.

After checking his watch for the fifteenth time, he was just about to reach into his pocket for his phone when he felt a pair of cool soft hands gently positioned over his eyes and the smell of strong intoxicating perfume filled his nostrils.

"Buongiorno Alistair," he heard her say from behind. He whirled around quickly to greet her.

"Sophia what a surprise! I thought you would be coming from the other direction," he blurted excitedly, his pasty complexion suddenly robust. "So glad you could make it." He greedily pulled her towards him and planted a wet sloppy kiss on each cheek.

"Yes," she said as she pulled away. "I am so sorry if I was a little late but I had a bit of trouble with Fifi. You see this morning, after the breakfast she couldn't make the Poo Poo and this is not like her."

Alistair worked hard to maintain a caring and concerned look, but secretly he was finding it hard to stop his racing mind, from returning to the moment when Sophia's amazing breasts had laid so delicately in his hands.

"So, I had to take the time to help her lose the Poo Poo. You understand? Of course, I learnt this trick back home in my country when I help my grandfather on the farm with the pigs. When the piggy can't make any Poo Poo's my grandfather, he put his finger inside the piggies, how you call it in English? 'Arsehole' and then after this the pig can make the Poo Poo without any problem."

Alistair was unwillingly jolted back to reality, after listening to this sordid little tidbit of tacky truth. Even though the anticipation of sensual delights was high on his agenda, he couldn't help feeling slightly disgusted by the images that were conjured up in his mind regarding Sophia's probing fingers and Fifi.

"But of course it is not the same with Fifi," she explained. "When I help her make the Poo-Poo, I always use the plastic glove," she smiled back at him.

"Well then, should we get going?" Alistair asked, eager now to change the subject. "I mean we wouldn't want to miss the museum now would we? Oh and I almost forgot, these are for you." He thrust the bunch of flowers towards her.

"Oh thank you, they are very wonderful," she took the sad, semi- wilted offering from him. "I am very surprised to see such flowers here," she said as she propped and prodded around the edges of the drooping petals. "In my country this kind of flower are only found near a church in the graveyard. I hope they do not die before I get back to my house," she laughed loudly, as she stashed them into her huge handbag.

"Oh that is interesting," Alistair smiled back weakly. "Shall we go?" He held out his arm for her to hold.

They walked most of the way to the museum together in a semi comfortable silence only making a few little comments here and there about the weather and the rising cost of things in Pastacula. However, by the time they reached the museum on the other side of the town, Alistair was finally starting to feel relaxed.

Despite the fact that things had gotten off to a shaky start, he was beginning to feel optimistic about the day and firmly believed it could only get better from now on. They climbed the steep stairs to the Magnificent old Museum arm in arm and were about to enter the ancient building when Sophia's pink diamante phone rang.

Even though she was speaking in a foreign language, Alistair could tell by the tone of her voice and also by her facial expressions that something was not quite right. He felt his heart sink when he realized, something was definitely wrong and his hopes of getting to know her better, started to take a nose dive. Sophia ended the call tersely and turned back to face him.

"Alistair I am so sorry but unfortunately I will not be able to see the exhibition with you today, I need to go home right away," her face suddenly looked pale and drawn.

Alistair felt his heart plummet further as he listened to her strained voice, 'So close and yet so far,' he lamented 'Why me?' He anguished. 'Why was life so cruel? …. Taunting him with the chance to be with a beautiful woman only to take it away again.'

He opened and closed his clenched fists until he could feel his nails dig deep and hard into the soft sweaty palms of his hands. Realising he needed to say 'something' but not quite sure WHAT he finally responded. "Oh no, that is a terrible shame. I was so looking forward to seeing the exhibition with you."

Sophia gazed back at him with a blank expression.

Realising 'even more' now, that she was going to be GONE in just a few minutes, he groped around in his nebulous mind for something reasonable to add. "Is there anything wrong, I mean is there a problem? Perhaps I could help you," he offered. He tried hard not to sound too eager as he leant his body in closer.

Sophia looked at him, gratefully, rapidly batting her thick long lashes up and down. She was making a gallant effort to prevent the tears that were swelling in the corner of her eyes, from falling. "It's Fifi," she said in a strained voice barely above a whisper. "My neighbour, she just called to me and she tells me, Fifi is crying too hard and scratching for a very long time at my apartment door, I knew I should never have left her alone today."

"Oh I see," Alistair replied sympathetically, his feeble mind was operating in complete overdrive now, as it made a determined effort to salvage what possibilities may still exist to make use of this 'Golden Opportunity.'

"Yes, yes, that is terrible news, you must be completely beside yourself is there anything I can do?" He asked, feigning concern as much as he could.

"I am so sorry but I need to go home now, maybe Fifi will need to go to the animal doctor in the next town. This, I know can take the whole day, because today I don't have any car with me and I will need to catch the auto bus." She started to make her way towards the steps.

"Wait," Alistair called out. He was on the verge of hysteria as he rapidly moved after her. "Don't go yet, I know we can't go to the museum today but perhaps I can help you anyway," he looked deeply into her eyes. "You said you need a car Right? Well I have a car at my house and if you need me to, I would be more than happy to drive you to the vets," he offered.

Sophie breathed a deep sigh of relief as she allowed herself to be comforted by this very good piece of news. "Oh Alistair, that would be wonderful," she said, "but we really must go now, Fifi will be getting herself into how you say a 'panicked attack' and I don't want to wait any longer. Please can you walk with me now, my house is not too far away."

Alistair walked briskly with her down the stairs and through the cobbled streets and up into the tiny narrow laneways until they finally reached a delightful medieval building in the heart of the "Centro Storico."

After walking up the small flight of stairs to the first level Alistair, feeling slightly elated now, but still a tad over concerned, waited patiently whilst she reached into her bag and pulled out the key. Placing her ear to the door she listened carefully for a few seconds before she inserted it.

"Please come in," she ushered to him as she turned the key and opened the door into a bright sunny room. Once inside Sophia wasted no time checking up on the status of Fifi. She quickly scanned the room for her beloved pet and raced across to the other side and diligently checked the petite doggie basket over by the window. Finding it empty she urgently called out the dog's name before entering the adjacent room. "FIFI, where are you Darlink? Please come to Mamma."

As soon as he entered the room Alistair felt strangely lightheaded, almost as though he was at a "loose end" and if truth be told, he didn't really know what to do. He had just decided to close the door behind him when he heard Sophia talking excitedly in the next room.

Sitting down in the chintzy patterned armchair situated next to the door, he waited in anticipation for what he thought would be bad news, he hoped against hope that the 'overstuffed fur ball' wouldn't need to see the vet, because the truth of the matter was, there wasn't any car available after all.

A few moments later Sophia sailed through the door positively beaming. Hugging Fifi tightly to her breasts, she crooned strange little girly noises in a foreign language to no one in particular.

Alistair almost fainted with relief when it appeared as though the "Doggie Disaster" had been averted. Not only that, he couldn't help feeling quite chuffed with himself. After all, even though 'technically', they were still on a 'First Date Basis,' he was actually sitting alone with her in her apartment. 'Don't botch it up now', he lectured himself, 'if you play your cards right, you could be in like Flynn.'

"Oh I am so happy," Sophia declared, "Fifi, she is really OK. I found her sleeping like the baby on my bed," she snuggled her face into Fifi's furry little body and then walked over to the basket and lovingly placed the sleeping dog down amongst the myriad of doggie toys and pet snacks that also inhabited the basket.

"My God, that's Brilliant," Alistair swooned. "I was so worried about her, I even rang up my housekeeper to make sure she had the car on standby." He let out a loud sigh and fell back into the chair.

"Yes thank you, it was very kind of you to offer your help to me. I am so sorry we didn't get to see the exhibition together. Ooooh, she suddenly, squealed in delight. "This really must be my lucky day." She bent down in front of him, conveniently providing a pleasant view of her shapely lower body packaged neatly in the pencil thin skirt. "I found my missing earring,"she exclaimed as she straightened up again and stretched her arm towards her ear, causing her large breasts to suddenly dominate the scenery.

Alistair continued to stare back at her in a 'frozen, dry ice kind of way'. He could feel his heart pumping as he rubbed his sweaty palms against the cool cloth of the cushion. After all, it had been a long time 'between drinks' and so it would only be natural for him to suffer from a slight case of shock.

Finally finished fiddling with her ear, Sophia asked sweetly "Are you OK? I see you look a little stressed," she queried as she ran her perfectly shaped hands through her luscious blonde hair. "Perhaps you are thirsty would you like a drink? Water, Orange Juice, maybe you prefer a glass of wine? This will help to relax you No?"

Alistair was thrilled beyond belief by this new turn of events. When he first started out on this venture he had hoped at best, he would be given the chance to get to know her a bit better but he had never in his wildest dreams anticipated things moving this rapidly.

"Yes please," Alistair replied automatically. He struggled to keep his voice even.

"Yes please for what?" She asked with a puzzled frown, "Water? Juice? Wine perhaps?"

"Oh, Oh Wine, yes I would love a glass of wine." He smiled back sheepishly.

"OK, I will be back in the jiffy. Just don't go anywhere, Handzome," she winked at him before she turned away and slowly sauntered off towards the kitchen.

Alistair sat staring into space for the next few seconds before the actual reality of what was about to take place hit him. Springing forward in his seat he quickly loosened his tie, took off his woolen cardigan and as an extra precaution, held his hand closely against his mouth, breathed into it heavily and checked his breath.

He was just about to sit back and relax when he happened to notice a 'hot pink coloured business card' with a picture of Sophia on the front of it, sitting on the table next to him. He picked it up and admired her image, before turning it over and reading the interesting little blurb about 'Translation and House Sitting; services, on the other side. The words *'I can come to you,'* printed in bright Purple and Gold ink jumped out at him. Scanning the card quickly he spotted a phone number right at the very bottom. Whipping out his mobile phone he hastily copied it down. 'Good, that will save me asking for it later' he mused. He had just about managed to slip into what looked like a fairly 'cool and confident' pose when Sophia returned with the drink.

She handed him the glass and looked at him with a just a hint of mischief in her eyes. "I hope you like red wine." She gently caressed his hand as she moved away. "This is a very expensive local wine, it was given to me by one of my Russian friends and I have been waiting for a very long time to open it."

"Thank you, thank you very much," Alistair blurted as he

took the wine in his trembling hand. "But what about you?" He asked, after noticing she had only bought one glass over. "Aren't you going to share a glass with me?" He suddenly felt disappointed.

"Yes, yes don't worry, I will, but first of all I will like to change into something a little bit more comfortable," she said as she kicked off her shoes. "Please, just relax and enjoy your drink, I will be back in a few minutes and then we can have a good chance to chat together," she teased. She placed her hand around the nape of her neck and flicked her long mane as she walked off towards the bedroom.

Alistair was not really a big drinker and given the fact he was already giddy with excitement the effects of the alcohol seemed to take place almost immediately. He sat forward stiffly in an attempt to remain alert, after all he didn't want to 'blow it all' now. Gulping down the liquid nervously, he couldn't help but wonder how fortunate he had been, 'but then again,' he chastised himself, 'Why shouldn't he be with a beautiful foreign woman? After all he was a very eligible bachelor and ALL the women who had had the pleasure of knowing him, had ALL agreed he was definitely a Great Catch.'

He was just starting to relish some of his fondest memories of his 'Casanova type Escapades' when Sophia reappeared at the door wearing what appeared to be NOTHING more than a lavish Hot Pink Mink coat and a pair of purple stilettos.

Alistair was absolutely, Jaw dropping, 'Gob Smacked', he could not take his eyes off her as she slowly sauntered across the room her long luscious legs coming closer and closer. Without so much as blinking an eye she sensually swayed her hips from side to side and smiled back at him seductively before she eventually sat down upon his weak trembling knee.

For some bizarre reason the theme song from the James Bond Movie, 'The Spy who loved Me,' suddenly sprang into his mind and the words 'Nobody does it Better,' played themselves over and over again as they surged through his poor dumb struck senses filling him with both wonder and delight.

Taking the glass gently from his hand Sophia took a tiny sip before placing it carefully on the table beside them. Alistair audibly gulped as she leant forward and then placed her full red lips on his mouth and kissed him long and hard.

At the end of the ravaging kiss, Sophia looked deep into his eyes and reached for the glass again. Holding it up against his lips she stroked the back of his head lovingly with her other hand. Alistair completely beside himself by now took the glass from her in anticipation of another steamy kiss but 'Alas' it was never meant to be. Just as he was about to place it back on the table. 'All hell broke loose.'

Fifi, unbeknown to both of them had woken up from her sleep, and had left her basket and was now standing next to the chair. After surveying the situation for the briefest of moments, the little dog took a sudden flying leap towards Alistair, sending the glass hurtling from his hand into mid-air where it twirled acrobatically for a few seconds before landing all over Sophia and the mink coat.

Sophia jumped up immediately and tried to snatch Fifi away, who was already, 'well into the process' of gnawing a great hole into Alistair's singlet.

She grabbed the dog's tiny rear end and pulled it hard towards her. However by doing this, she accidentally caused Alistair's rigid body to jerk forward too, and plunge face down into the cleavage of her heaving breasts.

Fifi, continued to squirm forcefully against Sophia's grasping hands as she growled and gnawed on the limp piece of fabric. Then finally, after a few more defiant growls she decided to let the sodden singlet go and Alistair instantly fell backwards, with a big 'Whoooosh', from the sheer momentum of it all.

Sophia spoke sternly to Fifi in Estonian as she held her firmly in her hands. Fifi on the other hand didn't seem in the least bit perturbed and started to 'Yap Yap Yap,' back at Alistair as she wagged her tiny fluffy tail up and down.

Looking over apologetically, at Alistair's frazzled state Sophia continued to chastise the small dog but this time in English.

"You are a very, very, bad girl Fifi look what you have done to our guest. That is not nice, say sorry to Alistair or

I am going to put you in the room."

Fifi sat angelically in her arms as though nothing had ever happened, not even the slightest hint of a bark or growl could be gleaned from the little dog. After a few terse moments Sophia apologized to Alistair and announced that she would be right back. Scolding Fifi in Estonian again she promptly took her to the bedroom.

Alistair didn't seem to be too upset as he rearranged his saliva, stained, singlet, back under the stiff collar of his shirt. Deep down he hoped that once the 'little blighter' had been removed that they would just pick up from where they left off.

After sitting patiently for what seemed like an eternity, Sophia eventually reappeared. She was fully dressed now in the clothes she had been wearing earlier and she was carrying the Hot Pink Mink coat over her arm.

Alistair could tell as she approached him, that she had been crying. Her face was all red and blotchy and her eyes seemed to be swollen and strained as she slowly walked over to him, looking forlorn and distraught.

"I am so upset Alistair. I really don't know what I can do about it. If I don't fix this problem very soon I will find myself in the middle of some big troubles," she said as she stood close to him.

Alistair was definitely disappointed to see she had already changed back into her street clothes. But not wanting to appear too annoyed, he decided to respond in a particularly benevolent tone, in the hope that something may ignite her steamy passions again. "Come over here and sit down Cupcake," he winked as he patted his knee lightly, "I don't want you to worry your pretty little head about it for one more minute. Look at me I'm as good as new. After all I am an Englishman and it takes a lot more than a little dog barking to take the wind out of my sails," he said with a lusty smile.

"No, No, you don't understand," she declared shaking her head from side to side. "It's about the coat. It's not mine and now it has a terrible stain all over it," she cried as she held it up in front of him to see. "It belongs to my girlfriend and she will be coming over this evening to pick it up, so she can wear it to the famous Russian Potato Festa in Pastacula tonight."

Alistair didn't know whether to laugh or cry or both. 'A Russian Potato Festival in rural Italy! What next?' He thought as he stared back in disbelief.

Sophia burst into tears and her loud sobbing suddenly brought him back down to earth as he wondered how things had taken such a turn for the worst in such a short period of time."I don't know what to do," she sobbed. "She will be very very angry with me if she finds out what We have done to this coat," she cried, she held the Mink coat out in front of him. "Do you know this is a very expensive coat it used to belong to a Russian movie star and now it is finished." She broke into a fresh new bout of sobbing.

"Alright, alright, calm down," Alistair issued sitting forward in his seat. "Why don't you think about getting it dry cleaned? Surely there is a dry cleaner in Pastacula that you could take it to?" He asked, in a slightly edgy tone.

"No, No, You don't understand, I can't drop it here in Pastacula, her friends, are also Russian, they own the dry cleaner's shop and I am sure they will say to her what has happened," she cried as she buried her face into the motley pink fur.

"Alright pull yourself together," he ordered. "There is no use crying over spilt milk that's not going to change anything. What about another dry cleaner? Somewhere else, like the next town? Surely they would be able to fix it up before tonight."

Sophia turned her tear stained face towards him. "Yes there is another express dry cleaner in the next town. I have used them before when some guests ruined my curtains. They are very quick and very good but also very very expensive, I think it will cost a lot of money to fix this problem," she said in a low voice.

"But would they be able to fix the coat in time?" Alistair asked.

"Yes I am sure they could manage it. That is why they call the name Express. They will always come to your house and pick up your clothes and drop it all off again in a few hours. This will be just enough time before my friend comes to claim it back," she sighed loudly.

"Well that's good news then isn't it?" Said Alistair, gleefully rubbing his hands together. "How about we ring them now and organise a pick up?"

"Yes that would be very nice but the problem is they only take cash and I don't have any money with me now. Also I can't go out to get any money from the machine because Fifi she will be too upset and cause many problems again," she said looking at him with wide fearful eyes.

Alistair, still hoping against hope that they could catch up from where they had left off, replied in a 'fervour of passion'. "Well I have some money with me and I am sure it will be enough to pay for the bill," he said pulling out a wad of notes from his wallet. "One hundred and fifty should be more than enough to cover the costs." He held the money out towards her. "No rush either, you can fix me up next time we see each other," he added, he followed this with a sleazy grin.

Sophia squealed in delight and moved even closer towards him, the coat still dangling off the end of her arm. "Ooooooh thank you Alistair," she cried as she grabbed the money. "You are really the Life Saver," she crooned softly in his ear. She bent down and placed one tiny dry kiss on the top of his forehead.

Just as he about to reach out and draw her back onto his knees a horrible scratching noise shattered this truly 'special moment.' It seemed to be coming from behind the bedroom door and was followed by a bout of "yippy yappy" barks.

"Oh its Fifi, she must be so upset. I need to go to her now before she makes sick again in my bedroom. The last time when I left her alone like this she made a big mess all over my bed; it was a very bad smell in there for many days." She quickly looked back and forth from Alistair to the bedroom door. "I am sorry I must go to her," she said as she hurriedly made her way across the room, clutching the money in her hands.

Alistair's hopes finally started to crash and burn as the realisation that his 'lucky day' was all but over, started to sink in. However being a man who doesn't give up easily he still hoped he might be in with a chance. 'perhaps this was her way of drawing him into the bedroom,' he pondered. 'after all she was a modest kind of girl and surely she wouldn't want to appear, too eager.' Finally fed up with waiting, he quietly walked across the room and placed his ear flat up against the door. He had just about made up his mind to go in, when he heard Sophia speaking again in a loud cross voice.

"Oh no Fifi, not again, not all over my bed. I knew I should not have let you eat that left over cabbage last night. Come here my Darlink you need a bath."

Alistair felt his stomach lurch from one side to the other. Any previous thoughts and desires of making out with Sophia literally drained from his mind like the water from a bathtub. Not wanting to know any more about what was actually happening on the other side of the door he decided to call it a day, admit defeat and retreat. 'After all,' he mused, 'It was obvious the girl was clearly besotted with him and couldn't wait to get her clutches on him.'

Not to mention he had her phone number and so he could easily call her later when things had settled down.

After all she was 'obviously obliged'; due to the very recent circumstances to at least meet up with him again in order to pay back the money. So with that in mind, he rapidly made his way back across the room, picked up his country road cardigan and quietly left the apartment, closing the door behind him.

# 14 MAFIA AND THE MONEY EXCHANGE

Algernon jostled the heavy painting under his arm and puffed in and out heavily as he dragged it, and himself, up the narrow dark stairway and into the entrance of the brightly lit cavernous room; which was vulgarly decorated with an assortment of garish strobe lights and silver plated pole dancing platforms. In the middle of the room he could see a much larger raised platform with a crimson velvet curtain hanging flamboyantly towards the back of the stage. Added to this bizarre collection of 'Crass over the top Bling', was a huge sign made up of a set of flashing, multi coloured lights that spelt the words "Lolita's Paradise." The charmless sign was brazenly hung over a line of scaffolding that had been erected haphazardly across the back of the stage.

His Italian escort generously waved him through the gold plated entrance doors, which were conveniently flanked on either side by a pair of burly body guards dressed in identical black suits. Each suit was comically topped off with a red and white striped bowler hat. In the normal world they would have seemed completely outrageous but in this environment they blended in perfectly.

Algernon shuddered inwardly as he stole a quick curious

look around the spuriously decorated room. The walls of the room appeared to be painted in a faded shade of what originally may have been a deep terracotta colour. But it was the copper plated gold bar with the fake diamond glitter that snaked its way across the length of the room that really caught his eye. It glimmered sadly here and there where the lights hit the patches of glitter that still hadn't been worn away by the countless number of elbows sliding over it.

Although it was only mid-morning, there was no doubt about it, the club was well and truly bustling and open for business. Algernon had never seen a real life 'Topless Waitress' before and he had to look twice, just to be sure, before he quickly turned away.

One woman dressed in a flimsy sequined gown, with a pair of diamante studded stiletto's hanging from the back of her stool was slovenly slumped over the bar, sound asleep. So much so that she appeared completely oblivious to the extremely loud vacuum cleaner making the rounds of the room. After looking at her a few times, Algernon wondered, as he passed by her chair, if anyone had checked her recently for a pulse? As far as he could make out, she seemed to be enjoying the kind of sleep usually reserved for the dead!

Just below the stage, he could see another group of men, boisterously playing a game of cards. As he stood there watching them an evil looking wiry man quickly jumped up into a standing position. Looking positively murderous, he leant across the table and furiously shook his fist into the face of the man on his right. After delivering a tirade of Italian obscenities, he finally sat back down, making sure he carefully kept his cards pressed closely against his chest. Casting his eyes a little further afield, Algernon noticed, that the few burly bouncers, lurking in the corners of the darkened room, were also watching this little fiasco unfold. Then suddenly, as if out of nowhere, some male waiters, sporting chic Black Tuxedo's arrived. Each one of them was carrying a large silver tray piled high with bottles of champagne that were nestled in tall buckets of ice. As they navigated their way across the room, they stopped off at various stations to replenish the glasses of the more alert patrons, before continuing on toward the big open doors and finally disappearing completely out of sight.

Striding onwards, they passed several men of various ages and sizes who all seemed to be sitting in a trance like state. Some of them were still clutching their wallets as they sat amongst, what may have been, their last remaining chips, scattered on the floor below them.

After what felt like a long journey of crude awakenings they eventually reached a black shiny door situated at the far end of the room. Donato, pausing for just a moment, whipped out his mobile phone and made a quick call in Italian before he attempted to open the door. After getting the all clear from whoever was on the other side, he turned the large metallic knob. Algernon, just like a faithful pup, obediently followed him into the room. The truth was he didn't quite know what to expect once he was inside but at the same time he was becoming increasingly aware that this was certainly no ordinary type of Art

Dealer.

As they approached the chrome and glass desk, an elegantly dressed man, wearing a pair of baby blue John Lennon type spectacles, that made him appear much younger than he actually was, stood up and held out his hand. At first when Algernon shook it he was impressed by how soft his hands were but after looking again a little more carefully, he was completely astounded by the huge diamond ring, mounted on his little pinkie finger.

Once they were all comfortably seated the man proceeded to introduce himself, "Good Morning Signore," he said seriously. "It is a pleasure to meet you, may I introduce myself? My name is Enzo Pimponello and I am the manager of this very fine night club. I also have a small art business that I run on the side," he cast a sideways glance to Donato who nodded back attentively. "Donato tells me you have bought a magnificent painting for me to see today, could you please show it to me now?" He asked.

Algernon, suddenly feeling quite dry in the mouth and slightly nervous, cleared his throat loudly before responding. "Errrmm, Yes of course. I have it with me here," he said as he started to bring it up onto the desk. "But as I mentioned earlier to Donato it is not exactly for sale. I would simply like to have it valued," he explained in a firm voice.

"Signore please, just relax you are amongst friends. There is no need to make any hasty decisions at this very moment. There are so many ways we can help you, but before you decide anything it is important for you to trust us," he said sternly, looking ever so slightly down the end of his nose as he lowered his head towards Algernon.

Algernon felt his face flush as the rush of hot blood surged across his cheeks. Suddenly feeling very light headed he loosened his wide flowery Cravat and scratched vigourously around his neck. "Yes quite and that is precisely why I am here. Donato tells me you are a reputable art dealer and in light of that I would like you to take a look at this painting and give me a professional quote on just exactly how much you believe it is worth."

"Certainly Signore it will be my personal pleasure to assist you but you must also understand we cannot do the evaluation here on the premises. To evaluate it correctly we will need to send it away to our workshop where we can have it appraised professionally by one of the many experts on our team."

"Yes of course I am fully aware of how this works." Algernon responded carefully. "But none the less I would like to ask you about the location of the workshop. I would like to know if it possible for us to go there today? Before I give you the painting? Could we go there this morning? I do have the time to go there now if it's not too far away," Algernon lowered the painting, just a little bit.

"Signore, our workshop is quite far from here. Perhaps forty to fifty kilometres away. I am afraid we cannot go there today. You would have to leave the painting here with us and then we would take a couple of days to return it back to you," Pimponello informed him with a piercing look. He leant back in his swivel chair and positioned his clasped hands behind his head.

Algernon shuffled his feet nervously under the desk. "Ahh so I see. You would like me to leave this painting here with you and then I should wait for you to tell me what it is worth. In a few days' time?" He sat forward abruptly, causing the heavy frame to hit the desk loudly.

"Ahh please do be careful," Signore Pimponello insisted. He quickly jumped up. Leaning forward across the desk, he reached his hand out and firmly grabbed at the top corner of the painting. He attempted to pull it up. "Signore Uberbite may I please take a closer look?" He asked holding onto the edge of the painting.

"Yes, yes, of course, obviously that is why I am here," wheezed Algernon. He reluctantly passed the painting over the wide desk.

Donato, who up until this point, had been sitting quietly during the entire conversation, automatically jumped to his feet and joined his colleague on the other side of the desk. As soon as they had laid the painting out flat he took a rather large magnifying glass from the top drawer of the desk and passed it across to Pimponello.

For the next minute or so, Signore Pimponello thoroughly inspected the painting from corner to corner, popping his head up every now and then to say something in Italian to Donato. Finally after giving the painting one more cursory look he stood up again and said in a very low voice.

"Signore Uberbite, I cannot be sure but I do believe this is the famous painting by the French Artist Greuze called the 'Epiphany.' Without consulting with my team of experts I cannot give you an exact figure but I do believe this painting to be very, very, valuable."

Sitting down at his desk again he continued, "You are a very lucky man Signore, to have such a famous painting. I know many people in the art world, who would very much want to own such an important piece of art. May I ask Signore, what is your future intention for this particular painting?"

Algernon was not really expecting this line of questioning and therefore was slightly lost for words. He loosened the thick ugly cravat just a little bit more and scratched the skin around his dry crinkly neck. "Well I would have to say at the moment I would simply like to have it valued. Then after I receive a professional evaluation I will be obliged to consider my options," he stated boldly. He started to tug the edge of the painting back across the desk.

"Si Signore Uberbite I completely understand your situation and my team of experts would be very happy to help you satisfy this option. My next question Signore IS what kind of arrangement would you like us to make for you?" Pimponello asked. He cautiously pulled the edge of the painting back towards him again.

Algernon, starting to feel relieved that the entire process was now in its final stage, released his grip on the painting, ever so slightly. He cleared his throat loudly. "Ehhhmm, I do believe a cash deposit totaling 10 to 15 percent of the value of the painting is usually issued to the owner. Particularly when somebody decides to leave a valuable painting such as this," he said. He stared back boldly into the face of the nightclub owner. "However before we go any further, Signore Pimponello, I would like to ask you a question."

"Certainly, Signore Uberbite and I will answer you if I can." Pimponello replied, leaning back, confidently in his slim line designer chair.

"What exactly do you get out of this? I mean the Art evaluation? Surely, you wouldn't go to all this trouble simply as a favour to the Art World?"

"Signore Uberbite, let me begin by saying, Art is truly my greatest Passion, it is something I have always loved and wanted to be a part of. But if you ask me what I should gain from this little transaction, it is quite simple. After we give you the money as a deposit for the artwork we expect you should pay us ten percent interest when you return to collect the Artwork."

"Oh I see, well that answers my question then. I suspected there must be something a bit more lucrative in it for you besides your simple love of art. As for my part of the bargain, I don't mind relinquishing ten percent of the overall value as long as I get my painting back in the end."

Signore Pimponello remained completely stony faced for the next few seconds as he considered Algernon's reply. Then he turned towards Donato, who had been relentlessly fidgeting with his mobile phone and spoke passionately and rapidly to him in Italian.

Donato, didn't appear to be listening at all and simply nodded his head as he continued to text. Only looking up occasionally to punctuate Pimponello's more breathless moments with the obligatory, "Si."

Pimponello finally turned his attention back towards Algernon. "Signore Uberbite," he began. "It has been a pleasure to do business with you. Now if you would just be so kind, to wait a few minutes more, my colleague Donato, will take you to our board room next door, where we will finalise the transaction."

## 15 BIRDS AWAY

Cornelia stood rigid in the courtyard as she haplessly watched Sebastion make his 'Debut Flight' towards the regal looking Oak tree presiding lovingly over the pretty country garden.

Sighing heavily, she was just about to take a consoling sip of wine when she noticed a lone white feather had drifted into her glass and was maliciously bobbing up and down in the intoxicating liquid.

She was so engrossed with getting it out, that she hadn't even noticed, that Winston and Churchill, had made a mad dash to the fence and were currently attempting to scale the metre high gate. It was only the sound of Alistair's rather terse high voice that brought her attention back to the present situation.

"Get back, you pair of useless Gits," he shouted as he tried to open the gate. "Trust me I've just about had an absolute gutful of man's best friend for one day."

"Alistair Wait!" Cornelia shrieked. "Please don't let them out. I really couldn't take any more drama."

After hearing the sound of Alistair's voice, the excited pair of dogs continued to throw themselves at the gate even more enthusiastically, only ever halting their frantic barking, when they occasionally started to choke on their own saliva.

Cornelia shuffled over in her frilly satin negligee, she was still diligently trying to pluck the feather from the fluted glass. When she eventually arrived at the gate, she commanded the dogs to 'S*it and Wait'* as she pushed past them and opened it.

Alistair sucked in his midriff and squeezed himself through the gap between the fence and his mother. By the irritated expression plastered across his face it was clear to see he was in no mood for any nonsense. He took one look at his mother's inappropriate attire and immediately broke into a sneering grimace.

"Who let the dogs out?" He asked sharply as he looked from the dogs to her and back again. "And what on earth are you doing outside in your night dress Mother? I mean look at the time surely you intend to get dressed at some point today?"

"Well yes of course Alistair, don't be ridiculous I don't usually saunter around all day in my bed clothes but due to this most recent disaster I haven't had a chance to change yet," she replied. She raised the glass to her lips after finally ridding it from the offending feather.

It was at exactly this moment that Winston and Churchill unanimously decided to resume their frenzied barking. After all, the opportunity to sit this close to both their Master and Mistress did not present itself very often and they were determined to make the most of it.

"Shut up will you, Shhooosh, shoosh," Cornelia demanded as they continued to bay at the top of their lungs. "Ali do be a sport would you and lock them away before I completely lose my mind. I haven't had a moment's peace since I let them out this morning."

"Whatever possessed you to let them out in the first place Mother? You know only full well father is the only one who can control them."

"Yes, but let's not waste time arguing about that now Ali. Please just take them away and come back as quickly as you can, I am really at my wits end. Honestly, I don't know how much more of this I can take." She sighed, dramatically before draining the last few drops from her glass.

"All right, calm down there is no need to act so pathetic," Alistair sniped. He grabbed the heavy leather collar of each dog and dragged them both towards the van.

Cornelia, feeling much more relieved to see them go, turned her attention now towards the large Oak tree that Sebastion had taken refuge in. She peered intently into the long spindly branches hoping to spot his brightly coloured feathers but was soon deterred from making any progress due to the glaring sun.

"Sebastion," she called out feebly. "Are you there?" She followed this question with a round of whistling, which unfortunately caused the two dogs to begin their incessant barking again.

"Mother," Alistair roared out at the top of his lungs as he shoved the wriggling rear end of Winston, back into the caravan. "Have you completely lost your senses? Can't you see I am having enough trouble getting this pair of Blighters to co-operate without creating any more unnecessary drama?" He pushed his shoulder up hard against the door. Just to make sure it was tightly closed.

Cornelia walked closer to the tree and attempted to grab the nearest hanging branch. She had just managed to grab it by the tips of her bare fingernails when the shrill shriek of Sebastion's, 'Sqawwwwk' filled the air again. Unfortunately, her first instinct was to let go and as soon as she did, she automatically fell down backwards onto her thin bony bottom with her lanky legs straggling high in the air above her. She wasted no time getting back onto her feet. She anxiously looked up into the tree again and eventually spotted Sebastion bobbing up and down, just a few branches higher.

She was so relieved to see him, that she broke into a new bout of exceptionally bad whistling, which in turn caused the rather confused bird to rise up high, onto his steely stick legs and stretch his wings out as far as they could go on either side of him.

"Mother, what did I tell you about making that shocking noise?" Alistair asked as he joined her at the foot of the tree. Sebastion, determined not to be overshadowed dutifully let out another long ear splitting screech before settling back down again onto the branch. "Do you mind telling me exactly how did this happen? I mean what on earth is he doing out of his cage in the first place?"

"Oh Ali, please don't go on. Can't you see I am truly beside myself with worry? This morning when I woke up he was making such a racket in the room that I decided to put him outside for some fresh air and of course, to relieve my poor ears from his dreadful screeching."

"Hmm I see." Alistair, peered up at the tree. "But how does that account for him being all the way up there?" He asked, pointing at the branch.

"Well the point is Alistair, once I took him out into the fresh air I started to think about the two dogs. I know we both know, that I don't really enjoy having them around, but for some foolish reason, that I now regret, I was feeling rather sorry for them this morning. Considering they had been cooped up in that little van for the past few days."

"And so you let them out? Is that what you did Mother?"

"Yes, but I never thought for one minute they would go berserk did I? I mean usually your father manages them. How was I to know they would make a beeline directly to the bird cage?"

"So, wait a minute Mother. Let me try and get my head around this ridiculous scenario. You let the dogs out and they knocked over the Bird cage." Alistair continued his inquisition. He tapped his foot to the side impatiently. "Is that how it happened? Is that the way Sebastion got out Mother?" He glowered back at her, his face black as thunder. He folded his arms tightly across his chest.

"Yes, precisely and here we are standing here gazing up at the ridiculous creature. Frankly if it was up to me he could stay there for the rest of his life, which mercifully may not be too much longer. In any case I have just about had enough of this nonsense. It is well and truly past 'Elevenses' and in my opinion I think I deserve a drink." Cornelia turned to walk away and as she did Winston and Churchill let out one final blood curdling howl, followed by a relentless muffled whimpering.

"Mother! Pull yourself together; we just can't leave the bird here. Do you have any idea how much he is worth? Father will be livid!" Alistair screamed after her.

"Well if you are that concerned about the oversized Dodo, then YOU can stand there and keep an eye on it until I think of something better to do," she said as she walked back towards the villa.

"Oh for crying out loud Mother! Don't be absurd, Sebastion is not a Dodo," Alistair sneered. He shook his head in disbelief. "Surely you know a Dodo bird can't fly? I remember father teaching me all about the birds of the world when I was about ten."

"Then surely you know Alistair dear, when somebody is being sarcastic or not? I know full well the hideous creature is not a Dodo but I also happen to know the word Dodo originally comes from the Portuguese word Doudo meaning foolish, perhaps I should have called you the Dodo instead. Furthermore if you are such a self-proclaimed expert on the topic of birds, then I have absolutely no qualms whatsoever about leaving any bird in your capable hands," she snarled as she reached for the door handle.

"Hang on a minute Mother, you just can't leave me here in the lurch, I mean what am I supposed to do now?"

Winston and Churchill let out a long woeful howl, which no doubt triggered another round of raucous screeching, compliments of Sebastion.

Cornelia was halfway through pouring herself a stiff gin and tonic when the front door bell rang. Deciding to ignore it and 'down the drink" instead, she threw the liquid to the back of her throat and was reaching for the bottle again, when the bell rang for a second time, followed by a loud set of knocking.

Thinking, it may have been Magdalena, returning to clean the house, she decided it may be in her best interests to at least take a look. After all Magdalena knew the bird better than they did and therefore she may have some idea of how to get it out of the tree and back into its cage.

Mustering up as much composure as she could, she carefully walked over to the door and opened it. However she was quite surprised to discover it wasn't Magdalena at all. Standing there instead was a rather tall, dark haired man, dressed in a bright Orange service uniform.

"I think you may have come to the wrong house," Cornelia stated in a brittle voice.

At first the young man deliberately averted her gaze. He quickly lowered his head and directed his eyes towards the ground. Perhaps he was feeling embarrassed for her, considering she was standing there in her nightdress, or perhaps it was her bright pink hair that frightened him or perhaps it was the peculiar combination of both. However despite all that, it seemed as though he must have had a change of heart, when all of a sudden he lifted his head up and introduced himself. "Buongiorno Signora," were the only two words Cornelia understood as she listened to him babble on and on in Italian for the next minute or so.

Realising the futility of the situation, Cornelia began to close the door directly in his face. "I am sorry. You are wasting your time. I don't speak Italian," she said as she pulled the door towards her.

"No Wait, Signora," the young man said holding up his hand. "I can of course speak English. It is part of my training here in Italy," he added proudly. "If you like, I will speak very slowly and very clearly for you, Okay? We can start again!." He took a deep breath and launched back into his speech. "Buongiorno Signora my name is Luca and I say to you just now, that I am a coming from the Vigili Del Fuoco. It means the fire brigade Signora, and I want to ask of you, Eeef it is Okay if we," he threw his hands out to the side of the road. "My crew and I burnna some of the field next door to yourra Ouse?"

"Hmm I see," said Cornelia, opening the door just a little wider. "So you need my permission to burn the field next door? Is that what you are asking?"

"Si Signora, we cannot just a burn without first of all telling to all the neighbours what we will do." His sunny smile beamed from one side of his face to the other.

Perhaps it was his lovely bright smile or perhaps it was his simple sincerity or perhaps it was a combination of both, that made her change her mind. But, knowing the situation at hand and knowing the type of woman Cornelia was, it was more than likely due to the fact that she was desperately in need of something.

"Well of course I am sure it will be all right but before you begin, I wonder if you could do something for me. Do you have a very long ladder in your truck?"

"Si Signora, we always take the long ladder with us. Why you needa this?" He asked, splaying his large hands in front of him.

Cornelia had fully opened the door by now. She stepped out towards the front of the terrace in order to take a better look at the truck. Opening her eyes as wide as she could, she peered out until she finally spotted the bright shiny ladder stored on the roof of the vehicle.

She rapidly turned back to Luca. "Pay attention," she insisted. "This is important, I will speak slowly and clearly so you can understand me, all right? Now watch me carefully. "I", she pointed to herself, "have a problem with a tree," she pointed to the entrance of the house and then back again to herself, "And I need to fix it up before my husband comes home," she tapped her watch. "Will you come with me?" she pointed at Luca and then to the open door, "And take a look at it?" She pointed at him and then back again to her and then towards the entrance of the house, "And let me know if you think the ladder is long enough or not?" She used both hands to give the impression she was measuring something long and straight.

Luca looked back at her with a puzzled expression he wasn't quite sure exactly what she wanted him to do but he knew it had nothing to do with the field next door.

"Signora," he stated bravely. "I think you no understand what the Fuoco Del Vigili do." He clasped both his strong sun tanned hands together and stretched his two arms out in front of him, he looked as though he may have been playing a game of charades and was impersonating an elephant's trunk. Then he bent his knees slightly, leant his body back on a tilt and looked back at her earnestly and said. "Signora watcha what I do I willa explain everything to you. Signora whenna there is a fire, we my crew and me take theesa very long hose," he swayed his two outstretched arms in front of him from side to side, "And we make the fire go away with the aqua," he started blowing loud gusts of air through his puffed cheeks. "You know it is the wet thing that comes fromma theesa hose." He swayed his outstretched arms from side to side. "Signora we don't do nothing with a tree," he said seriously. He straightened up again and placed his arms back down by his side.

"Yes, yes, there is no need to explain, I am fully aware of what you do," Cornelia sniped impatiently; her shoulders shaking slightly as a cool breeze whizzed by. "But I am trying to tell you, I have a problem with a tree in my back garden and I would like you to come with me and have a look to see what can be done about it." She reached out and tried to grab his arm.

"Signora," Luca gasped. He hastily side stepped her grasping hand. "I am a very sorry to tell you, but for theese problem I cannot a help you. But eef you like I will give to you the phone number of my cousin. He is a tree doctor and he will come to yourra Ouse to take a look at yourra tree." He raised his eyebrows with a knowing smile.

"Look you silly man, I don't have time to waste. My husband will be home soon and I don't want him to find out, so we need to get on with this NOW." Cornelia grabbed him by the wrist and forcefully yanked him towards the door. "Would you please come with me?" Luca momentarily lurched forward and then instinctively pulled his arm back again. He stepped back in fright.

"Signora please," he pleaded in a shaky voice. "You are of course a very beautiful woman, even for your age. But Signora I think you no understand, I am a very happy man," he said shoving his hand out in front of her; he wriggled his ring finger under her nose. Luca continued, apologetically. "Signora, I know sometimes it can be very lonely living here without your friends and family, for this situation, I cannot imagine." He paused for a moment before reaching for his phone. "Signora eef you like I will give to you the phone number of my other cousin, he lives at home with his mother and he is a single Okay?"

"Don't be ridiculous, clearly it is you who doesn't understand," retorted Cornelia, completely outraged. "I don't wish to meet any of your cousins or their mothers for that matter. I am simply trying to get you to take a look at the size of a tree in my back garden that a bird is caught in."

Luca wasn't sure whether he had been insulted or not. "Signora I am a little confuse, did you just tell to me now, you have a bird who has the problem, with the tree in the garden of your Backside?"

"Yes that's what I have been trying to explain to you for the past ten minutes," she replied exasperated. "I NEED, you to bring your ladder around to my back Garden," she emphasised the word garden. "So we can try and get the bird out of the tree before it flies away, do you understand?" She shouted.

"Ohhh Signora why you didn't mention theesa little bird in the first place?" He was clearly relieved, his face, now shining like the sun. "Si of course, we can take a look at thissa for you." He waved his arm out to the truck again. "Signora the Vigili Del Fuoco is also working very hard to keep the safety for the birds and the small animals too."

"So you will ask your Men to come around the back and

bring the ladder with them?" She asked.

"Si Signora we will come now, it will be our pleasure to take the ladder and meet you in your backside," he rubbed his two hands together enthusiastically.

"Very well, I shall go and tell my son you are coming." Cornelia started to close the door.

"Si Brava Signora and Errr Signora, just one thing before you go. I don't know how to say to you in the nice English, but I think it will be good manners if maybe you put some clotheses on," he looked at her sheepishly before continuing. "I think my crew; they never saw a foreign woman in her night clotheses before now, so for thissa reason it will be better if you wear your daytime clotheses, Si?"

Cornelia felt herself flush from head to toe when she realised she had been standing there the entire time in her night dress. For just the briefest of moments the idea of being a distraction to a group of strong young firemen was really quite flattering. The truth was she hadn't really thought of herself in 'that way' for a very long time. Then again, now was not the time and place to consider such frivolity. Actually right now, what she needed to do was to remain focused. Like it or not she was a woman on a mission and time was of the essence.

"Yes of course we wouldn't want to distract them from their duty would we?" She replied, with just a ghost of a smile. "Now, could you please excuse me? I really must speak to my son as soon as possible …… and of course …… get dressed," she said, as she curtly closed the door.

## 16 THE FESTA

Algernon let out a loud exasperated sigh as he rapidly swerved the silver ghost over to the side, in a gallant effort to avoid the massive pile of fallen wood that had taken up most of the narrow road that led up into the heart of the historical village.

Winston and Churchill yelped sharply as they both slid uncouthly from one side of the wonky van to the other. Algernon, already feeling more than a bit rattled, shot a quick darting look into the rear view mirror just to make doubly sure they hadn't fallen out.

"Father," Alistair shrieked. "Was that necessary? I mean I am really starting to lose faith in your driving. Surely to goodness you didn't need to react that Abruptly!"

"Excuse me Alistair, when I want your opinion on how to drive I shall Bloody well ask for it. In the meantime would somebody be so kind as to tell me where we are going and whom exactly we are meant to meet?" He puffed.

"Algernon, please don't get into one of your awful Paddies. As I have already told you we were obliged to come here. After all, if it wasn't for these people, that wretched bird who has caused nothing but trouble would still be stuck up in that tree," Cornelia intervened.

Algernon concentrating hard now, slowly edged the car through the grandiose Roman arches that heralded the beginning of the tiny picturesque village of Pidginonia.

"Blasted Italians and their never ending brick work," he muttered under his breath as he swerved along the tiny cobblestone streets that endlessly twisted up and down and round and round in every possible direction.

"Mother is quite right father, if it wasn't for Luca's Uncle Luigi, Sebastion would still be caught up in that tree."

"Hmm this looks as though it may be the main parking square," Algernon muttered again, as he drove the car towards a wide open area filled with an assortment of fiats and brightly coloured motorcycles.

"Algernon are you all right?" Cornelia quipped. "I don't think you have listened to a word we have said."

"No I am not all right," Algernon snapped. He pulled the hand-brake up hard. "Truth be told I would much rather be back at Horatio's Villa enjoying a good drop of quality scotch before retiring for the evening. Instead, here I am floating around some God forsaken outpost, looking for a fireman and a self-appointed Bird Whistler."

"Truth," spat Cornelia. "You're a glowing example of the truth aren't you Algernon? Correct me if I am wrong but I do believe it was your incessant lies that led us here in the first place. If it wasn't for you and your badly orchestrated cover ups about a holiday in Tuscany we wouldn't be here at all. Furthermore, I am convinced that there is more to this little sojourn than meets the eye."

"Oh for crying out loud could you please stop your bickering for five minutes? At least whilst we are in public." Alistair peered out towards the car park. "What's more, if I am not mistaken I do believe the two gentlemen in question are approaching the car right now."

All three of them sat in a stony stifled silence as they watched Luca and a wizened old man, who was dressed rather unseasonably in a three piece woolen suit and a traditional Italian cap, walking towards the car.

"Let's just get this over and done with shall we?" Algernon said with military precision. He looked sternly from left to right before opening his door to greet them.

Cornelia had made a little more effort than usual with her choice of clothes for the evening. After all it wasn't every day that she got to sit next to a strapping young 'Hunk' of a man like Luca. Besides most of the clothes she had packed were now slightly unsuitable and clashed terribly with her new brightly coloured 'Do.'

However after rummaging around in the upstairs wardrobe that afternoon she actually managed to find a very nice Orange and Baby Blue, Nylon Kaftan, featuring a large technicolour swirl on the front. She was also very pleasantly surprised when she discovered, not only was it wonderfully comfortable but it also fitted her perfectly.

Checking her face in the sun visor mirror, she hurriedly smoothed out her iridescent locks before alighting from her side of the car. With just a hint of a smile and a slight lilt to her voice, she bid them both a good day before placing two tiny dry kisses on either side of Luca's clean shaven face.

"So these are the two brave men you were telling me about dear," Algernon inquired as he looked on in surprise. "Would you be so good as to introduce me to them," he said, looking quizzically at his wife. "After all it is not every day I get to meet a real life hero is it," he finished, as he held out his hand.

"Grazie Signore," Luca responded, eagerly shaking Algernon's hand. "But I am not so sure we are as you say 'the real life heroes', but in any case I am very pleased to meet you," he smiled brightly as he let go of the hand. "But Signore, I must to tell you, Eeef anyone should be called a hero it should be my Uncle Luigi here," he said as he gestured towards the small wrinkled man whose mischievous grin, resulted in a grandiose display of a toothless cavern.

"Ah I see," Algernon replied casting a superficial look in the direction of the imp.

"Signore, this is my Uncle Luigi and he is very famous in theesa villages as the man who calls the birds home, how you say in English, to roots."

Algernon spluttered back a cough of surprise before shaking the shrivelled old hand of the bird whistler.

Cornelia, fearing the discussion may invariably take a

turn for the worse, jumped in with an explanation.

"I think what Luca means to say is 'to Roost' as in come home," she corrected. "And he is quite right if it hadn't been for Luigi and his dentist appointment we may never have seen Sebastion again." She gave Alistair a slight nudge with her elbow.

"Yes, yes, mother is quite right," Alistair joined in, looking up from his mobile. "I have no doubt Sebastion would still be up that blasted tree if it wasn't for uncle Luigi here and his brilliant bird whistling skills."

"Oh I see," replied Algernon, slightly confused. "But I thought it was the firemen that rescued him, I mean Sebastion. With all due respect I don't wish to appear rude or ungrateful but I can't help thinking Luigi is a little too old to belong to the fire brigade," he stated. He raised his bushy eyebrows unevenly.

"Algernon please show a little bit of gratitude," hissed Cornelia. "Of course, he is not a member of the fire brigade. However fortunately for us he had a dental appointment this morning."

"A dental appointment?" Algernon spluttered. He looked intensely at Luigi. "But how did that change anything. I thought it was the fire brigade that saved the day. Next minute you will be telling me it was his toothless grin that won Sebastion over in the end." He laughed loudly, his rotund girth swaying from side to side as he rocked back and forth on his heels.

"Father please would you stop with all the questions, can we just move on now?" Alistair asked, in an overly loud whisper. "Surely you understand these people are just simple country folk and have no idea what you are getting at," he said. He flashed a tokenistic smile in the direction of the two men.

"Signore," Luca began, in a slightly injured tone. "I can explain for you. My Uncle Luigi was at the dentist today and needed a way back home to his village, Thissa village Pidginonia. So I pickka him up because after you'rra house my crew and I are going to burn the grasses around Pidginonia, you understand?"

"Yes Yes, it's as clear as mud. No need to say anymore," Algernon declared. Clicking his tongue he looked around with a bemused expression.

"I really think we should get going now?" Cornelia warned.

"Signore," Luca continued. "My Uncle Luigi is a very famous around here in the San Pocolo Mountains for a speaking and whistling at the birds. Today after I pickka him up from the dentist I bring him over to the garden of your backside to whistle at the bird who doesn't want to come."

"Oh I see," Algernon responded looking slightly more confused.

"Signore," Luca began again, this time he was waving his hands as well. "I try once a more to explain to you. Today my uncle," he pointed to Luigi, "Lose one of his tooths at the dentist," he pointed to his mouth and tapped his front tooth with his finger. "After this, Luigi could make a very nice whistle to your bird in your backside."

Algernon quite convinced now that there was always going to be a slight loss in translation decided that they really had gone as far as they could with regard to understanding one another.

"Yes, yes, I see Jolly good hockey sticks then. I say wasn't it good that you were able to bring old Luigi in to save the day," he chuckled. He gave the little man a slight tap on the shoulder.

As soon as he had finished chuckling, they were interrupted by a few loud bangs that sounded as though they were coming from behind the village wall.

"I think we really should get going now," Alistair insisted. "It definitely sounds as though something is going on over there." He pointed to the wall and slid his phone back into his pocket.

"Yes, yes, please come, they have begun the celebrations already if we don't walk now very quickly we will miss the Dishplay," Luca warned, urging the group to follow him.

"Fireworks in Broad daylight?" Algernon muttered loudly under his breathe. "How on earth are we meant to see anything?"

"Oh for goodness sake, Algernon stop complaining.

Where is your so called sense of Adventure?" Cornelia issued. She sped up her step in a deliberate effort to catch up to Luca.

"That's a change of heart if ever I saw one," said Alistair as he sidled up to his father. "She usually loathes fireworks let alone long drawn out dinners with Contadini, how unusual. I must say the outfit she has chosen is a little sparkly and bright to say the least, don't you think Father?" He choked back a snigger as he looked at his mother's brightly clad body, prancing just ahead of them.

"Perhaps she has finally seen the light," Algernon puffed as he slowly plodded his way towards the foot of the ancient sandstone stairs.

After reaching the top of the stairs, Algernon decided it was time to stop for a moment and take a well-earned break. As he stood there puffing and panting and breathing in the cool fresh air he couldn't help feeling slightly elated when he contemplated the wondrous mountain views that surrounded the little village.

Also being an avid car enthusiast, he was mildly impressed by the assortment of antique fiats in the car park that were no doubt, still in good working order. Casting his eyes further afield he took advantage of his elevated position and scrutinised the car park carefully hoping to spot one of his favourite cars, a vintage Maserati.

Peering down intensely, he was just about to turn back and join Alistair and Cornelia, who were waiting impatiently in the square, when something glinting and shiny caught his eye.

Looking as hard as he could into the brilliant setting sun, he thought he could make out the shape of a man sitting on top of a dark coloured car. He seemed to be looking up at them through a pair of binoculars. "That's all very odd I think that chap over there is looking at us," he muttered. "Alistair, come over here and take a look at this."

"Oh for crying out loud Father, what are you moaning about now? Can't you see you are holding us all up Mother is about to blow a head gasket. Could you please just get yourself over here as soon as possible? Honestly I am ashamed to say your behaviour of late is nothing short of appalling."

"Ease up on the insults there Lad, I hardly think that level of attack is called for. Besides you know full well I can't see very far without my glasses. I simply wanted you to come over here and double check something for me."

"Algernon, I think it may be a good idea if Luca and I and Uncle Luigi went ahead," Cornelia called out sharply. "After all we wouldn't want to miss all the excitement of the fireworks would we?" She said with a sly smile.

"All right dear, Alistair and I will join you shortly. Make sure you keep a seat for us," he instructed.

"What? Don't tell me you have spotted another one of your phantom ghosts?" Alistair said sarcastically as he approached his father.

"Don't be facetious Alistair. It really doesn't suit you." Without waiting for a response he turned back again and threw his arm out diagonally across the car park and asked, "What do you make of that?"

"What? What exactly am I meant to be looking at?"

"Oh Darn, where has he gone?" Algernon asked. He leant forward and peered out intently. "I could have sworn he was there just a minute ago."

"Who Father? I have no idea who you are talking about. Perhaps a bit of a hint may help."

"I was almost certain there was a man sitting on top of a car watching us with a pair of binoculars. But now it appears as though he has gone."

"Ha ha ha ha , Oh my God, Father that is classic! I've heard it all now. I have to say that is the stupidest thing you have ever said. Come on, we really should be getting you out of this sun, clearly it is doing you some harm." Alistair grabbed him under the elbow and tried to steer him back towards the square.

"But I am sure he was there. I mean I know my eyesight is not what it used to be, but that doesn't mean I can't make out basic shapes and sizes. I tell you there was a man sitting on top of his car staring up at us."

"Hmm yes Father, and Pigs can Fly," Alistair replied. He laughed again. "Now if you don't mind I really think we should be making our way back to Mother. I am sure she will be wondering where on earth we are and if I were you Father, I wouldn't mention a word about any strange man and a pair of binoculars."

"Thank you Alistair, but if you don't mind I think I am more than capable of making my own decisions as well as walking by myself." Algernon stated gruffly as he pulled away from Alistair's grasp. He cast one last hopeful look towards the car park before turning away.

"Suit yourself, but I am going to start heading over. I wouldn't want to miss the spectacular fireworks display now would I," he laughed loudly again. "I daresay, it will be the first and the last time I will happen to see one in Broad daylight."

"Come now, Alistair you shouldn't make fun until you have tried it. Aside from that this is their country and obviously they will do things their way and as the old saying goes. When in Rome you should do as the Romans do," he said as he took out his large oversized handkerchief and wiped his sweaty brow again.

<table>
<tr><th colspan="3">INSTAPOL POLICE REPORT</th></tr>
<tr><td>Agent<br>Guido Ventosi</td><td>Day:<br>Three/Afternoon</td><td>File Number<br>1200/12/20098</td></tr>
<tr><td>CASE</td><td>LOCATION</td><td>Report No</td></tr>
<tr><td>Uberbite<br>Surveillance</td><td>Village of<br>Pidginonia</td><td>4</td></tr>
<tr><td colspan="3">Persons of Interest<br>Algernon Uberbite, Cornelia Uberbite, Alistair Uberbite</td></tr>
<tr><td colspan="3">ACTIVITIES</td></tr>
<tr><td colspan="3">16.30 Uberbite family arrives to Pidginonia.<br>16.40 Uberbite family speaks with two men.<br>17.00 Uberbite family go to the Village Piazza.<br>1710 Suspect stared at me in the car park.<br>1720 Suspect walked with his son to the Festa.</td></tr>
<tr><td colspan="3">COMMENTS</td></tr>
<tr><td colspan="3">The Uberbite Family arrived in the Village of Pidginonia at around 4.30 pm. They were greeted by a handsome young man and a very nice old man in the parking lot. When I saw the lovely clothes they were wearing I think these two men looked like they are Italians.<br>They had a very big discussion in the Car Park. It didn’t look like it was a very friendly discussion the son kept playing with his phone.<br>They all walked towards the village square. I am sure they were waiting for the Fantastic fireworks display and a wonderful Festa.<br>The wife was walking separately, far away from her husband and son. She seems to like Italian men very much.</td></tr>
</table>

| INSTAPOL POLICE REPORT | | |
|---|---|---|
| **Agent**<br>Guido Ventosi | Day:<br>Three/Afternoon | File Number<br>1200/12/20098 |
| **CASE** | **LOCATION** | **Report No** |
| Uberbite Surveillance | Village of Pidginonia | 4 |
| **Persons of Interest**<br>Algernon Uberbite, Cornelia Uberbite, Alistair Uberbite | | |

**Comments:** The family in question the Uberbites still appear to ave bad manners, hostile and unfriendly. They didn't bring any gifts of wine and cheese or even flowers for the people who had met them in the car park. The primary suspect Algernon Uberbite did not seem very happy to be there. He walked very slowly with no passion or feeling. He stayed behind the main group and stopped three or four times on the staircase on his way to the square. The son Alistair Uberbite was also very rude, he played with his mobile phone the entire time, I think he must be missing his girlfriend.

**Other Notes about other Suspects**

So far there has been no sign of the two dangerous men working for the foreign bank in question. It seems they must not have arrived yet in Pastacula. I am sure the locals will let me know when they do.

**Expenses** One new pair of long range binoculars, I lost the old ones at the local beach. One new, Gucci sports jacket, I didn't want the family in question the Uberbites to recognise me.

The smoke of my own house is better than another man's fire.

# 17 THE WITCH HUNT

*'A woman should be Obscene and not Heard', Groucho Marx*

Even though the tiny walled village of Pidginonia was best known throughout the remote and steep countryside surrounding Pastacula for its famous virgin olive oil, it was also well known for its delightful charming medieval square. Despite the fact it was referred to as a square or a piazza it was actually shaped like a triangle with a well preserved Palazzo Communale presiding at the very tip and flanked on either side by a charming pair of Romanesque monastic churches that featured some very impressive ancient frescoes. Added to this quaint rural charm were a series of medieval buildings that adorned the tree lined streets forming the main Viale, where most of the inhabitants of the village amicably strolled up and down every evening as they bid Buonasera to each other, before retiring for the night.

Luca had done a splendid job as far as settling them all in and making them feel comfortable and before they knew it they were seated down at the VIP table with some other expatriates who had come over to the village to attend the festival. Even Algernon despite his earlier misgivings found himself warming to Craig and Donna, retired school teachers from Melbourne Australia who had been living in the pretty little village next door for the past few years. Craig was an aspiring writer and had written several books of poetry which he hoped to publish sometime in the near future. Douglas and Vivian, from Los Angeles were also part of this little entourage and wasted no time expressing their sheer delight about living in the area and jubilantly recounted how they had spent the last few years restoring their ancient farmhouse. Douglas a retired Lawyer eagerly shared with Cornelia how relieved he was to have finally left the rat race and how fortunate they had been to buy their house before the property Boom had hit.

A little while later they were joined by another couple, Ryan an American and Fey from Thailand who were travelling in the region and had heard about the festival from a friend of theirs who lived in Pastacula. After taking a quick look around the table Ryan, slightly younger than all the others, spotted Alistair sitting all alone. Assuming he would have a lot more in common with someone his own age, he wasted no time making his down way to sit at the other end.

Overall they started out as a very cosy little group and initially, for all intents and purposes they appeared to get on quite well. However, 'Sad to Say' appearances can be misleading and unfortunately before long, things rapidly took a turn for the worse. One could almost say they hit rock bottom as the memorable night progressed.

Luca, full of national pride was at all times a perfect host and took his time to carefully explain to the group that the food and wine was typical of this particular village and even though it was quite provincial he believed it was well worth eating. He spoke about it with such a deep level of affection and sincerity that he almost had Cornelia convinced, about trying something new. In fact she even blushed a little and was quite possibly flattered, when he looked over at her, as he attempted to explain, how some members of the Royal family had also sang the praises of such delectable regional delights.

Feeling a lot more confident now he took the liberty of ordering all the courses for the evening as well as two large Carafes' of red and white Vino Della Casa which were, he assured them the best in the house. Algernon was also a lot more relaxed now and feeling particularly generous. Of course not wanting to be outshone, he ordered three bottles of the best Prosecco in the house for all the guests to sample. When they tried to thank him for his generosity, he shook his head and dismissed their praise, and humbly explained his actions as a simple gesture of good will, to mark the marvellous Italian occasion that had bought them all together.

Once Algernon had poured everyone a glass, he then proceeded to make a toast in honour of Luigi and Luca, who had undoubtedly saved the day by rescuing Sebastion from the tree in the first place. He then promptly sat down again, no doubt feeling very satisfied with himself.

The other expatriates were absolutely intrigued after

listening to Luca relay the story, and begged him to share a few more of the details.

So Luca, positively beaming, recounted the entire story again in his best possible English and then finished the exciting episode with a toast. Holding his glass out high in the air he called, "Salute," to Luigi and then again to the table. There was a little more excited chit chat and light laughter about the daring rescue mission before Luca, in very high spirits now, announced to the group, that it was time for Luigi and him to leave.

"Allora," he began. "I am so happy to see you all together enjoying the wonderful wine of this region. But now Luigi and I must to go very quickly from here before the procession begins. The reason we must go now is because Luigi and me are going to help the Commune to make the strong wooden stand for the Effigy. The truth is, When we  have this wooden stand we can help the Effigy very much to stand very tall and, so when we make it theese way we need to make sure we have made the very strong Erection.

Holding his hands up in front of him, he made a few demonstrative grabbing motions into the air before he continued. "This I think you know is a very important job and so we need to be very careful how we put theese wooden stands together," he announced seriously. "After we are finished our part with this important job, we hope we will come back and join with you, for the watching of this very nice procession."

A short interval of muffled silence descended upon the group as they digested the bizarre but nonetheless innocent connotations made by Luca, who was already standing up, ready to leave, completely oblivious, to any linguistic blunders he may have caused.

"Splendid idea," Algernon finally boomed from his seat. "We shall all look forward to your return and until then Cin Cin," he declared heartily, raising his glass high into the air.

The rest of the group, seemingly relieved and infused now with new found enthusiasm, partly due to Algernon's rescue speech but also due in part to the splendid quality of the alcoholic beverages, all followed suit and jubilantly raised their glasses in unison to the departing heroes, before settling back into animated pockets of conversation.

Alistair, finally came up for air after an exceptionally long bout of texting and noticed Ryan and Fey sitting next to him. Swiftly taking into account his actual proximity to such an attractive exotic woman he wasted no time striking up a conversation with both of them. "Alistair," he stated, shooting his hand out to Ryan. "Actually I saw you arrive earlier but with all the fireworks and speeches going on I didn't quite get your details," he announced.

"Hi I am Ryan and this is Fey," Ryan said, smiling back at him.

"Hmm so you are American, what about you Fey are you an ABC?" He laughed loudly as he looked across the table and winked at her.

"I'm sorry; I don't know what you mean?" She replied.

"ABC," Alistair said loudly, "American Born Chinese. That's what we call Asian people who are not really American, but live in America," he explained.

"Actually I live in Thailand, this is the first time I have travelled out of South East Asia," she said. She blankly stared back at him.

"Ahhh, so you're not American? Who would have guessed," Alistair said, followed by a high pitched chortle.

"No Fey is from Laos. I met her whilst I was working in Thailand."

"Ohhh I see, one of those arrangements is it," he sniggered as he shot a sneaky sideways look at Fey.

"Fey and I have been together for Five years, this is our first trip to Europe, and we are visiting a friend of mine that lives here in the region."

"Ahh, I see so you and Fey are Together-Together as in an Item." Alistair asked, looking very surprised.

Ryan silently glared back at him and took a long sip from his glass.

Realising he may have put his foot in it, Alistair decided to change the topic. "By the way, I was sure I heard, you mention something before about Pastacula. This friend of yours, the one that you are visiting, does he live in

Pastacula?" He asked. He stole another sneaky look at Fey's rather low cleavage.

"Ahhh it's a She actually," Ryan replied coolly. He looked Alistair up and down as he lit a cigarette. Blowing the smoke out to the side, away from the table he pulled his chair back slightly and sat up straight and tall.

"Oh, so your friend is a She? Oh I see, so is She with anyone?" He asked, slightly hopeful.

"Yeah, she has a really nice girlfriend called Olga, she is a Swedish Masseur, they've been together for almost ten years," Ryan replied. He stared back at him with a flat face.

"Oh I see so "SHE," he said, making quotation marks in the air to exaggerate the word 'she,' "lives with her girlfriend in Pastacula?" He sniggered again. "What a waste," he said as he shook his head. Raising his eyebrow quizzically he nodded his head and winked at Fey.

"Yes, yes she has been there for a few years she speaks Italian quite well," said Ryan. He took another sip of his wine.

"Actually, I was there myself, just this morning on a Hmmm," Alistair paused for a moment, "What can I say? Very Hot Date," he winked at Fey. Using both hands, he lewdly drew the shape of a woman's body in the air, making sure to punctuate all the imaginary shapes with a crude whistle, "And she was very nice too," he leered back at them.

"Really, so you are a bit of a player then? A bit of a ladies man if you like," Ryan laughed. He nudged Fey under the table with his foot. "Well I think a steamy holiday romance is always good for making the trip a bit more exciting isn't it? Did you meet her here?" A sarcastic smirk played across his face. He gave Alistair a playful punch on the shoulder.

"I most definitely did." Alistair puffed his chest out. "As a matter of fact I had only just met her the day before in a local café. You know the one in the main square of Pastacula, I think it's called 'Bar Caperoli'. But, Hey- Ho that's fairly standard for me. You know how it is foreign women just can't resist my British accent. Actually this one was all over me like a rash, right from the Get-Go," he leered at Fey again.

"Hmm really, I hadn't actually noticed your accent but now that you mention it I can understand why." Ryan replied sarcastically. He shot a sly look over towards Fey, who had lost interest in the conversation by now and was busily chatting away with Craig's wife, Donna. "Actually I think I know the Café you are referring to, if it's the Bar Caperoli we were there this afternoon, just before we left to come here. It's a small world eh!" He exclaimed giving Alistair another, slightly harder, playful punch. "Clarissa, the friend of ours who lives in Pastacula, always likes to go there she thinks it is a bit quieter than all the other bars. Funny I should say that though, it wasn't very quiet this afternoon. Actually there was a bit of a drama going on while we were there. The tourist police were called in and everything, Man it was full on."

"Really what happened?" Alistair asked as he cautiously nibbled on the end of a piece of hard cheese.

"I am not really sure exactly what it was all about. Fey knows more about it. You know how women are, they can't keep their nose out of other people's business," he laughed. "Hey Fey," he leant across the table. "What was that drama all about in the café this afternoon Babe?"

"Sorry," she said, as she reluctantly broke away from her conversation with Donna. "I wasn't paying attention. What were you asking?" She scowled, back at him.

"Remember what happened this afternoon, when we were at the coffee shop with Clarissa and the owners of the cafe were chasing out that Romanian girl with the tiny dog."

"Which café? We went to two today."

"Oh yeah, Ok, no it's not the pokey smoky one down by the Park. I was talking about the big one. The one that's in the middle of the square. The one Clarissa likes I think it's called Bar Caperoli."

Fey paused for a moment to think about the question before she replied. "Ahh yeah that's right, now I know what you are talking about," she said in a hushed tone. "That woman with the cute fluffy dog. Yes it was, the Bar Caperoli. Oh my God it was so awkward wasn't it? I didn't know where to look," she blushed, pulling the edges of her cardigan a little closer together.

"Yeah it was really bad," Ryan exclaimed "the owner of the café was totally going, Psycho. He was screaming and shouting at her. He was practically throwing her out onto the Square," he added. He leant across the table excitedly and scooped up a handful of pistachio nuts and greedily popped a couple into his mouth.

"What do you mean the owner was throwing her out? I mean what had she done was it because she had a dog with her? What kind of dog was it?" Alistair inquired. He was starting to feel slightly uneasy.

"I don't know but it was some kind of tiny toy poodle or something, you know like one of those little rat dogs. It was like watching an Italian version of cops. It was Awesome man," Ryan laughed. He took another gulp of his wine.

"Well, what was the problem? I mean what exactly were the police accusing her of?" Alistair asked. He sat forward and looked intently at Fey.

"Well, to tell the truth, we didn't really understand much of it because it was all in Italian but our friend who speaks Italian could understand everything. According to Clarissa, the Romanian woman, had been using the café to pick up tourists, well more to the point, men. Apparently she was taking them back to her home and conning them into paying her money for something or rather, I think it was some sort of scam job. I think Clarissa said it had something to do with a mink coat and dry cleaning," she laughed out high and loud and looked at Ryan and then back to Alistair.

Alistair had turned a deathly shade of pale as he turned the petite thin stem of his wine glass around and around in his fingers. It would only need a little bit more pressure to make the stem completely snap off.

"So it had nothing at all to do with the dog then?" Alistair asked, listening intently for their responses.

"No I think the dog was involved in it too somehow, wasn't it Hon?" She shot one of those 'Get me out of this', kind of looks across at Ryan.

"Do you mean at the café or at her house?" Alistair squeaked. He leant further across the table.

"Ummmm, well I am not really sure ….. Yeah I think it was at the house…Yeah that's right, the woman was using the little dog as part of the scam," Fey pulled her cardigan in, even closer.

"But that's ridiculous. It doesn't make sense. I mean how would the café owner know about what was going on in her house?" Alistair's voice was getting louder.

"Well according to Clarissa, the Tourist Police had warned him about it only a couple of hours earlier."

"The Police!" Alistair stood up alarmed. "What would they have to do with it? I mean surely they have better things to do than worry about someone's dry cleaning bill!" He pushed back the long piece of lanky hair that had fallen flat across his forehead.

"Well I don't really know all the details as such," Fey said. She shot another anxious look at Ryan and gave him a sharp little warning kick under the table. "I mean we really didn't spend too much time discussing it but I think it had something to do with her friend, didn't it Babe?" She raised her eyebrows expectantly.

"Yeah Fey's right," Ryan interjected, finally getting the hint. "We didn't really talk too much about it but apparently the hooker's friend owned the mink coat and she had been asking her to give it back for about six months. So she finally went to the Tourist Police and told them the whole story. I suppose the cops thought it was a good idea to warn everybody. Anyway who wants another drink?" He picked up the carafe of red wine.

The long awaited for food, mercifully arrived directly after this  candid convoluted conversation and everybody famished by now except for Cornelia and Alistair, tucked into it with gusto. Lashings of rustic bread and olive oil, plates of tripe, mixed with cheese and scrambled egg and breaded eggplant with chili olives and basil were placed in front of them. There was also an assortment of pastas, and grilled mutton chops and large chunks of tasty fried potatoes.

Cornelia had been on her best behaviour whilst Luca had been around. But now it seemed as though she had decided, she was entitled to a well-deserved drink or two. Realising there was not a great deal on offer she quickly helped herself to several glasses of wine, before picking up a couple of pieces of bread and what looked like a piece of potato and placing them ever so carefully, on her plate.

"So what do you do, Cornelia, do you work?" Vivien asked cheerfully, hoping to strike up a new friendship. "I must say I really like the colour of your hair, it kind of gives the impression that you work with something to do with the Arts. Am I right?" She smiled. Tiny neat laughter lines crinkled at the corner of her eyes.

"Good heavens no. I have never worked a day in my life and I don't intend to either. As for the hair colour, that I can assure you is nothing short of criminal in my opinion. Nothing at all to do with the Arts and if I had my way I would close down the blithering buffoons that were responsible for creating this hideous monstrosity in the first place!" Cornelia snorted.

Turning herself away from Vivien's somewhat surprised expression, she addressed the other guests with a question. "So does anybody know exactly how long this procession goes for?" She picked up another piece of hard crusty bread and placed it on her plate. While she was at it, she carefully examined the piece of food she had picked up earlier; she turned it over and over with her fork. Still not convinced it was actually potato she examined it a bit more for any signs of life, before looking up.

"It's hard to say really. Each Festa is different but they usually go on for at least an hour or two. It really all depends on the importance of the patron Saint and what other activities the Village has planned around the Festa," Craig explained politely. He reached out and grabbed a sumptuous piece of mutton.

"Hmm, I see, but that doesn't really tell me a lot does it? In fact I have been told virtually nothing about this Festa. Does anybody know what it is all about?" She asked stabbing the morsel with her fork.

"Well I am not sure any of us know much about it either," Dianne laughed; she swung her long thick black hair from side to side. "We did come to it last year didn't we Craig? But to be honest, I don't remember the actual details too well. I think it was because we went to so many Festa's last year, I tend to get them all mixed up. Maybe a bit too much of this," she laughed, as she held up her glass. The rows of brightly coloured metal bracelets lined up and down her slender wrist made a loud Clinky- Clanky noise as she pulled the glass up to her lips.

"Yes, it was fantastic last year. It was a much bigger turnout too. Come to think of it I don't think tonight's Festa is about a Saint at all, actually. I am fairly sure it's all about the burning of a witch," he said, popping a juicy black olive into his mouth.

"A witch," Cornelia gasped, "how ghastly." She tossed a piece of crusty bread under the table.

"Yes but it's not really a witch, it is one of the village woman I suppose," Douglas interjected, "And from what I have heard she is tied to a stake at the top of the town square and has to wait for the religious Effigy to be paraded through the streets before they can burn her," he laughed out loud and hard. "If I recall correctly, the effigy is paraded through the streets on a wooden platform, which has each of its corners resting on the shoulders of the strongest and most virile men from the village. It should start from the bell tower on the other side of the village," he announced confidently. He looked around the table, just to make sure they had all taken notice.

"Yes it all sounds a little barbaric," said Vivian. Obviously she was trying very hard to put their earlier little misunderstanding to the side. Giddy with excitement she looked at Cornelia and continued, "But of course it is all just for a bit of fun," she explained, her pretty bright eyes wide open. "No one really gets burnt it's a simple re-enactment of some kind. Actually to be honest we don't really know too much about it either, other than the procession usually ends after they burn the witch. But it's all very exciting isn't it?" She said as she nudged Cornelia with her hand. She laughed heartily, making strange snorting sounds as great gusts of air rushed in and out of her nose.

Alistair, who up until this point, had appeared to be lost in thought and literally miles away, suddenly looked up from his texting. "Oh good God, it sounds perfectly charming" he sniped, rolling his eyes. "Just as appealing as this appalling food," he added picking up a piece of tripe and turning it over on his plate. "Is there anybody here, I mean in this village that may know exactly how long this event will go on for." He looked around indignantly. "I for one don't want to be here any longer than I need to. Frankly I have some very important matters I need to attend to back in Pastacula." He turned to the side and sniffed.

"Well I am sure it won't go on for too long," Algernon interjected from the far end of the table. "Mind you Ali, once the actual parade begins in full earnest, you will probably wish it would last much longer. Craig and Donna here, tell me it is really quite entertaining." Algernon greedily sucked the ends of his fingers. He rolled his eyes in ecstasy as he savoured the flavour of the several chunks of grilled salty mutton, he had just consumed.

Cornelia, finally tired of turning the morsel of food perched on the end of her fork, cautiously poked it into her mouth and within less than a nanosecond; she had lapsed into an explosive session of spluttering and gagging. Most of her tepid drink was sent cascading over the top of her glass, rapidly creating a set of red splotchy patches all over the white linen tablecloth.

Douglas, who had been observing her latest display of hostility, with a keen interest, secretly felt delighted about her plight. The truth was he had taken quite a disliking to her by now and deep down he thought she deserved to splutter and gag. However as the seconds ticked by, Cornelia turned from a deep shade of red to almost purple. Feeling afraid she may actually choke to death and of course ruin the entire evening, he quickly jumped up and clouted her firmly on the back.

"Cough, cough, coughfitty, Cough." Cornelia, threw her heaving head back and drank in huge gusts of the fresh country air. "For…or….or God's Sa…a…a…kes, would you sttt..o…o…o…ppp belting me, you foo…oo…oo..l," she demanded as soon as she had caught her breath. "How on earth can anybody be expected to… oo…oo' she coughed, coughed coughed again, "Eat this filthy foo... oo….ood," she squeaked, in-between intermittent bouts of coughing. Dark black mascara stained tears ran down her face. Snatching up the plate of tripe sitting in front of her she added, "I must say I doubt very much if even the dogs would eat it," and in a moment of rage, she vindictively flung the plate under the table. "Surely there must be an alternate menu for people who have a more sophisticated palate." She threw the last few drops of her salvaged wine, down her quivering throat. Her mascara rimmed 'Panda Eyes' were making her look slightly demonic.

Douglas, was feeling terribly humiliated by now. He tucked his shirt in and skulked back to his seat. However after he had been sitting there quietly for a few minutes, he picked up his fork and in a deliberate act of defiance, he started to scoff down the large plate of tripe sitting on the plastic plate in front of him. He smacked his lips loudly as he looked back over at Cornelia and gave her the universal "thumbs up" gesture of appreciation.

Vivian, suddenly sporting a terse drawn face, no doubt caused by Cornelia's cruel, ungrateful remarks, decided to take Cornelia to task. "I am not quite sure I would be so hasty if I were you to judge the culture and customs of people who have been eating this kind of food for centuries," she protested wryly, flicking her eyes around the table for any added show of support. "We always make it a point to try something new when we come to another country and I think it would do you good if you tried adopting that policy too," she stated through gritted teeth as she twisted her napkin around and around her hand.

"Well yes quite," conceded Algernon. "I am sure Cornelia would agree whole heartedly. As a matter of fact she usually enjoys the challenge of a new culture and all it has to offer. Don't you dear?" He nodded his head in her direction and looked at her sternly from beneath his bushy eyebrows. Cornelia, unaffected by Vivien's outburst and rather drunk at this point, stared down at her bag in silent indignation as she sifted around for another cigarette.

"Well quite frankly Father, in this case, I would have to agree with Mummy. From my experience I would have to say the quality of food in this country is rather ordinary and in MY opinion the sooner we leave and get back to a more civilised country like Spain the better." Alistair moved around in his seat as he tried to pick up a signal for his phone.

"Spain," Craig exclaimed. He laughed loudly. "I hardly think the Spanish diet could be considered sophisticated, especially when you compare it with Italian food. When I was there last summer all I could get was Paella, Paella, and more Paella. I couldn't wait to get back home and eat some decent food again."

"Back home!" Cornelia sneered belligerently. Clearly she had decided to re-join the conversation. Shooting a smug look across at Alistair she added. "Surely you are not suggesting Australia has better food than Spain or even Italy for that matter. For heaven's sake what would an Australian know about good food?" she cackled cruelly. "As far as I know most Australians consider a meat pie to be a delicacy with the occasional 'Roo Burger' thrown in for good measure." She squinted her eyes as she lit a cigarette.

"Now just hang on a minute," Craig retaliated. "Just for the record, we no longer call Australia home. We have been living here in Italy for the past few years and this is our home now. But that doesn't mean we think anything less of our country or the food there for that matter. For your information Australia is known to have some of the finest cuisine in the modern world and even though most Australians appreciate a tasty meat pie we most certainly would never consider them to be a delicacy." He picked up his glass and quaffed down the remaining fluid.

"I think you are on the money, there Craig. I can't really talk from personal experience but my nephew who has lived in Australia for the past two years raves about the quality of food over there. He believes it is second to none." Douglas declared, boldly.

"Well yes Precisely, I have to say I agree whole heartedly with Craig," Algernon boomed, from the far end of the table. He shot a sharp warning look at Cornelia.

"Hah, I hardly call that a recommendation, especially coming from an American. Everybody knows you don't have the slightest inclination when it comes to food. The next minute you will be telling me you speak the Queen's English too," she cackled loudly again, revealing an ugly, dark, wine stained tongue.

"I beg your pardon! Did you just say we don't know how to speak English?" Vivien jumped in, her eyes narrowed into angry slits her tight lips pursed together.

"Well this is turning out to be another fun night isn't it?" Sighed Alistair as he fiddled impatiently with his phone, He held it high above his head.

Ryan and Fey, had already stood up to leave. They rolled their eyes and exchanged secret glances, as they packed up their bits and pieces and made their way to the front of the table.

"Ahhh I think I can see Luca," Algernon boomed, placing his hand across his sweaty forehead. He leant his head down a bit lower as he tried to block out the bright light, bouncing off the gaudy decorations hanging from the trees."

Thankfully a momentary truce was established between them as they strained their eyes towards the darkness and desperately searched for a much needed distraction.

Just like a Saviour, Luca magically appeared, dressed impeccably in his Fireman's uniform only this time he was accompanied, by a lovely young woman, who he was gently escorting by the elbow, towards the tables.

"Buonasera at last I come back," he announced jubilantly. "Please let me introduce you to my very lovely girlfriend Natasha. I am sure you will be able to talk English with her perfectly because she is a fantastic English teacher." He beamed a besotted love struck smile into the young woman's face.

Cornelia glared scornfully at the new arrival, before she turned her head away. Snorting loudly into the air she reached for the almost empty carafe and poured herself, yet another drink.

Stupefied silence reigned over the disgruntled little group for the next few moments and may have remained like that for some time, had it not been broken by the loud, 'Boom Boom Booming' of a brass band approaching them.

Apparently the procession had already begun at the bell tower and was making its way slowly towards the main square. It was only a matter of time before it would pass by their table on its way up to the hill.

Douglas, ever mindful of keeping up appearances and aware of the need to make new friends stretched out his hand towards Natasha and introduced both himself and Vivien. Craig and Donna, although feeling slightly hesitant, did the same and awkwardly stretched past a very drunk Cornelia and introduced themselves. Ryan and Fey had reached the other end of the table by now and briefly introduced themselves too, before bidding everyone good night and making a hasty retreat to their car.

Algernon, no doubt concerned that things may be escalating towards another social disaster, suddenly stood up at the end of the table and asked Luca and his girlfriend to come over and take a seat next to him. He "click clicked" his fingers into the air and summoned the wandering waiter to come back and replenish the dwindling supplies of wine.

However, just as things seemed to be settling down again, Cornelia decided to make an announcement that was ultimately responsible for opening Pandora's Box and sounding the 'death knell' for any possible peacekeeping deals. "I am terribly confused," she declared loudly with a belligerent swagger. "Have I missed something vital here this evening?" Scowling down towards the end of the table she carefully singled out her latest victims. "Luca did you just say your friend was an English teacher? How interesting, perhaps she could shed some light on the conversation we were having earlier."

"Scusa Signora but I don't understand what you ask of me. What conversation are you meaning?" Luca asked looking back at her, with a puzzled expression.

Douglas, clearly sensing Luca's confusion, jumped into the rescue. "Well it doesn't really matter does it? After all, we are all global citizens aren't we?" He chuckled lightly and looked at everyone a brave grin plastered across his face. "You know the funny thing is, even though English might be the most widespread language in the world, I still find it amazing that there is no, Ham in Hamburger, No Egg in Eggplant and neither Pine or Apple in Pineapple,

Go figure!" He exclaimed, before taking a satisfied sip of his wine.

"I hardly find that amusing," sniped Cornelia. "Furthermore your obscure reference to fruit and vegetables only made you sound even more idiotic than you actually look. But of course, that sort of thing is to be expected from an American, who insists on wearing his cap on backwards."

Silence prevailed, for the smallest of moments before complete Pandemonium struck!

"Oh for crying out loud woman, don't you think it's about time you gave it a break? I, and I am sure I speak on behalf of all the others here, have just about had a gutful of your overbearing Imperialism for one night," Douglas declared as he threw his cap down onto the table and helped himself to the newly arrived carafe of red wine.

"Yes mother, Do sit down, the parade will be coming this way in a few minutes and we won't be able to see it if you are blocking the view," Alistair hissed through semi clenched teeth.

"Excuse me Alistair, mind your manners. I will be perfectly happy to sit down when somebody is able to answer my question," she shrieked as she took a long deep drag of her cigarette. The great Multi-coloured Kaftan, billowed out boldly behind her.

"I am sorry, I don't think I understand. Did you say you have a question about the English Language?" Natasha asked timidly.

"Hah, just as I suspected," snorted Cornelia triumphantly, blowing great gusts of smoke all over Douglas and Vivien. "I can tell by your horrible foreign accent that you're not even English. So how on earth could you possibly be an English teacher?"

"Oh, I have heard it all now," lamented Vivien, shooting a quick bemused look around the table. "You really do take the cake don' you? So let me ask you then," she stared directly into Cornelia's mocking eyes. "Does that mean you have to be a Paint Brush to be an Art teacher?" She laughed loudly as she turned back to face the others.

"The Biscuit, my dear I believe you mean the Biscuit. That is of course if you wish to speak the language correctly. However bearing in mind, you are in fact, American. I strongly doubt you would have any idea what I am referring to!"

"Cake or Biscuit, Get over it Lady, that's the way the cookie crumbles." Douglas shouted back at her. "To be honest nobody really gives a hoot. Why don't you give us a break and sit down, we are all trying to enjoy our night and we don't really give a damn about whether or not you think we can speak good English," he snarled. He pulled open the top button of his shirt.

"Precisely my point," Cornelia shouted passionately. She leant in towards him. Her long spindly body was hunched halfway across the table by now. "It is because of people like you," she screamed at him, "and You," she pointed at

Craig, "Who don't care enough, that we allow people like "Her," she pointed at Natasha, "to teach a language that is not even their own," she yelled stretching her body tall and upright, she thumped her fist down hard.

"Oh my God, I can't believe you just said that," laughed Dianne. "I have never heard of anything so ridiculous in all my life," she let out another jittery uneven titter as she looked around the table. "I really didn't want to say anything before just in case I offended you, but right now I really don't care what you think. Actually I think you are one of the rudest people I have ever met in my life," she was shaking and trembling all over, from the sheer emotion of it all.

"Well of course I would expect an Antipodean like you to make such an ignorant statement." Cornelia snarled, finally going in for the kill. "I mean isn't it your own countrymen and woman who perfected that truly horrid phrase, Shee'll be right mate! I shudder every time I hear it," she shrieked. Flexing and waving her scrawny arm as she sucked in another long line of smoke.

"Shhhhhhh, Quiet Everyone," Algernon issued gruffly. He gingerly held his hand up around his ear. "I think I can hear the procession approaching. Yes, yes here they come," he added expectantly. He gazed out into the darkness.

Luca, had been quietly watching the entire fiasco up until this stage, but now he had decided it was time to speak up. "Signora, I no understand too much what you try to say to us here about your English Language, but I do know that the peoples here come from many different countries and even so they still like very much this wonderful life we have here," he said with a faint smile.

"You tell her mate with a bit of luck she might listen to you," Craig called out as he grinned over at the others who had now turned their attention to the oncoming procession.

"Yeah that's right Luca You tell Em Luv," Dianne, turned back and gave him the thumbs up gesture.

Natasha had also been listening carefully to all the strained conversations and at this point it would be fair to say she was completely confused. Leaning forward, from the other end of the table, she held her head up high into the night air and called out to Cornelia. "I am sorry but I am not sure if I am following this conversation very well. Can you please tell me what exactly you meant when she said it was people like me that couldn't teach a language that was not their own?"

Cornelia was horribly, horribly drunk as she stood at the end of the table, swaying back and forth. She looked like some kind of giant skittle. She clearly had no interest in anybody else's opinion. However not wanting to be beaten, and just like a dog with a bone, she continued. "Well of course it doesn't surprise me that you can't understand what I am getting at. After all you are a foreigner and English obviously is your second language, therefore you couldn't possibly comprehend a word of what I am saying."

"Signora, I theenk you not understand." Luca interjected, "Natasha she is a very good English speaker much more than me. She is one of the best English teachers at the University in Roma."

"University," Cornelia shrieked like a banshee wailer, "the mind boggles, it's no wonder then that this country has fallen into a state of rack and ruin." She took another puff of her cigarette, which was perilously close, to spilling the end of its spent ashes, onto a plate of discarded tripe.

The procession was in full swing now and everyone at the table, except for Natasha, realising that nothing could be done to deter the ongoing feverish attack, gratefully turned their full attention to the brightly coloured Effigy that was being carried towards them, by a solemn little group of young men.

"I apologise for any misunderstanding Cornelia; that is your name isn't it?" She, crossed her legs and adjusted her sitting position and leant in a bit closer. "I am afraid Luca is very enthusiastic, when it comes to me, and he may have gotten things somewhat confused. The truth is I am not exactly an English teacher in the traditional sense of the word" Natasha offered coolly.

"I knew it!" Cornelia interrupted loudly, maniacally banging her fist down hard upon the table again.

"Actually, I am a Professor of Psycholinguistics, specialising in Second language acquisition and I am currently involved in a research program involving Adult learners and Word Choice," she said in a very matter of fact tone. She crossed her arms.

The community brass band was just starting to pass by their table and for the next few moments the loud 'Oom Pah Pah, Oom Pah Pah', blaring from the nearby trombone, should 'Ordinarily' have blasted away the possibility of any further discussions.

"PRECISELY," shouted Cornelia at the top of her lungs, she drew her arms in and beat her chest hard with her closed fists, causing her to stagger back and forth on her spindly splayed legs.

"You couldn't possibly be an English teacher. It's not even your language, but I on the other hand COULD because it is MY language, it is MY mother tongue." She beat her chest feverishly with her fists. "What you fail to understand Natasha, is that very few people on this earth can truly lay claim to speaking the Queens own English, and as such it belongs utterly and solely to those loyal subjects that can," she declared, flailing both arms out to her side in a flamboyant display of passion and fury.

Coincidentally, or rather unfortunately, as fate would have it. This particular episode of passionate 'Arm Flailing' happened to occur, just as the sacred Effigy, was passing by their table.

SO, the results were nothing short of catastrophic, when one of Cornelia's outstretched arms collided in the most 'Spectacular Fashion' with the back of the religious Effigy, and in one foul swoop, sent it hurtling forward onto the terrified torch bearers, 'Immediately setting it Ablaze.'

Everybody looked on in horror as the ghoulish pantomime unfolded in all its gory detail before their very eyes. Cornelia, still virtually oblivious to her diabolical actions, continued to gesticulate wildly as she ranted and raved about the virtues of being English.

Alistair, had finally managed to come up for air between his tandem texting and sulking and literally shrunk back in horror, when he was confronted by the results of his mother's outrageous behaviour. Strangely enough at the height of his fear he felt an uncontrollable surge of exhilaration race through him as the sudden urge to jump up and sing the Robbie Williams song, 'Let me Entertain You,' threatened to overcome him.

Winston and Churchill were both rudely awoken from their fitful sleep and were full of vigour. Sensing the impending danger, they immediately lapsed into a bout of hysterical barking, almost resulting in a near death choking experience and a slight case of strangulation; which no doubt was caused by their overly tight collars as they made a series of unsuccessful attempts to catapult themselves into the besieged procession. Algernon, completely astounded by this horrific turn of events but at the same time realising the community would soon be baying for blood, took advantage of the bedlam, created by the disaster and decided to act quickly. After reaching the other side of the table he wasted no time gathering up his precious dogs and screaming wife. He made a desperate grab at her contorted, torso with his free hand and with Alistair on one side and he on the other, they promptly 'frog marched' her as fast as they could across the square towards the darkened car park.

# WINSTON'S WOES

*"When a man's dog turns against him it is time for a wife to pack her trunk and go home to mama." Mark Twain*

The young handsome vet looked as though he had just stepped off the front cover of a Vogue magazine. To call him an Adonis was probably going too far but to suggest he was every bit the epitome of Italian style and grace would not have been an exaggeration. He had thick black curly hair slicked back into a neatly bobbed tail, an angular jaw line with fine boned chiselled features and a long slender well-toned body. This was coupled with a passionate, 'can do' attitude, positively reinforced by the white medical gown that casually hung untied all the way down to his white leather shoes, which were a perfect match for the ultra-white walls of the examination room.

His pale blue eyes looked intensely, from the dog on the table and back again to Algernon without blinking once as he dutifully scribbled into the designer notebook he was holding. Every now and then he reached over and prodded Winston in the abdomen or just below the ribs and felt his nose for moisture, he firmly held his hand over the dog's nose one more time before writing down his observations.

Just before he had finished scribbling his last entry, the young secretary who had greeted them earlier in the reception area, burst into the room without knocking and spoke to him in Italian. Judging by the way the Vet repeatedly replied, "Si Capito," whilst casting several anxious looks across the room at the dog's owners, one could safely assume they were talking about a rather serious matter. After they had finished this little "tete a tete" the secretary silently made her way out of the room, making sure she avoided any eye contact with Algernon and Cornelia as she walked past.

Then in one single action, the young vet, sharply inserted a thermometer into Winston's rear end, which caused the poor dog to jerk forward and yelp loudly. He then turned his attention back again to the disconcerted owners.

"Scusa Signore, Can you help me, I just want to ask you, how old is the bitch?" He looked over at them from the metal examination table.

"I beg your pardon. I am not too sure what you are getting at?"

"The bitch, how many years is she?" He looked at Cornelia now, hoping she could provide the answer.

"What I mean is, she doesn't look very young and for that reason I need to know what I could do with her, if I had to keep her with me for one night." He looked down at the quivering dog.

"Excuse me for saying so but I hardly think this is the time and place to speculate about such matters," Algernon replied gruffly.

"I am sorry but this is a very important matter to me. I don't get the chance to see too many bitches from the UK and when I do I need to know what is the best service for them. It can all depend on the age of the bitch and how often she would need my service," he said as he pulled the thermometer out efficiently and briefly looked at it.

Cornelia, still looking like death warmed up and clearly suffering from a hangover, immediately lapsed into a long coughing fit that left both eyes streaming. Her left over mascara, the only remnant of the 'pre-disaster glamour' from the night before, ran down her cheeks, creating soft dark lines that made her look more like a tragic clown from an Italian opera.

Even though Algernon was still feeling very angry with her, due to the current 'dog situation,' he couldn't help feeling a certain level of pity for her as well. "I beg your pardon. I know it was very foolish of her to give him Foreign food in the first place, but putting that aside for one minute, I really must say that is no way to speak about my wife," he said sharply.

The young vet looked back at him silently perplexed. Taking his gloves off he turned away and proceeded to wash his hands thoroughly before turning back to reply.

"Signore .... Uber... Uber... bite," he stammered as he read the name from the medical card, hanging at the end of the table. "I am not so sure about what you say or what you would like me to do with your wife, but I must warn you now, I am an animal doctor and so I don't ever touch the human being."

"Yes," Algernon replied irritably. "I am fully aware of that and that is why we have bought our dog here to see you. I know my wife may not look her best this morning, in fact she is not feeling too well, but that certainly doesn't give you the right to make cruel jokes about her age," he finished. He stole a quick glance at Cornelia, who had dozed off again and was slumping halfway down the chair.

"What you mean I make the cruel joke? Scusa Signore, I No say anything about your wife, I just ask you how old the bitch was so I can think about the best treatment for her," he protested, waving his arm over towards Winston, who was busily chewing the pair of gloves that had been left on the side of the table.

"Oh I see," Algernon replied sheepishly, finally realising he had been talking about the dog. "Well in that case I would have to say HE," he stated, emphasising the word HE "Is about ten years old, quite old really for a dog of HIS breeding."

"Well in any case Signore Uberbite, it doesn't really matter what it is, a he or a she. After I finish to examine your dog I think she is suffering from a bad case of indigestion. Also I find some strange marks around the neck which can be from something too tight or perhaps something like a spider has bitten the bitch. In my personal opinion at this moment we cannot be too sure."

"Is it Serious?" Algernon asked anxiously. He suddenly jolted forward, causing Cornelia to fall forward too and wobble around ungraciously from left to right before she woke up with a start.

"Signore, as I tell to you before at this exact moment we cannot be too sure what the real problem is to cause thissa dog to vomit up all Hizza food. But to be perfectly sure it is nothing too serious, I think we should keep your dog here for one night. This way I can make many more examinations of this bitch."

Cornelia, wide awake now, sat demurely in the chair. After listening intently to what the young man was saying, for the briefest of moments, she appeared to be genuinely concerned for the fate of poor Winston. However taking into account the kind of woman she was and bearing in mind the difficulties she had recently endured, it was only to be expected that she would undoubtedly feel the need to defend her actions.

"Well I must say," she started in a shaky voice. "I had no idea the silly dog would actually eat the food I was throwing under the table. As a matter of fact, I didn't consider it edible for either man or beast and that is precisely the reason why I threw it there in the first place."

"Si Madam, I understand what you say," the young vet replied pitifully. "But of course you are British, therefore it's true, you do not understand too well the difference between the food for the animal and the food for the human being," he advised. He folded his arms tightly across his body.

"Well let's not get too carried away with the how and the why, shall we?" Algernon interjected. "I think the most important thing to consider here, Is what we shall do now?" He lifted the lower regions of his great girth up for just a moment before plunging them back down again with a whoosh. "If you believe the dog would be better off to stay here for the night then I am only too pleased to abide by your wishes. After all, Winston's health and well-being is of paramount importance to me and I shall do whatever it takes to make sure he is in safe hands."

Almost like clockwork, Winston sent out a blood curdling howl that caused them all to automatically shudder and exchange startled looks of concern.

"Theese I think would be the best solution. Eeef you like, I will also call to my colleague now and make the arrangements for him to come here today. I will ask him to tell me his idea about what is causing the red marks around the neck. This way you can be sure we will cure the problem very quickly. In the meantime you can leave the dog here with me and I will take care of its every need." He walked back over to Winston and officiously wrote something down on the chart.

Algernon, visibly relieved that the critical situation was beginning to settle down, jumped up from his chair and waddled over to the examination table. Shaking the vet's hand vigorously he thanked him several times before he turned his attention to Winston and gave him a generous wobbly all over body rub, finally finishing it off with an affectionate tug of the dog's ears, before turning back again to face his wife.

"Well it appears as though we have narrowly avoided a tragedy thanks to some quick thinking on my behalf and some brilliant intervention by this young man here," he said beaming robustly towards the young vet. "But next time we may not be so lucky," he warned. He pointed his finger at her. "Perhaps you had better think twice Cornelia, before you take it upon yourself to feed the dogs food they may not be accustomed to," he Wheeeeezed loudly.

"And perhaps you may think twice Algernon, before you put me in a position where I am subjected to primitive eating habits that literally make my blood curdle," she spat out tartly. Snatching up her handbag she stood up, ready to leave.

"Scusa Signora, I am sure you must be mistaken," the Vet objected. "The food from thissa part of Italy is very famous and some people even think it is the best in the entire country." He crossed his arms tightly against his white coated chest before continuing. "But, it is true, thissa kind of food should not be given to the dogs, it is too strong for them but of course, you don't really know about these very important things." He gave them a patronising smirk.

"Excuse me," countered Cornelia. She took a step

forward, “I really beg to differ. It’s quite clear by the evidence set before us, that not only is it not fit for Humans; it really isn’t suitable for animals either. What’s more, I haven’t slept a wink all night due to a dreadful stomach upset. I for one shall not be entertaining the idea of ever eating such a ghastly selection of ‘awful offal’ again,” she finished. She turned towards the door.

“Oh come dear, it really wasn’t that bad. Actually I thought the mutton was quite tasty,” Algernon replied, he walked over to her as briskly as his gammy knee would allow. “In fact this situation reminds me of the famous quote made by Mark Twain. ‘The only way to keep your health is to eat what you don't want, drink what you don't like and do what you'd rather not,’ he flashed a flimsy smile over at the Vet.

“Yes and wasn’t he the fool who also said that Sacred Cows make the best Hamburgers?” She snarled as she pulled open the door.

“Si Signora and this is why I say you no understand what I try to explain to you before.” The young vet shook his hands about him passionately; he was clearly becoming more agitated with every passing second. “Scusa Signora, thissa situation is just like when I try to tell another Italian friend, about that famous American food called the ‘Hot Dog.’ Signora please, let me explain to you,” he pleaded. He rubbed his hands, over his slicked back hair. “It is really impossible for an Italian person, who has never been abroad, to understand that a Sausage, that no looks like a Sausage,” he shrugged his shoulders, “And is made from the most Orrible parts of the animal, can be eaten with a sauce, called the tomato sauce that has no Tomatoes in it. Signora, I explain to you, that for an Italian, this is incredible," he exclaimed. He drew his hands up around his ears and stared back at them, the whites of his eyes standing out dramatically against his red flaring nostrils.

"Surely you don't believe for one moment that I or any other British person would even begin to consider a Hot Dog to be passable as food," Cornelia hissed. She bristled as she turned around to face him.

"Yes, well that's all very interesting, but we really should get going now," Puffed Algernon. He hurriedly pushed Cornelia through the open door, obviously hoping to avoid any further conversations regarding Food, Dogs and Americans, but not necessarily in that order.

"Signore Uberbite," the vet called out as he walked over to the door. "Wait please, before you go, I just remember I needa to give you a message about a man who came to the office before looking for you. He told my secretary that it is important for you to know that he will be sure to meet with you later. Just a moment while I read the note he give to her." He fished around in his pocket for a couple of seconds before bringing out a piece of paper.

"Signore, Eeef you like, I will translate it for you O'Kayyyy. In Italian it says, Quando IL migliore amico DI un uomo è IL cane, quel cane ha un Problema and in English, I cannot be totally sure but I think thissa means, "When a man's best friend is his dog, that dog has a problem." Signore Uberbite when I hear such a thing like this it sounds a totally crazy, but I am sure because you are so wise you will know what this message means." He shrugged his shoulders as he handed the piece of paper over to a bewildered Algernon.

As soon as Algernon took the paper from the vet his phone rang in a long shrill tone, causing him to instinctively jolt up against the open door. Instructing Cornelia to go on ahead, he took the phone from his pocket and scowled hard at it for a moment. Placing it closely against his ear he issued a rather 'Harried Hello' before he heard it click off at the other end. Looking perplexed at the phone again he turned towards the Vet and asked, "Is it usual to receive random phone calls in this part of Italy? I seem to be getting quite a few over the past few days."

"Signore Uberbite, I don't know how to answer this question but I think anything is possible when you are on vacation. Perhaps you have a secret admirer somewhere who wants you to know they are thinking of you," he replied politely as he stood at the open door.

"Yes but I don't know anybody here and I can be almost certain I don't have any admirers. Besides, this phone belongs to a friend of mine. He lent it to me, to use whilst I am here," Algernon blustered pushing his large frame through the narrow door.

"And what's more," he said holding the phone up to the Vet, "whoever is making these calls, is definitely a foreigner."

"Well of course, you are in Eeetaly. In this situation it will be natural for the Italian language to sound foreign to you if you don't understand any Italian."

"No, No, I don't mean that, I mean 'Foreign,' you know, like somebody else from one of those other strange countries. Take a look at the number, it doesn't look Italian to me," Algernon explained. He held the phone directly under the Vets nose.

"Hmmmm Si, You are right this is not an Italian number. I can't be sure but I think it might be from somewhere in Africa or some other place like this," he said. He stepped back towards his office.

"Africa! Why would anybody be ringing my friend Horatio from Africa? As far as I know he doesn't know anybody in Africa."

"Well in that case Signore Uberbite perhaps your friend would be the best person to ask about such things," he said as he started to close the door. "Now I am so very sorry but If you would excuse me I really should be checking back on the dog, it is time for me to take her temperature again," he looked down at his watch.

"Oh yes of course, don't let me keep you. After all it's Winston we should be concerned about," Algernon replied hastily. "By the way, Old chap, I would just like to thank you again for taking care of Him, he really does mean the world to me and I would hate to think of what could have happened if we didn't bring him here," he cleared his throat loudly.

"Prego Signore, believe me it was a pleasure. You can be sure your dog is in the best of hands," he said. He pulled a pair of surgical gloves out of his pocket and started to stretch one over his broad hand.

Just then the phone rang loudly again and as Algernon bumbled around in his pocket, the vet took the opportunity to bid him 'farewell' and promptly closed the door.

"Hello," Algernon issued. He strained his ear for any sound that might seem familiar. However, just like all the other calls, after a few moments of silence the caller abruptly hung up. "Who the hell is it?" He pondered. He stared intensely at the phone resting silently in his hand. "Surely to goodness nobody would intend us any harm," he said out loud, much to the surprise of the young secretary who was keeping a safe distance behind the desk.

"Oh for crying out loud Algernon can we please get a move on," Cornelia demanded as she poked her head through the open door of the office. "How much longer do we have to hang around here worrying about that imbecile of a dog?"

"Don't be like that Cornelia you know how much he means to me. I really don't know how I would go on without him. In this case the old saying, "a dog is a man's best friend" is true." He jutted his large 'double chins' into the air.

As soon as Algernon had uttered the very last syllable, the pitiful sound of Winston's high pitched yelping, echoed towards them with an 'Eerie Haunting Resonance.'

**INSTAPOL POLICE REPORT**

| **Agent** Guido Ventosi | Day: Four/ Midday | File Number 1200/12/20098 |
|---|---|---|
| **CASE** | **LOCATION** | **Report No** |
| Uberbite Surveillance | Veterinarian Surgery Pastacula | 5 |

**Persons of Interest**
Algernon Uberbite, Cornelia Uberbite, Alistair Uberbite

**ACTIVITIES**

11.30am Suspect and his wife go to the vet.
11.35am Two bad Men go into the vet.
11.40am Two bad Men leave the vet.
12.30 pm The Suspect and his wife leave the vet.
12.35pm Suspect and his wife have a loud fight.
12.45pm Suspect walked away quickly from his wife.
12.55pm The suspect went for his lunch in the Piazza.

**Expenses**

One new Apple Macintosh laptop. I needa to buy this. My computer it doesn't work very well in the old building of the Pensione. It must be the thick walls. Also it is more stylish. One electronics toothbrush. The personal hygiene is very important for meeting new people.

I hope you are happy now with the reports. I try very hard every night to study my dictionary. There is nothing else to do in Pastacula.

Every Dog has it's Day Ogni cane ha il suo giorno

| **INSTAPOL POLICE REPORT** | | |
|---|---|---|
| **Agent**<br>Guido Ventosi | Day: Four/<br>Midday | File Number<br>1200/12/20098 |
| **CASE** | **LOCATION** | **Report No** |
| Uberbite Surveillance | Veterinarian<br>Surgery Pastacula | 5 |
| **Persons of Interest**<br>Algernon Uberbite, Cornelia Uberbite, Alistair Uberbite | | |

| |
|---|
| **COMMENTS** |
| .Algernon Uberbite and his wife Cornelia Uberbite took a very ugly looking dog to the Local Vet in Pastacula. When they came back out again they had a very loud argument and they walked away from each other. I theenk they must be arguing about who will pay the money for the vet. The wife doesn't seem to care to much for the sick dog. For this reason I think her husband is not very happy to be with her.<br>Algernon Uberbite walked off quickly towards the main town and left his wife on her own.<br>Cornelia Uberbite walked off towards the Park alone.<br>I also saw two very rough nasty looking men go into the Vets just after the Uberbites family arrived there. They looked like they bringing something to someone. They left in a big hurry in a sports car after five minutes.<br>I asked at some of the local shops if they have seen any strange persons in Pastacula. They told me the only strange person they have seen is the Horrible old British woman with the Pink hair. I will keep a strong eye out for the men from the Foreign bank in Question. I am sure they will arrive to Pastacula soon. |

## 19 MAY THE BEST MAN WIN

*There is no Rose without thorns Non c'è rosa senza spine*

Alistair was absolutely positive beyond the shadow of a doubt that Sophia couldn't possibly be the woman Ryan and Fay had been referring to. After all she wasn't even Romanian, to start with. It was true that she hadn't answered ANY of the texts or phone calls he had made the night before, but that didn't mean she didn't want to talk to him. Not to mention she was probably run off her feet, tirelessly looking after Fifi. Bearing in mind what a sweet and loving woman she was, he was quite sure she would be doing whatever it took to get Fifi back on the road to good health again.

Besides that, if the truth be known, she may not even have received any of the text messages he had sent. He recalled how Ryan had informed him only last night, just before his sudden departure, that the reception in those mountainous villages was always a bit sketchy, even at the best of times, let alone during a Festa.

Nonetheless, despite all the evidence, he still felt slightly heavy at heart and even though he didn't want to admit it, he did harbor a few possible misgivings about the longevity of their new "relationship." Bearing all this in mind, he decided that the best plan of action would be to go around to her home and pay her an unexpected visit. He was convinced that this would be the best way to dispel any insecurity for once and for all. Besides he was quite sure she wouldn't mind, "After all, she was only too pleased to invite him in the last time he was there," he recalled, lustfully.

Alistair hoped against hope she would still be at home as he walked briskly along the quaint little cobblestone streets that led up to the main road. All he had to do once he got there was cross the street, go into the main building and ring her apartment intercom. He was quite sure she would open the door as soon as she heard his voice. He had mentally rehearsed the entire 'Surprise Scenario,' over and over again, as he lay tossing and turning in his bed last night. Finally in the wee small hours of the morning he had made up his mind to go and meet her bright and early. The initial plan was to meet up with her for a "Surprise Breakfast" and then all going well, as he imagined it would, stick around for what other 'Delights,' may be on the Menu.

However, with all the drama of the dog being sick this morning, he really wasn't able to get away before now. Besides, he did feel slightly guilty about poor Winston, considering it may have been the Chili Olives that he threw under the table last night that triggered this sudden onset of illness. But to be fair he didn't really think the stupid dog would eat them in the first place, after all he had only just finished wolfing down the huge plate of tripe that Mother had thrown under there as well.

Alistair winced with shame and the tips of his ears burned as he recalled how he and Father had to hightail it, as fast as they could through the village square, before the townsfolk had a chance to look for them. It wasn't that easy either, considering Mother was really quite 'Legless' and literally had to be dragged away kicking and screaming. Not to mention the blasted dogs, who both continued to howl at the top of their lungs as though they were rehearsing for the lead role in the 'Hound of the Baskervilles.'

Anyway enough of that nonsense, he thought to himself. There was no use crying over spilt milk. He needed to get on with his life. Right now, all he cared about was seeing Sophia again and nothing and nobody was going to stop him. He was just about to cross the narrow street running adjacent to Sophia's building when he noticed that the Black Citroen Sedan that had been slowly idling down the road had promptly pulled into the curb and parked only a few metres away from him.

He turned his gaze back across the street and stared long and hard at her building. He was completely lost in thought, as to whether or not he should broach the subject of the money he had lent her for the dry cleaning, when he heard a man's voice call out to him.

Looking again to the side, he noticed the man in the car had wasted no time exiting the vehicle and was rapidly approaching him as he called out something in Italian. He also noticed he was holding a parcel and a white sheet of paper.

"Scusa Signore," the man called out, "Mi potete aiutare sto cercando UN indirizzo."

"I am sorry I don't speak Italian." Alistair impatiently dismissed him with a flick of his hand, as he turned back to cross the road.

"Ok no problem," said the man, who was standing next to him by now. "I can speak English. Signore I need to deliver Thissa parcel, to a person who lives here but somehow I have become lost and I don't know how to find theese address," he said. He held out the piece of paper.

Alistair, had no intention of becoming caught up with this man's problem, but at the same time he felt a slight obligation to at least look as though he were giving a helping hand. Not to mention Sophie may be looking out her window, so it was important for him to 'look good' at all times. He quickly glanced down at the white piece of paper and was just about to excuse himself again, when something familiar caught his eye.

"Oh, wait up, that's all very strange," he said, staring hard now at the paper. "I actually know that name. That is my father's name," he stated. He looked up at the man and back down again at the parcel.

"You're Father; you mean this name is the name of your Papa?" Then of course, you should know where he lives."

"Yes but why would you need to know that?" Alistair asked, he was beginning to feel slightly uneasy. "I mean, as far as I know my father is not expecting any parcels. So, tell me, who are you? How did you get this address? And what exactly do you want with my father?" he demanded.

"Oh scusa Signore, I beg your pardon, witha all theese activities I forgot to introduce myself. OK, I will tell you now. I work for the Postal Courier Services and I have a parcel here for thissa man yourra Father," he smiled broadly. "The other workers at the Post office, no recognize thissa name and so they aska me when I go to the countryside to take it personally to theese address, thissa one written here, but now I am a leetle lost."

"Oh I see, well perhaps you could leave it with me then. I will make sure he gets it all right," said Alistair. He quickly whipped his head around to the side and back. He needed to keep an eye on Sophia's house just to make sure she didn't leave.

"Grazie Signore, but that is impossible. I needa the person who owns thissa Parcel," he explained, holding up the small neatly tied box. "To make a signature on thissa paper," he said holding out the piece of paper with his other hand.

"Well I do know for a fact my father isn't actually home at the moment. You see one of our dogs or more to the point HIS dog was sick this morning and so he took him to the vet. I think he also had some other errands to run as well. I don't think he is expected to be back until around seven o clock this evening," Alistair offered cautiously.

"Oh Bravo Signore that will be perfect. Theese means I have the time to go back to the office and look on the computer for exactly how I can get to hizza house. Thissa way, I can be sure to deliver it to him in person, after Seven pm," he smiled gratefully.

"Hmm yes, that would probably be the best solution. After all we wouldn't want anything valuable to fall into the wrong set of hands now would we?" He looked down at his watch anxiously. Ever mindful, that with every passing second, the morning would have slipped away, taking with it the better part of his energies.

"Yes, like the willing body of a young woman, I understand whatta you say. Theese, for a man, is one of the most important things to remember," the stranger said. Looking wistfully into the distance he continued. "We have a very old proverb in Italy that goes like this, Una cosa Bella e presto presa. In English thissa means "A pretty thing is soon taken," he nodded. A flash of sadness passed over his solemn eyes.

"Ohh how very interesting," Alistair nodded back. "But I am afraid if you don't mind I really MUST get going now. I have a few people to see before the day is over," he said looking down at his watch and tapping it lightly before he looked up again.

"Si Signore you are right it is getting very late now," the man said, after he checked the time on his mobile. "It is very good luck for me that my next appointment is only across the street," he added, tucking in his shirt with his spare hand after dropping his mobile phone into his pocket.

"You mean here? Directly across the road, from here?" Alistair asked, an unwelcome twinge of suspicion gnawed at the corners of his mind.

"Si Signore, I just remember now. I have a very, very, nice appointment with a young lady in thissa apartment just over there," he pointed with his spare hand over towards Sophia's building. "Do you know thissa girl Signore? Many people here know her. She is not an Italian, she comes from Estonia," he stated harshly. He sniffed into the breeze.

Alistair felt his stomach lurch up into his throat and his pulse skipped a beat. The discussion he'd had with Ryan and Fey last night came flooding back and bumped cruelly against his pulsating temples.

"Oh I see! So you mean you have to deliver another parcel over there?" he asked. He threw his arm out randomly towards the road. "But surely dropping off a parcel wouldn't count as an appointment. What I mean to say is, surely delivering a parcel would only take a few minutes," he stated sharply, his fists clenching up into tight hard balls.

"Signore I see you are a gentleman. In this case I would like to say it to you nicely. Thees kind of appointment you understand is not for a business it is for a pleasure," he confessed. He winked crudely at Alistair. He sniffed into the air again and casually pulled up his trousers, causing them to sit up much higher on his waist. "You know Whatta I mean?" he asked. He smiled broadly and made a few vulgar gyrations with his hips. "But don't worry Signore; I will still have the time to go back to the office to finda yourra house. I am sure that I will finish here before Seven pm because I think thissa Donna has a many more appointments after me." He licked his lips and shot a sleazy smirk at Alistair.

Alistair's face went bright red, almost purple as the blood rushed like a raging torrid towards the top of his pointy head. Both his eyes bulged painfully in their sockets as he gaped back in disbelief at the man. "Now just wait a minute," he commanded. He poked his finger into the man's face. "You just can't run around saying whatever you like about the women in this town. I happen to know the young lady who lives over there," he threw his arm out to the side of the street, "And I can assure you she is perfectly respectable," he shrieked in a tight shrill voice.

"Si Signore," the man added, quickly putting his hands up in front of his face. "I don't mean to say such a bad thing about thissa girl. Really Signore, she is a very good girl and very town should have a girl like her for the man like me who has lost his a love and feels very lonely. You understand what I mean?" He asked as he waved his hand in a downward motion across his nether regions.

Alistair felt his heavy heart dive as the realization of the whole sordid situation finally started to sink in. There was no point denying it. Sophia was definitely the girl in the café Ryan and Fey had told him about. Standing there feeling like an absolute fool he burned inwardly as he felt all his wants and desires drain out of him. Just like a balloon that had lost its air, he immediately became hopeless and deflated. Fighting back the tears and feeling totally dejected, he half-heartedly shook the lucky man's hand, bid him a vague farewell and turned back towards the lonely little laneway.

"How could he have been such a fool?" He berated himself bitterly. "Was he really that much of an idiot?" At this precise moment he really didn't want to know the answer to that unfortunate question. Recklessly kicking an empty soda can along the narrow laneway, he chastised himself yet again for being so desperate. There was only one thing for it now he fumed. 'come hell or high water' he was still going to make it to Spain. Fortunately for him, the height of summer wasn't completely over and with a bit of luck he could get there before the weekend. "After all there would still be plenty of talent on offer," he consoled himself, "Especially for a well-travelled Sophisticate like him!"

## 20 PRAYING IN THE PARK

Cornelia couldn't help feeling more than a tad upset by the cruel remarks Algernon had made about her before he stormed off to visit the bank. There was no doubt he was still feeling slightly upset about what had happened at the Festa and now on top of all that there was a problem with the dog. But surely that didn't give him the right to call her a 'Despicable old Witch,' she mourned, as she sat down on the pretty park bench to catch her breath. Staring forlornly at the colourful flowerbeds, she tried hard to make sense of exactly WHY he had been so angry with her. At the same time however, she checked herself for being so sentimental. Normally she would get over this kind of outburst quite quickly, it would simply be like water of a duck's back, but there was something about the way Algernon had looked at her this time that had undoubtedly cut her to the core. 'It was almost hateful,' she thought as she sadly recalled how he had spat out those, nasty, nasty, words. As far as she was concerned there was no denying it, they were definitely well intentioned. Not only that, the way he had marched off and left her in the middle of nowhere, without the slightest care for her well-being, only confirmed it. There was no mistaking that kind of behaviour, she lamented. It was nothing short of 'Malicious!' But was she really that bad? She wondered.

The hot stinging tears, that had welled up in her eyes, soon became great heavy torrents and for the first time, in a long time, she let them stream down her tired old face, unashamed and unfettered. 'I mean everyone gets a little upset here and there and of course she was no exception to the rule. But to suggest she was a 'Raving Alcoholic' and that he was ashamed to be seen in public with her was just a bit too harsh she felt. She swiped sadly at the sudden puddles of salty water that had pooled beneath her nose. 'It wasn't as if she was drunk all day every day and truth be told they probably would never see the people from the Festa again. So why should Algernon be so annoyed with her?' she puzzled as she blew her nose long and hard. 'There were far more serious things that had happened over the years compared to the events of last night. Like for example the time she had forgotten to pick up Alistair from the train station when he was still at boarding school. Admittedly it was a terrible experience for him to spend the night in a juvenile detention centre when he was only seven, but look at him now, it really hadn't done him any harm,' she concluded as she lit up the end of her slim line cigarette.

Sitting all alone, literally miles away in thought she hadn't actually noticed the two young men quietly approaching the park bench. Obviously she had far bigger things to worry about. Hurriedly finishing off the last of her cigarette she was just about to get up and leave, when one of the young men walked over closer and asked her a very strange question. "Excuse me Madam," he said in a deep, heavily accented voice. "Do you mind if we sit here?" He waved his large hand towards the seat.

Cornelia, only just re-emerging from her doldrums, felt slightly alarmed by the proximity of his broad smiling face and she immediately checked the surrounding area from left to right, just to make sure there weren't any other benches available, before answering him.

"Thank you Madam," the young man said. He casually sat down on the seat before she could give him a definitive answer. "May I introduce myself to you? My name is Samuel and this is my brother Joseph." He gave the other tight lipped young man, standing next to him a light tap on the hand, signaling that he should also sit down.

Cornelia, no doubt surprised, by this unwanted intrusion glared back in silence. For once in her life she actually appeared to be completely lost for words. However despite appearances and of course, unbeknown to the two young men, the truth of the matter was; she was really quite Livid! 'How dare they think they can just come over here and try to take my seat,' she fumed. 'Who the hell do they think they are? But more to the point, what on earth do they want? Well I certainly won't be hanging around to find out, I am in no mood for any chit chat,' she thought. She narrowed her eyes into a pair of suspicious slits and gave them an irritated scowl.

"Oh, I see," said Cornelia, still scowling."But it looks as though you have already helped yourself to a seat doesn't it? I mean I can't exactly stop you from sitting here can I? But you could have at least waited until I answered. Actually, you can have the entire bench to yourself if you like. I was just about to get up and leave," she announced, as she began to return her cigarettes and lighter to her bag.

Choosing to disregard this deliberate episode of 'Bristle and Chill,' Samuel held out his hand, beamed a magnificent pearly white toothed smile and asked, "And what is your good name Madam?"

"Cornelia," she automatically answered in a brittle voice. Ignoring the outstretched hand, she stared back at his wide eyed open face. "Why do you want to know my name?" She questioned. Her eyes were almost closed now as she tilted her head back and lifted her long nose into the still air between them.

But before he could give an answer, Joseph grabbed him by the bottom of his shirt and tugged at it hard. He spoke loudly to Samuel in a strange language and hit himself in the middle of his forehead, with the palm of his hand. Initially Samuel answered back quite cheerfully but within a few short moments both their voices had escalated, until they had become rather high and loud. Joseph sprang up from the bench. He turned away from them both and shrugged his shoulders. It looked as though he was trying to shake something heavy off his back. He swaggered away from them and took out a shiny metallic mobile from the back pocket of his baggy jeans and made a call. He turned his head around a few times during the course of the call, and glared angrily at Samuel. That was when

Cornelia noticed the long nasty scar running all the way down the left hand side of his face.

"Please don't worry about this, Madam," Samuel said, looking back over at his brother with a worried frown. "There is nothing wrong here. My brother and I, we just always like to know what is the name of the people we share our message with, sometimes we don't agree about some things. Madam, do you know about your name?" He gaped back at her; the whites of his eyes were becoming as big as a small saucer. "Cornelia, Madam, this is a truly blessed name," he continued apprehensively. "It means the devoted mother of the revolutionary reformers. Madam, did you know, this name takes it roots from ancient Rome?" Joseph walked back over to the seat and quietly sat down. "To tell the truth Madam It makes us so very happy to know your name," Samuel added. He stole a hasty glance at Joseph and gave him a nudge in the ribs before continuing. "And, the most important thing is, if we know your name Madam Cornelia, it is much easier for us to remember you, when we make our evening prayers at night. That is all Madam, I tell you. There is no need to be alarmed, about that." Samuel assured her, he gave his brother another sideways glance.

"Prayers but why would you pray for me, do I look as though I need prayer? Besides you don't even know me." Cornelia retorted, as she self-consciously flattened out her wrinkled skirt.

"All of God's children need prayer Madam. Even Jesus, asked his disciples to pray for him in the garden of

Gethsemane," Samuel added earnestly. Cornelia looked back at him with a bewildered, 'rabbit in the headlights' expression.

"Yes but that has absolutely nothing to do with me," she said as she turned her head away. Turning back again quickly, she added, "If you must know, I have never asked Jesus to pray for me. As a matter of fact I don't even believe in all that kind of thing. Now if you don't mind I really must get going. I have a family to shop and clean for and no doubt they will be wondering where I am," she stated as she started to stand up.

"A modern family Madam, how fortunate. This is truly one of the biggest blessings you can receive from the Father, isn't it Joseph? How old are your dear children Madam?" Samuel asked with childlike innocence. He nudged Joseph with his elbow.

"Actually, I don't have any children as such, not that my family status is any of your business anyway. What I mean to say is, I only have one son and he is not a child. Although I must say he most certainly has been acting like a child recently."

"A son, my goodness Madam, the Almighty has truly bestowed a blessing upon you. You must be so proud and so dedicated to him. Tell me Madam, does he live happily at home with you and your husband?

"Well yes, we are. Of course he does, but I am afraid I don't see how that has got anything to do with you. As I told you before and as you quite rightly noted, I am a very busy woman and have many things to do. Now if you will excuse me I really must go," Cornelia replied firmly, as she stood up to leave.

"Every person from your country is always too busy. I don't think you even care too much about what is happening in the lives of all the other people in the world," Joseph blurted. He glared back at her with hard, coal black, eyes.

Samuel muttered something quietly under his breath, before he directed his attention back towards Cornelia. "Yes, yes, Madam we know you are working so very hard. Madam, you must do a lot to dedicate yourself to your loving husband and modern family. This we know is one of the highest duties asked of you from the Almighty. But Madam I appeal to you please don't leave us at this hour. Truly we don't want to cause you any trouble," he stole another hurried look at his brother before he continued. "Madam Cornelia we only want to share the truth of the Almighty with you," Samuel said, nodding his head over at Joseph, who was now looking for something in his rough hessian shoulder bag.

Cornelia tapped her foot impatiently. She was trying very hard to zip up her bag without actually taking it off her shoulder. She eventually looked back at him and said, "Well yes I am quite sure that is the case. But nonetheless I am afraid to say, I don't have the slightest interest in the Almighty or any of his 'Airy Fairy' friends. What's more as I have already told you, very politely, I have some very important things to do and so I can't possibly stand around wasting my time, chatting. Do you understand? I need to go NOW." She stamped her foot down hard on the stony ground as she fidgeted irritably with the straps of her bag.

"Truly Madam we do understand, but please before you go, would you be so kind as to take from us one of our very important holy tracts? They are for showing each one of us the word of God. We had them made in Italian and in English too. Madam this one that I give to you is especially for the Salvation of the Lost Souls of this world," Samuel advised solemnly. He handed her the crumpled piece of paper that Joseph had finally retrieved from the bag, his broad shiny face looking almost angelic as he blinked his big soulful eyes at her.

Cornelia looked down her nose at him. Then, quite unexpectedly she snatched the thin piece of cheap paper that he held out towards her. It seemed as though she must have had a miraculous change of heart. Perhaps she felt obliged due to the very recent spate of unfortunate events to appease these two young men. In any case, it would be fair to assume, she didn't want to stage a repeat performance of the previous night's behaviour. "Very well I will read it," she said in a clipped tone. She looked down at them impatiently whilst she diligently kept her other hand firmly placed across the entrance of her handbag.

Samuel was elated, when she took the paper; his large face glowed from ear to ear. Joseph on the other hand, continued to stare back at her with sullen eyes, drawing the hessian bag, back onto his lap he hugged it closely into his chest.

After, a short period of respectful silence, Cornelia, completely 'out of the blue,' broke into a deep, raucous belly laugh. Not only that, as if to add insult to injury she literally stood there, shamelessly swaying backwards and forwards, hysterically laughing as she read what was printed on the flimsy piece of paper. She was laughing so hard she almost doubled in two. In fact it seemed at one point that if she leaned down just a teeny bit more she may actually keel over in front of them.

Samuel and Joseph gawked back at her, their mouths hanging wide open. Considering, their convictions it would be safe to suggest they couldn't possibly imagine what could be so funny. After all, they had given her one of their best and needless to say, well produced tracts; it was clearly no laughing matter. Yet right in front of their very eyes, this ungodly woman was disrespectfully laughing at them. They sat in a mortified state of silence, no doubt shocked, by the reaction of this strange foreign woman.

Finally straightening up, she wiped the tears away from her laughing eyes and turned her attention back to them. However after taking one look at the confused expressions, plastered across their almost white faces, she realised they had absolutely no idea what she had been laughing about. Cornelia made a snap decision to read, what was written on the paper. Surely then they would find it just as funny as she did.

"Would you like me to read it to you then?" She asked, her eyes brightly flitting back and forth at them. Noting their stupefied muteness as a sign of consent she began to read. "It would be easier for a Caram," ……. Cornelia lapsed into laughter again. Her shoulders shook and her belly jiggled as squeals of laughter literally poured out of her. She stood there swaying as she clutched the crumpled piece of paper in her hand. It was almost as though she were afraid to let it go.

As if that wasn't enough, to add further insult to injury. Just when Cornelia's laughter was at its most boisterous, a heart stopping cacophony of pitiful baby howling was added to this unholy mix. The compliments of the group of young babies, who were being pushed up and down the Viale in their strollers. Samuel and Joseph hung their heads, low, hoping somehow they wouldn't be noticed by these curious onlookers.

"Look, I really am sorry," Cornelia giggled, "but I have to say this is by far the best laugh I have had for years." She puffed in and out as she tried to catch her breath. However after noting the continued stony silence glaring back at her, she heartily cleared her throat and with far greater composure this time, she tried once more. Taking another couple of deep breaths she began to read what was written on the paper. 'It is easier for a Caramel to pass through the Eye of .. a…a.. Noodle," she pushed down the giggles that threatened to overcome her, "than for a Rich man to enter the Kingdom …. of .. A Heathen," she laughed quite loudly again.

As soon as she regained her composure, Cornelia realised, that the humour, she had so devilishly relished had not even managed to make the slightest dent in the world of Samuel and Joseph. It was clearly obvious by their reactions that something very crucial had failed to hit the mark. Feeling wonderfully refreshed, but at the same time guilty about the possibility of causing further offense, she tried hard to explain it from her point of view.

"Don't know why I am laughing?" she asked. She shook the paper up and down in front of their frozen faces. "The verse you gave me," she shook the paper a bit harder. "It is completely full of spelling mistakes. Instead of Camel, you had Caramel you know as in the sweet," she giggled. "And ... and ... instead of needle you had Noodle, you know, the food that Chinese people eat," she laughed and clapped her hands together in glee.

Realising that the 'lights were on but no one's home' look, was still registering within their eyes, she continued. "Ahhemm," Cornelia cleared her throat and took on a sober expression. "And finally instead of Heaven you had Heathen. I must say that's quite a serious spelling mistake isn't it? Because as you know, everybody knows, Heathens can't possibly make it to heaven. So why on earth would there be a kingdom of Heathens?"

Samuel and Joseph broke into a heated argument as soon as she had finished delivering her very flippant explanation. Cornelia couldn't possibly understand what they were screaming about because, naturally, it was all in a foreign language but she did think it was about something quite serious by the way they were poking and prodding at one another.

After hastily rearranging his black and white polyester checked vest, which was now all askew, Samuel was the first one to speak. “Madam,” he began in a shaky squeak, “You must understand, we are trying with all our Heart and Soul to bring the word of God to the Lost and the Sinners, but Madam we cannot help it if the Lost and Sinners cannot understand what the ‘English’ word of God is saying to them.”

“Yes, yes, and that is exactly what I am trying to tell you,” said Cornelia. “It is because there are so many spelling mistakes …..”

Joseph jumped in before she had a chance to finish. “Madam, I think you should know that the holy verse my brother and I gave to you was translated by some very clever experts from our country. Believe me, when I tell you, these kinds of services are very expensive in my country and for this reason I am sure there are not any spelling mistakes.” He stared hard at her.

“Madam Cornelia what my brother says to you is very true,” Samuel offered. “We have been working so hard with so many people for so long to make sure everything that is written on these tracts is one hundred percent right,” he shook his head.

“But, that is not all. It is my solemn duty to tell you, that you have truly offended us,” Joseph added. He barely moved his lips. “Nobody has ever been rude enough to laugh at these things before," he hissed as he jiggled one of the tracts, up and down in front of her.

Cornelia was starting to feel slightly exhausted by now, probably from all the laughing, not only that she didn't really like the tone of Joseph's latest little contribution. It seemed to take all the fun out of everything. "Very well, I think I can understand most of what you are trying to tell me. And if it helps to make things right then I am prepared to make an apology," she said as she relaxed the grip on her handbag. "And perhaps, as a way of apologising, I may be able to help you somehow," she offered rather matter of factly.

Joseph was busy making another phone call. Samuel however, still sitting up as straight as a poker, blinked his bewildered eyes back at her in surprise. "Help Madam? I don't understand what you are saying. In what way could you offer any help to us?" He looked up at the sky and back again.

"Well, I realise now, by the way you are behaving that I may have possibly upset you both, when I laughed at what you had written on that piece of paper. So if it makes you feel any better than I am ready to make it up to you by giving you some help."

"How could you help us in any way?" Joseph, had finished his call and had turned back to challenge her.

"Madam, I don't think you understand, but YOU are the one who needs OUR help," Samuel instructed.

"Me why should I need any help from you? What Piffle! Without wishing to sound rude I think I have far more than you could ever dream of," she checked her watch and frowned.

"Madam Cornelia, we know you have many modern things but that doesn't mean you have what WE have," Samuel replied, suddenly all wide eyed again.

"What exactly do you have then?" she asked.

"Don't try and confuse my brother's mind with your, big mighty ways. What Samuel means is, WE have much more in our hearts than you or any of your family will ever know."

"What Poppycock! You have never met any of my family, so how do you know that? Cornelia was starting to get cross.

"Madam, what Joseph says is not only about you and your family. It is about all the people here who live their life like you do. The life that is ruled only by the money and time. This is what we mean when we say we can help you. We don't like to live our life like this way Madam. This is why you need OUR help."

"Well I am not sure that I entirely agree with you. It seems to me that there are many people from where I think you might come from, who would love to have my kind of life. But that's a completely different story." She looked at the shocked expressions still plastered across their faces and decided to change the topic. "Now listen up, it's getting late and I don't have the time to explain it all to you now. But here is my address," she wrote it down on the back of the piece of paper they had given her. "Why don't you come around for Supper this evening at around Seven pm? I think I could give you both an English lesson and then you could have some supper with us. That way you will see for yourselves that the people from where I come from do indeed have very happy lives." She handed them back the paper.

"Do you mean you are inviting us to your house, the house where your husband and son live?" Joseph blurted. He shot a wild sideways glance at Samuel.

"Well yes, in a manner of speaking, but it is not really my house."

"But Madam, do you mean, if we should come to this house for supper tonight, that this will be the same house of your husband and your son and they will be there, with us too." Samuel asked, his eyes were goggling so wide that it looked as though his pupils were in danger of popping out and rolling all the way down the road.

"Precisely, but as I told you before it is not my house, actually it is a small cottage. Oh… and before I forget I suppose I should ask you. Is there anything you would like to eat or should I say, would rather not eat?" She frowned hard at them both and then quickly checked her watch.

"Madam, I have dreamt about it but many times but I have never tasted the fruit of the Apple that has been baked in a pie. I have been told by many people that have been to your country that this food is truly the food of the Gods. I think we could both feel so happy with you if you made this food for us tonight," Joseph declared.

"Yes my brother is right," Samuel added. "Madam we are going to be so happy just to come to your house and meet your husband and son. It is true, like Joseph said we can forget about all the laughing from before. And, I am sure we can eat any of the food and drink you put before us, especially the French Fries."

"Well yes of course it goes without saying. I mean you would be completely foolish not to appreciate an invitation to visit my house. Besides that I am sure I could manage an Apple Pie amongst other things." Cornelia replied curtly. She looked back at them with a slight hint of disdain. "Very well then, it appears as though our plans for this evening are settled." She looked at her watch again. "So if you will excuse me now, I really should get going. I shall see you again this evening at seven PM sharp, Shall I?"

"Yes Madam Cornelia you can be sure we will be there," Samuel replied tipping his baseball cap towards her. "It has been a pleasure to share the word of God with you. We will look forward to meeting with you and the rest of the family when we come to your house tonight."

"Well Yes, Yes, Cheerio then," Cornelia started to walk away.

"Madam Cornelia, Wait!" Joseph called out after her, "Please, just remember, it's dangerous out there, so take care," he warned.

"Oh don't be so dramatic, Joseph. Next minute you will be telling me I am being followed by undesirable characters from the local mafia. Really you need to get out more often." She turned away and walked back towards the village square, laughing.

# 21 ALGERNON'S GELATO

Algernon wasn't really all that worried about the missed phone calls. After all he was in a foreign country and these types of misunderstandings were bound to happen from time to time. It was probably somebody from India trying to get him to join a new Telephone company or something like that. Also bearing in mind Horatio's exotic taste in friends it could quite possibly be another Artist from a faraway country. But nonetheless he did still harbour some niggling doubts. If the truth were told the sudden increase of strange calls and wrong numbers he had received over the past two days did give rise to a certain element of alarm. 'Still,' he reasoned to himself, 'the phone did belong to Horatio and therefore it was quite normal for the caller to hang up once they knew it wasn't him.' However he was more than a tad concerned about the note that the vet had given him or rather the content of the note. Considering it did mention a dog, perhaps it was MORE than a bit of a coincidence then, particularly when he factored in the current condition of poor Winston. 'Come on Old Boy,' he warned. "You're letting your imagination run away with you. Nobody knows you are here and why would anybody want to harm Winston? "Pull yourself together Old Chap," he said out loud, much to the surprise of the rowdy group of Italian school children that were passing by. 'There are far more important things to think about.'

Striding in a determined fashion, across the square, he felt unusually energised, almost exhilarated as he recalled the recent heated exchange that he had just had with Cornelia. Frankly it was to be expected and doubtless quite long overdue, bearing in mind her outrageous behaviour the night before. 'What shall he do now,' he pondered as he suddenly stopped mid square. He didn't feel like going back to the Villa and he most certainly did NOT want to bump into Cornelia. As far as he was concerned she could 'Jolly well find her own way home!'

Feeling somewhat peckish he looked up at the big clock residing proudly on the front of the town hall and realised it was almost past his lunch time. Just to be sure he wasn't over reacting with the hunger pangs, he double checked the time on his faithful old Fob watch. After confirming that it was indeed well after midday he decided it was high time he looked for something to eat. Algernon didn't normally have a sweet tooth, he usually preferred savoury foods especially at lunch time but for some strange reason he felt a real desire for something sugary. Setting off again through the square, he spotted a little bar on his right and as he got closer, he noticed a long refrigerated stand, boldly displaying a variety of multi coloured ice creams. Looking intently at the huge tubs of delectable delights he suddenly felt in the mood to consume one, or even quite possibly two.

"Scusa," he said loudly to the pretty young girl behind

the counter, "I would like to buy an ice cream."

"I am sorry but we don't havva' any Ice cream," she answered in a flat voice. Mercifully she could speak good English.

"Don't be ridiculous of course you do. What do you think that is in front of you?" he asked, pointing at the stand.

"That is gelato," she replied in a sluggish tone, as she slowly twirled, the end of a long drawn out piece of bubble gum, the origins of which were stuffed somewhere in her mouth, around and around her middle finger.

"Oh I see," Algernon replied gruffly, not so sure now, if he was still as keen to eat an ice cream.

"Whatta flavour do you want?" She asked in a lazy drawl. Twirling the gum out, even further.

"What sort of flavours do you recommend?" He scrunched up is eyes and peered deeply into the stand and tried very hard to decipher the Italian words, that were written beside each tub.

"We have chocolate, strawberry, vanilla, banana and many, many more," she informed him. She stood poised over the stand with a large gelato scoop in her hand; she languidly reached for a cone with the other. "You wantta the cone or the paper cup?"

"Go on then give me a cone." Algernon clapped his hands and rubbed them together in glee. "I may as well go the whole hog I haven't had one of these in years," he answered, smiling.

"Scusa, I don't understand Whatta you mean? We donna sell the 'Whole Hog' here." She looked back at him as if he had grown two heads. "We just a have the cone or the cup," she replied curtly shoving the cup out in front of his face.

"Ohh never mind, it's just a figure of speech too hard to explain I am afraid. Very well give me a chocolate cone," he instructed. Acutely aware that all the fun of the situation may soon be spiralling towards an imminent state of meltdown, Algernon proceeded to hum away to the little tune gaily tinkling on the shop front radio. He was even more delighted after he recognised it to be a popular song he knew from years ago when he had danced the night away with some good old friends along the seaside promenade. If his memory served him correctly it had something to do with the words, 'Tintarella and Luna' and it featured an attractive Italian woman doing a very provocative dance that they called the 'Twist.' Oh those were the days, he recollected fondly, when life was so simple and the well-known song 'Oh I do like to be beside the Seaside,' was never far from anyone's lips.

Algernon didn't actually notice the two burly looking men approaching the Gelato stand as he stood there waiting for his ice cream. He was quite busy checking how many possible flavours he could have when he inadvertently caught sight of them out of the corner of his eye.

As the young girl handed him his very generous multi flavoured ice cream he heard them say something quietly to her, in Italian. He felt quite sure by her 'husky voiced' laughter and by the way she kept taking, sly, little looks back and forth, that they had actually said something quite vulgar about him. Feeling slightly uneasy and not wanting anything to spoil this happy spur of the moment occasion, he strolled over to the floral plastic table and chairs that were parked beside the bar and sat down. He was still humming away to the happy tune as he munched voraciously into the huge mound of ice cream, when the two men walked over to him.

"Scusa me, how ya doing? Do you mind if we take a seat," one of them said in a rough gravelly voice with just a hint of a New York accent.

Algernon looked up and was quite surprised when he realised it was the two men from the bar standing there. They were both holding a huge double headed ice cream that was neatly wrapped at the base by a white paper napkin. ' She didn't give me a napkin,' he thought bitterly. He licked at the drips of ice cream that were sliding down the cone and starting to form murky brown puddles around his wrist.

"Certainly, these seats are spare and as far as I know, I am not expecting any company," he said. Concentrating hard, he made another avid dart with his poky pink tongue, at the dollop of cream that was about to topple off the top of the wobbling mound.

"Thank you, that's very kind of you. Let me introduce myself to you, my name is Bruno, Bruno Condeesi and this is my cousin Vinnie he don't speak much English," he said. Pulling the chairs out roughly they rapidly flipped them around and sat on them backwards, so that the backs, of the chairs, were now facing Algernon.

Algernon not quite sure what to make of this bizarre type of behaviour decided it was best to simply humour them with a few harmless questions, whilst they finished eating their ice creams together. "So I noticed your English is quite good are you from around here or do you hale from elsewhere?" He inquired, dabbing at his moustache with his handkerchief, hoping none of the ice cream had congregated into sticky congealed clumps.

"No, I come from Brooklyn New York and Vinnie here," he said waving his hand over towards the other grinning goon, "Is a local boy. I don't know where the hell elsewhere is," he replied. He looked back with a strained kind of curiosity.

Vinnie nodded eagerly in agreement and took a large chunky bite of his ice cream, briefly revealing a solid gold tooth that glinted boldly in the bright sunlight.

"Well yes, of course I am fully aware that Elsewhere is not exactly a post code. It's just another way of asking if you come from another place."

Bruno stopped munching his ice cream and gawked at Algernon with a mixture of emotions, not unlike a feral cat in mid fight. "Hey Pal, are you talkin to me?" Bruno asked. “Cos if you are, let’s get one thing straight before we go any further, Pal. What’s with all the questions? What are you some kind of wise guy? I’m the guy around here who asks the questions,” he snarled as he looked across at Vinnie who was now cracking his knuckles, as well as keeping a steady eye on the ice cream, he had wedged between the salt and pepper shaker and the ashtray.

“Dontcha know who we are?” He asked impatiently. He viciously swatted a fly that had been feasting on a droplet of ice cream.

“Well yes you are Bruno and that’s your cousin Vinnie you introduced yourselves earlier,” Algernon replied uneasily. He squirmed restlessly against the hot plastic seat, trying hard to push down his feelings of doubt, but truth be told, deep in his waters, he knew something was not quite right.

“Look Pal, I don’t know what kinda game you are playing at, but from where I come from people like you,” Bruno angled his two middle fingers sideways at Algernon; “Show guys like us a bit of respect,” he growled. “Now listen up Pal and you better listen up good to what I am about to tell you,” he said pointing his fingers in a menacing way at Algernon.

Algernon gulped as the last of the blob of ice cream that had been melting in his mouth gushed its way down his thick tight throat.

“The truth is, this ain't no accidental meeting, you

understand? Vinnie and me, we came here looking for you. Because we got some business to do Wit you." He nodded his head over towards Vinnie, who bit savagely into the side of his ice cream before cracking his knuckles again.

"I want you to listen very carefully to what I am about to tell you." Bruno pulled his chair in closer towards Algernon and lowered his voice. "It looks like you have gone and upset a very good friend of ours. Not only that, this friend of ours, he told us he trusted you like his own son, Know what I'm sayin? He tried to help you. He says he was gonna make a very good business deal Wit a nobody like you. But since then I heard on the grapevine that this good friend of ours is very upset wit you because you tried to make a monkey out of him. I think you know what I am talking about Pal," he growled. He took another huge bite of his ice cream.

"I have absolutely no idea what you are referring to," Algernon squeaked in an anxious tone, as he helplessly watched the rivulets of sugary cream, surge all the way down his wrist and disappear beneath the sleeve of his checked jacket.

"OK Let me spell it out for you Pal." He sighed loudly as he moved his face even closer to Algernon. "This important friend of ours, let's just call him Mr X, he made a deal wit you about some old painting, he told me he gave you a lot of money in good faith you wouldn't double cross him. Last night when I was visiting him and his lovely family at his beautiful home, he told me privately in his office about how upset he was that you had tried to pull the wool over his eyes. Know what I am saying?"

"I still don't have the slightest idea what you are talking about. Yes I made a financial arrangement with a possible Mutual Acquaintance of yours regarding a painting and its value but as far as I am concerned everything was above board," he protested, his eyes bulging. He wiped his sticky face with the sleeve of his jacket.

"Hang on a minute Pal it's not that simple. I think you need to show a little more respect. We both know there's a lot more to this story than meets the eye. I know for a fact that after Mr X passed over his hard earned cash, that you forgot to inform him that the painting you handed over is nothing more than a Fake," he shouted loudly. He paused for a moment, shook his head sadly and looked intensely into Algernon's face. "Nobody treats a friend of mine like that, Pal especially Mr X." He prodded Algernon in the chest. "Let me explain it to you, Mr X is how can I say it, the 'Capo di Tutti,' in my family's language this means 'the Boss of all Caps.' You know what I mean? Like the Godfather, and Vinnie and Me we go completely crazy when we hear about somebody who tries to knock the Cap off the top of the Boss' head."

Just then, as if on cue, the double headed Ice cream that had been wedged so uncouthly between the salt and pepper shaker and the ash tray dramatically fell forward and decapitated itself. Algernon gulped, as the remains of the ice cream rolled towards him; splattering him with hundreds of tiny multi coloured spots before it fell to the ground with a plop.

"Look, I am gonna make it very simple for you. Let me spell it out one more time," Bruno insisted in a menacing tone, moving his face even closer to Algernon. "Like I said before, our good friend Mr X is no ordinary guy he is a very busy man," he stretched his two clasped hands out in front of him. "So he requested me and Vinnie here to come over and talk to you. Know what I am saying?" He asked, his face was only centimetres away from Algernon. "He don't want no trouble, he just wants to give you one last chance to make amends." He stared directly into Algernon's blotchy startled face as he cracked his knuckles.

"Well I ….. I am not exactly sure what you would like me to do," Algernon replied, his eyes flitting backwards and forwards as he looked earnestly into their faces. He edged back as far as he could go into the cheap plastic chair.

"Look Pal, I understand we are all busy men here, so let's not waste any more of our precious time. Listen up, It's very simple. You are gunna give back the money plus fifty per cent interest by the end of the day or we are gunna have to come around to your house and pay you a visit," he announced with an intimidating snarl. He cuffed Algernon sharply on the back of the head as he stood up to leave.

The crass sharp sound of Bruno's phone ringing no doubt ruined any opportunities Algernon may have had to negotiate his way around this unexpected problem. A fearful cold chill started ran from the nape of his neck and all the way down his spine when he realised the conversation that Bruno was having in English was more than likely about him.

"Yeah that's right Mr X you don't need to worry no more, Vinnie and me have taken care of the whole situation. Yes Boss I am sure he understands," he looked over at Algernon. "He says he is very sorry to have caused you any trouble and he told us he will do whatever he can to make it up to you."

Too terrified to make any sudden moves Algernon had no choice but to sit there and stare back at Vinnie, who was smugly staring back at him, as he busily cleaned his fingernails, with his shiny, black, flick knife.

Snapping his phone shut, Bruno clicked his fingers at Vinnie, before turning his attention back to Algernon. "That was Mr X and he wants you to know he was very happy that we had this little talk. Looks like it's your lucky day Pal. Mr X is willing to forget the whole thing ever happened after I told him you agreed to pay back the money along with the interest."

"But .... But that's not right, I haven't agreed to anything yet," Algernon protested. He suddenly felt quite small as he looked up at the two bulky frames that were casting long wide shadows over him.

"By the way, that's a very nice watch you have there. Do you mind if I take a closer look?" Bruno reached over and grabbed at the antique Fob watch pinned securely to

Algernon's jacket. Yanking the chain roughly he snatched at the watch and in the process, ripped an unsightly hole in the front pocket as he pulled the watch away from the fabric.

"I think it's a good idea if I ask Vinnie here, to take care of it as a favour for you, just to make sure it doesn't get lost. But let's just keep this between us. Nobody else needs to know. You know what I'm Sayin? That way nobody gets hurt," he sneered.

"But you just can't take my watch." Algernon pleaded. Long salty lines of hot sweat dribbled down his legs. "I don't think you understand, it is a very valuable family heirloom. It belonged to my great grandfather. It's been in my family for years," he squeaked, as the final dregs of his ice cream slowly but surely collapsed into an oozy glug onto the palm of his hand.

"No need to worry about that Pal. Vinnie here will take good care of it, he has a very good reputation for looking after things that belong to the family, don't you Vinnie?"

Vinnie nodded his head up and down as he skillfully bit into the end of the watch with his heavy gold tooth. Looking back over at Bruno he stuck his right thumb up vertically before turning his gaze back towards Algernon. Vinnie leered at Algernon like a mad man with his eyes squinting; half open and half closed. He jumped up and down maniacally as he pulled at the tufts of hair that were sticking out from behind his ears. He let out a long crazy loony laugh that seemed to start from the soles of his feet and end in his smirking eyes.

"Alright, it's been very nice doing business wit you. I am glad we could work something out together but now Vinnie and me, we gotta go. Like they say no rest for the wicked the boss wants us to have a chat wit some other people just like you. But don't worry Pal after we have taken care of business we are going to come back here and meet up wit you again. Just remember we won't ever be too far away," he gave Algernon a little punch on the shoulder. "By the Way Pal; I forgot to ask how is your dog feelin now? Don't worry, he is in very safe hands and if everybody does what they are supposed to do, then its Gunna stay like that, No what I am sayin?" He gave Algernon another quick cuff across the back of the head. Bruno clicked his fingers again at Vinnie again. It was obviously time to leave.

They both turned their backs on a 'Shell Shocked' Algernon and walked back over towards the bar. As they passed the gelato stand, Bruno casually tossed a ten euro note at the young girl who was busily painting her toenails. Then they both disappeared, into the long dark shadows that had now cast themselves over the old brick building.

## 22 ESCAPE FROM PASTACULA

Algernon burst through the pair of kitchen doors causing them to swing back on him violently only to find Cornelia anxiously hovering around the stove in one of Magdalena's large floral print aprons. "Cornelia; go upstairs and pack your things immediately. We have to leave here as soon as possible," he commanded. He rapidly moved towards the window on the other side of the room. Carefully peeling back the edges of the lacy old curtain he cautiously peered out onto the front courtyard before turning back to face her again. "Cornelia did you hear me? I asked you to go upstairs and pack," he bellowed at her pointy bottom that was poking up at a peculiar angle as she bent down to check the oven.

"What on earth are you babbling on about now Algernon?" She said as she straightened up and turned around. "Surely you can see I am in the middle of doing something?"

"Yes but I am afraid it will have to wait. There is absolutely no time to waste, as I told you a minute ago we need to leave here as soon as possible. Cornelia would you please pay attention this is a very serious matter?" He pleaded. He shot an anxious hurried look towards the closed door.

"Well, I should like to inform you Algernon, that I have no intention whatsoever of packing my bags or anything else for that matter. As a matter of fact I am expecting guests this very evening and frankly I would appreciate it if you didn't keep interrupting me. Can't you see I am in the middle of preparing some supper for them? God only knows when they will get the opportunity to eat some proper English food again."

"Guests, what guests, Who, How? What I mean to say is, how could you be expecting any guests? You don't even know anybody here." Algernon stepped towards her urgently as she turned away to attend to the pot on the stove.

"It's a long story Algernon and one that I don't particularly have time to go into now," she replied irritably. She yanked hard at the edge of the apron that had managed to creep its way up her long skinny torso. "I am already running completely behind schedule. It took me absolutely hours to walk around those measly shops looking for all the ingredients I needed. As it is I still didn't manage to find everything. It's most unfortunate but it looks as though I am going to have to go without the kidneys for the steak and kidney pie," she briskly stirred the gluggy concoction that was merrily bubbling on top of the stove.

Just then the familiar sound of a dog barking rang out from the back garden. Algernon, alarmed 'tippy toed', over to the kitchen window and tentatively pulled back the curtains. He slowly bent down and kept his body as low as he could, his great rolls of hair were the only parts of him that were sticking above the window sill.

"Algernon what in God's name are you doing? Have you gone completely Mad this time?" Cornelia asked.

"Shhhh, be quiet woman," he hissed, raising his index finger up towards his lips. "I think somebody is coming to the house. Get down quickly in case they see you," he issued, waving his hand down low towards the ground. As soon as he had finished giving this order, they heard a heavy set of footsteps approaching the front entrance of the villa and make their way up the stairs towards the door.

Cornelia, not quite sure what was going on but suddenly alarmed by Algernon's strange behaviour, surprisingly followed his advice and promptly dropped down onto her knobby knees. Staring up from her position on the floor, she helplessly glanced at the pot, which was now merrily spluttering bits and pieces everywhere.

The clock on the wall ticked over loudly as the pot on the stove continued to bubble. Algernon too afraid to move remained in his comical stooped stance as he listened intently to the approaching footsteps which were now inside the villa.

The dogs in the back let out a blood curdling howl as the footsteps got closer and closer.

"Hello, anybody Home," called out Alistair as he pushed open the kitchen door. "For God's sake Mother what on earth are you doing down there?" He shouted. He quickly jumped back in fright. "Can't you see there is something boiling all over the stove?" He sneered at her pathetic crouch.

"Oh it's only you Ali," Algernon said. Breathing a great sigh of relief he attempted to stand up again. "Ahhhh my back," he groaned. Wobbling his head from side to side he had no choice but to remain in a squatting position, frozen to the spot, on his huge "ham like" haunches. "Oh Blast, I can't move. Get over here and help me up," he growled through gritted teeth. Grabbing onto the window sill he steadied himself and panted heavily.

Alistair and Cornelia, responded with remarkable speed as they dashed across the room to assist Algernon's crunched up, crumpled frame. Grasping his elbows on either side, they pulled him up as hard as they could and finally yanked him into a standing position. Algernon in the meantime continued to bellow obscenities at the top of his lungs as his crooked old backbone was stretched to its limit like a piece of stringy elastic.

After assessing that all was back to normal and double checking that his father was not going to keel over anytime soon, Alistair wasted no time firing questions at his apparently insane parents.

"Would either of you care to explain to me what exactly you were doing down on all fours when I came into this room? Oh no …… Wait, Stop, Please don't tell me it was some kind of ritual foreplay. Ewwwww, that just doesn't bear thinking about," he said, turning his head away in disgust.

"Don't be ridiculous Alistair," Cornelia chided. "Your father and I no longer engage in that type of behaviour, not that I should have to explain that to you. Good heavens what's that awful smell?" She asked pointing her long nose upwards; she sniffed at the air. All at once the hapless trio shifted their gaze towards the ancient oven on the other side of the room. As it started to 'belch out' great billows of smoke that had rapidly wafted towards the ornate ceiling and were defiantly clinging to the edges of the dusty chandelier.

"Oh darn," wailed Cornelia as she rushed across to the oven. "It's the Apple Pie, its burning," she flung open the door, just in time to reveal a blackened mound of pastry, that had burst at the seams and spewed its contents all over the oven walls.

"I thought you said you were cooking a steak and kidney pie," said Algernon gruffly as he rubbed the small of his back, with both hands.

"Yes Algernon, but that doesn't mean I couldn't be cooking anything else at the same time," she snapped. Pushing her head down into the oven, she tried to survey the damage. "Alistair, don't just stand there, you fool. Pass me that towel will you?" She demanded, as she straightened up again. "Can't you see this dish is awfully hot and dare I say, completely ruined? Thanks to your father and his mad ravings. What on earth am I going to give my guests for supper now?" She wailed, wringing her scrawny hands together.

"What guests? Why would YOU be cooking supper for anyone Mother?" Alistair looked at her incredulously as he passed her the linen tea towel. "The last time I remember you cooking anything was at my ninth birthday party, when you helped the cook make some icing for the cake."

"My point precisely," Algernon interjected. He limped over towards them. "Besides that, as far as I am concerned there won't be any supper for anyone. Because none of us will be here," he announced with a defiant clap of his hand.

"Well you've got that right father, I definitely won't be here. I am leaving this evening. I bought a ticket to travel to Rome with the last little bit of money I had. It took me all afternoon to find a travel consultant who could vaguely understand a word of English. I for one will be glad to see the back of this Beastly little town."

"I am afraid that won't be possible Alistair. When I said we were leaving I meant ALL of us, together and the sooner the better, we can't possibly wait until this evening."

"Leaving? All together? What are you talking about father?" I have just spent the better part of this afternoon organising somewhere to stay with a friend of a friend, in Rome. He expects me to meet him there in just a few hours."

"Algernon, I certainly do not intend to leave before the morning. As I have already explained to you I have two very nice foreign men coming around for supper at seven pm. Not only that, I promised them I would help them with their English. I just can't pack up and go. As it is I won't have anything decent to give them now." She swiped madly at the glugged up pools of gravy that had formed into hard gristly lumps on the bench top.

"What exactly do you mean by foreign? Who are these young men?" Algernon asked, suddenly breaking into a hot sweat. "And why would they need help with their English? Do they speak a foreign language?"

"I hope you are not becoming a racist Algernon. I am not exactly sure where they come from but it sounded to me as though they came from a country like Africa. Actually they were very religious."

"Africa! Why would there be any religious Africans in Pastacula? That doesn't sound right and what could they possibly want with you?"

"Nothing in particular Algernon, they were just being nice. People can be nice you know they don't always have to have an ulterior motive. Surely you are not getting jealous Algernon," she snickered lightly as she wiped away at the bench.

"So, these very nice religious Africans suddenly came up to you out of the blue and invited themselves here for supper tonight? Tell me, where exactly did you meet them Cornelia?" He frowned hard at her.

"I met them in the park. Just after you cruelly left me to wander alone in the town. They were very kind to me and they made me laugh. It was the first time in a long time that I'd had a bit of fun," she said. She picked up the burnt dish and took it over to the sink.

"Mother, you can't be Serious! Surely you didn't invite a pack of foreign strangers to our house? Especially those types. God knows what we could catch off them."

"Mind your manners Alistair, that's no way to talk about people you don't know anything about. I didn't actually invite them over, 'Willy Nilly.' I invited them over for supper after I had taken the time to have a very long chat with them I told them I would give them some help with their English. Not everyone has had a fortunate life like you Alistair," she sniffed.

"Hmm, very unusual if you ask me. Anyhow, I must admit, aside from all that nonsense, I do think mother has a point. We just can't pack up and leave." He picked up the spoon from the pot on the stove and gave it a big lick.

"Why not Alistair? If it's the dogs you are worried about there is no need to. I have already picked Winston up from the Vet and even though he is still a bit poorly, he is nonetheless quite fit for travel."

"Oh, but of course, let's make sure we get our priorities right," quipped Cornelia.

"No father, it has got nothing to do with the dogs." Alistair placed the spoon back into the pot. "The reason you can't leave tonight is because an Italian Postal worker is coming over here at Seven pm this evening to drop off a parcel for you. He told me you would have to be here in person to sign for it."

"A parcel, what Parcel? I am not expecting any parcel. How do you happen to know all this Alistair?" Algernon asked, as he 'tippy- toed' commando style back over to the window again.

"Because Father, I met him when I was walking in the town today. Look it's a long story but basically he thought I was an Italian and he parked his car next to me and asked for directions."

"Perhaps I could quickly whip up a nice lemon tart. I noticed there is a big lemon tree in the back garden. Ali, do be a dear and bring me in half a dozen lemons will you?" Cornelia pleaded, as she lit up another cigarette.

"Oh all right Mother but only on one condition", he held up his finger and waggled it back and forth.

"What Ali? Please don't make too many demands; can't you see I am already upset as it is?"

"That you stop harping on about this Bloody Supper. Honestly Mother the way you have been carrying on about it truly gives me the Impression that you really do think it will be your Last Supper," he sniggered cruelly, through a lopsided smile.

"Stay right where you are Alistair, you're not going

anywhere," Algernon commanded from his self-imposed Outpost. "Tell me, what kind of car was he driving?" He discreetly pulled a small piece of curtain back to gain a better view.

"What? Who are you talking about now, Father?" Alistair plucked at the long hairs that were standing up stiffly on the back of his arm.

"The Italian Postal worker, what kind of car was he driving. Was it a dark car by any chance?" He bullied.

"Well I….. I didn't take much notice of it, but now that you mention it, yes I believe it was," he replied. Alistair checked the time on his phone and blew out an impatient gust of air through his flaccid lips. He was running out of time and he still hadn't packed anything.

"And tell me Alistair, Exactly, how did MY name happen to be brought into the conversation?" Algernon wheezed heavily again as he turned back all ruddy faced. It was surprising how much he had seemed to age over the last twenty four hours.

"Oh for crying out loud Algernon, would you stop with all the interrogation? Can't you see you're upsetting the poor lad? Not to mention I need those Lemons as soon as possible if I am going to get this tart finished before the young men arrive, Quick- Sticks Alistair," Cornelia directed. She stubbed out her cigarette and turned back to check the ingredients she had left on the kitchen bench.

Alistair fidgeted with his mobile phone before

answering. "As I told you before father the man was lost and he thought I was Italian. So after he parked his car he came up to me, and asked if I knew anything about an address. But I don't see why that should be of any importance to you."

"So this man …… This, this, Postal worker, he could speak good English?" Algernon wheezed long and hard again. He clung on tightly to the edge of the window sill to steady his bulky frame, his shoulders shook up and down as he coughed.

"Well yes, as I said before, not at first, but after he realised I couldn't speak Italian, he spoke English to me. I don't understand what you are getting at, Father. What on earth has this got to do with me going to Rome? "

"Stop whining Alistair and answer the questions. How does the man know I am living here? Surely even you would have enough sense not to give a perfect stranger our address. Especially now whilst we are in this current state of transition," he nodded his head over towards Cornelia and raised his eyebrows to indicate, his usual secret signal.

"No ….. No of course not ... I'm not that stupid … I wouldn't just give our address to anyone. In fact I didn't actually give him our address, it was a co-incidence really."

"What do you mean a coincidence you blithering Idiot?"

"Well …. Well …… just hear me out please Father." He pushed his outstretched hands up and down in the smoky air as he desperately pleaded his case. "You see Father, when I looked down at the parcel he was holding I recognised your name on it didn't I? …. And … And that's how he knew where you lived."

"Ha! I can't believe how much of an idiot you are. Even a five year old child would know better than to 'Let the cat out of the bag," he thundered. He limped across the room and grabbed Alistair by the shoulders, "I am sure Albert Einstein must have been thinking of YOU, when he said 'Only two things are INFINITE, the universe and human STUPIDITY", Algernon bellowed, as he took his huge angry hands off Alistair's puny shaking shoulders. He turned away from them both and glared out at the window, completely content to be consumed by his own red hot anger.

"I think you have said quite enough, Algernon. After all the poor boy was only trying to help you," Cornelia cautioned, as she spun around to face them. "Now if you don't mind I really do need those lemons Alistair, if I am going to make a lovely tart for this evening's supper."

"Hold your foolish tongue for once Woman," Algernon issued. He turned back rapidly and shot her a dark look. "Alistair was not far wrong when he said it might be your last supper. Listen to me carefully," he commanded, raising his index finger towards both of them. "We are all in very grave danger and if we don't leave this house within the next half hour, I can't be held responsible for what might happen next."

<table>
<tr><td colspan="3">INSTAPOL POLICE FINAL REPORT</td></tr>
<tr><td>Agent<br>Guido Ventosi</td><td>Day : Four/ Night Time</td><td>File Number 1200/12/20098</td></tr>
<tr><td>CASE Uberbite Surveillance</td><td>LOCATION Villa of Horatio Windybottom</td><td>REPORT No<br>6</td></tr>
<tr><td colspan="3">Persons of Interest: Algernon Uberbite, Cornelia Uberbite, Alistair Uberbite</td></tr>
<tr><td colspan="3">ACTIVITIES</td></tr>
<tr><td colspan="3">Guido Ventosi Instapol Agent (me), Two Male representatives of the Local Mafia, Two Foreign Male Representatives from the Foreign bank in Question.<br>7.01 Pm I arrived to the Villa and Entered through the left wing (I was there first).<br>7.02 Pm The two Local representatives of the Local Mafia arrived at the Villa and entered through the right wing.<br>7.03 Pm The two Foreign Male Representatives of the Foreign Bank in Question Entered the Front Entrance of the Villa.<br>7.05 Pm The three Parties already mentioned above converged together at the same time in the smoking room of the Villa.<br>7.06 Pm There was an Electrical Failure and then there was a complete Blackout.<br>7.07 Pm There was a shootout involving open gunfire from all the Separate Parties already mentioned above.<br>7.09 Pm There was a mass exodus from the Villa involving all the Separate Parties mentioned Above (I left the villa last).<br>7.12 I run to the outside of the Villa and I see the strange helicopter in the sky. The two men from the foreign bank in question were sitting inside.<br>7.13 I run to the driveway and I see two men driving a car</td></tr>
</table>

| INSTAPOL POLICE FINAL REPORT | | |
|---|---|---|
| **Agent** Guido Ventosi | Day : Four/ Night Time | File Number 1200/12/20098 |
| CASE Uberbite Surveillance | LOCATION Villa of Horatio Windybottom | REPORT No 6 |
| **Persons of Interest**: Algernon Uberbite, Cornelia Uberbite, Alistair Uberbite | | |

| COMMENTS |
|---|
| The three separate parties arrived in a few Minutes of Each other including myself (I arrived first). Soon after I gained the entry to the Villa. There was a complete Blackout. At this time all the Separate parties who had now entered the smoking room fired at once into the room. Due to no light and the dangerous situation the Separate Parties quickly exited the Villa.Unfortunately in this chase I tripped over a large coffee table and fell to the ground. I suffered from a blackout for a short period of time. When I regained my senses I pursued the separate parties of interest but they had already escaped. I cannot be 100% sure but I believe the dangerous men from the Foreign Bank in question escaped in the big helicopter that I saw flying in the sky just above the Villa. I theenk the two male representatives from the local mafia escaped in their very nice Ferrari Sports car. I could easily identify by the noise it made as it sped up the driveway My brother used to own the same kind of car.<br>It is better to light a candle than to curse the darkness E'meglio accendere una candela che maledire l'oscurità. |

## 23 A CONFESSION

Guido had already packed up most of his things into the small overnight bag that he had placed on top of the lumpy lopsided bed. After looking around the room for a few extra moments, just to make sure there was nothing he had forgotten, he carefully picked up the fragile, framed, photograph of the scantily clad woman that had dominated the table next to his bed for the past five days. Pulling the dusty photo passionately towards his heaving chest, he slowly closed his eyes, threw back his head and let out a long and whispery sigh. Bringing it up closer, to his dry chafed lips, he moved his head forward and planted a delicate little kiss onto the cracked glass before placing it face down again into his bulging bag. He was just in the process of zipping up the bag again, when his mobile phone rang in a series of morose, lonely tones. Sitting back down on the bed he picked up the phone from where he had left it under the moth eaten pillow and checked for the caller ID. After noting it was Riccardo Martinelli ringing yet again for the third time he reluctantly decided it was about time he took the call.

"Pronto," he issued in a subdued tone.

"Agent Ventosi, this is Agent Martinelli calling you again for the third time; are you able to talk now?"

"Si …… Scusa ….. I meanna ….. Yes I have just woken

now, from a very long sleep. Because last night my head was hurting too much after I fell over the coffee table. To tell you the truth, I needa to take so many pain killer to help with this terrible pain. Of course after the very dangerous situation I have to face alone last night it was also so very hard to fall asleep again," Guido replied in a shaky voice.

"Yes I have noted in your recent report that you mentioned you had a small accident. For this situation, I am very sorry," Agent Martinelli's voice paused for a moment before continuing. "Agent Ventosi I see you also wrote in your report that you were unable to pursue the persons of interest due to this unfortunate accident. In any case, I need to ask you a very important question. Are you really sure all these people of interest have escaped?"

"Of course I am sure," Guido fired back, suddenly energised. "You must have read my report by now and from this you should know that these same people of interest are no longer in Pastacula.

"Si …… I mean yes, I received it this morning. But I wanted to hear from you exactly what happened. You write in the report that there was a blackout at the villa at the same time as the 'shoot out.' Then you say you tripped over a coffee table and so then you have your own 'Personal Blackout'. After that, you write you woke up and you run to the back entrance and you saw a helicopter in the sky just above the Villa and then you write that you saw a very nice Ferrari leaving the long driveway. Theese to me all sounds very strange."

"Of course it must seem very strange but you must understand Agent Martinelli, this is exactly what happened at the villa," Guido replied, as he tugged at the end of his ear. "I wrote the report after my blackout based on what I remember were the true events of the last night. It is important that head office is aware of that," he finished sharply.

"Yes of course, but you also need to be aware Agent Ventosi, and I very much regret to inform you, that as of today, your services with the Rome office of Instapol have been suspended until further notice," Martinelli advised efficiently.

"What are you trying to say? Are you telling me just now, I am no longer needed to work on this case? Why, what have I done wrong to you?" Guido asked, quickly jumping up from the bed.

"Agent Ventosi," Martinelli issued in a stern voice, "To tell the truth after reading your report I think there seems to be a few important points missing. Also there are some things that need a leetle bit more explaining. For this reason I would like to take this chance to ask you some more questions about exactly what happened yesterday afternoon before you went to the Villa. Also some questions about what happened after you went to the villa. But I must warn you now. Theese part of the conversation you do understand will be recorded for investigative purposes and therefore it will be advisable for you to answer the questions as truthfully as possible and in English."

"Yes I think I know what you are trying to tell to me." He reluctantly sat back down on the end of bed. "Don't worry Agent Martinelli even though my head hurts and I maybe am a leetle unsure, I will still try to answer your questions as best I can," he added flatly, as he fiddled with the frayed cotton threads that hung loosely from the end of his tie.

This little episode of mutual disclosure was followed by a rather long uncomfortable pause during which time Martinelli appeared to be unavailable. In the meantime Guido, could vaguely hear what he thought may have been the sound of an electronic device being activated. Then Martinelli's voice returned and he began his line of questioning once more.

"Agent Ventosi in your report you mention that you entered the Villa alone at 7.01 before anybody else. From theese point of view I must tell you I am a leetle confused," Martinelli cleared his throat loudly before continuing. "I must ask you to explain to me exactly why you were on your own at the Villa?"

"Scusa Agent Martinelli, as I already told to you before. I arrive there at the villa first, before the others. Of course after they arrive I was no longer alone."

"Agent Ventosi I don't think you can understand what I am asking you. Let me ask you another question. Which people, are you talking about when you mention the others?"

"I don't know why you can't understand me when I

mention to you the others. Surely you should know that I mean the other people of interest we have been tracking in theese case."

"Yes, Of course I know all about these people. The two hit men from the local mafia and the two African men, sent from the Foreign Bank in question, who were pretending to be missionaries," Martinelli replied tersely.

"Yes exactly, these are the people I tell you about when I mention about the others. So what can't you understand?" Guido asked. He tugged harder at the long threads of untidy cotton that were recklessly unravelling, from the bottom of his tie.

"But Agent Ventosi, you still haven't told me why you were alone at the Villa. I will ask you once again. Where were the others?"

"What Others, What, Others?" Guido screamed hysterically down the phone. "I don't know about any others. Do you mean the family in Question, the Uberbites? To tell you the truth they were not around when I arrived at the Villa."

"Agent Ventosi, tell me, Why, did you miss the rendezvous with the Back Up Team that was sent from Roma? According to our records an email had been sent to you earlier that day informing you that the back-up team would be meeting you in front of the post office in Pastacula at 1.30 pm."

"What are you are you talking about? I didn't know

about any back-up team, nobody contacted me," Guido shouted jumping up again. Pulling angrily at his tie he ripped it off in one foul swoop and flung it as far as he could across the room.

"Please, calm down Agent Ventosi, this is a very serious matter and one I would like to get to the bottom of. Also according to our reports, yesterday afternoon ten phone calls were made to your mobile number between the hours of 13.00 pm and 18.30 pm. Unfortunately; all of them were answered by the automatic voice mail of Guido Ventosi. These phone calls were vital to the investigation. My question to you Agent Ventosi is, why were you not contactable during all this time?"

Guido slumped back down onto the bed, his shoulders stooped like those of a defeated man. Looking miserably around the gloomy little room he imagined for a moment just how different his life may have been if he had been allowed to go to Monaco. Rousing himself back to the present situation he begrudgingly answered Agent Martinelli's Question. "As I told you before I don't know about any back up team and about yesterday, the truth is I had some very important personal business to attend to," he confessed. He held his head in his hand.

"So tell me this Guido, was this business you mention so important that it made you forget your responsibilities to your fellow colleagues and your country?"

"What do you mean? How can you say I am not thinking of my colleagues or my country," he shrieked. "As you know I came here to this very horrible town just to show everybody how dedicated I am to this job," he replied bitterly.

"Yes and up until now we have appreciated your efforts, but it grieves me to tell you that yesterday afternoon you were spotted by one of our local contacts entering the house of a well-known prostitute in Pastacula. The same contact informed us that you did not leave the house again until 6.30 pm that same evening." Agent Martinelli paused before continuing his conversation. "Agent Ventosi, I regret to inform you that in my opinion and in the opinion of your colleagues this type of activity cannot be considered as personal business and therefore you have willingly placed the whole of this investigation in jeopardy."

Guido held his drooping head miserably in his free hand. He stared down at the cold ceramic tiles that made up the dirty floor. Suddenly, out of the blue his shoulders began to jerk up and down as his body and upper chest began to heave in and out. This was followed by a succession of loud, choking sobs.

For the next few moments the only sound that could be heard between them was Guido's pathetic inconsolable sobbing, punctuated here and there by a deep rasping intake of air.

Eventually after what seemed like a lifetime, Riccardo Martinelli's brittle officious voice projected clearly from the other end of the phone. "Agent Ventosi are you alright, is there somebody else there with you? I think you sound a little distressed please can you answer me? Agent Ventosi, are you still there? If you are still listening I would like to remind you once again that this conversation is being recorded for quality purposes." He cleared his throat loudly.

Guido eventually stopped his pitiful sobbing and raised his face back up towards the tiny mouth piece of the phone. Madly swiping at the tears that had so readily strewn across his crumpled face he answered his estranged colleague.

"Dimme (tell me) Agent Martinelli," he began in a croaky voice barely above a whisper. "Do you know how it feels for a man to have his heart brutally ripped out and broken into a thousand leetle pieces? To be sent so very far away and cruelly separated from the only one you have ever loved." Loud soulful sighs offered up by Guido dominated the frosty cold air between them. "Let me tell you, thissa situation is just like the greatest love story ever told. Have you ever heard of the famous love story of Marc Antony and Cleopatra, Agent Martinelli? Thissa story is exactly like my love story. Do you know how totally crazy this can make a man feel?" Guido finished in a soft whisper.

Martinelli paused for the briefest of moments before answering. "Agent Ventosi I am so very sorry to hear of all your troubles but I have absolutely no idea what you might be talking about. Of course after listening to you it seems to me as though you are suffering from some terrible personal problems. Even so may I remind you once again, this conversation is being recorded? In any case I will ask you. Can you please stick to the Questions that I ask of you? At this point it is very vital to the investigation for you to tell me truthfully where you were yesterday afternoon between the hours of 13.00 and 18.30."

"Yes Yes Yesss, Believe me, Don't Worry I will tell you everything that you want to know," Guido cried out passionately, flinging his arms out in front of him as he steadied himself against the back railing of the bed. "Okayyyyy? Now I am prepared to tell you everything Agent Martinelli. So If YOU want to know the truth OK I will give you the truth," he panted breathlessly into the end of his phone. "The truth is Agent Martinelli I was forced to go into the arms of another woman. Thissa woman is the only one who knows too well the deep needs of such a lonely and a sad man like me," Guido screamed down the phone. Beating his hand to his chest he continued his unorthodox confession. "Only the saints in heaven knows how desperate and lonely I have been for the touch of my woman's love, Ever since YOU," he emphasised the word You, "Sent me here to Pastacula."

Another poignant moment reigned between them and was only remotely relieved by a fresh new bout of sobbing from Guido. Agent Martinelli finally broke the uncomfortable silence.

"Agent Ventosi," he began. "You will be required to return to Rome as soon as possible and hand in your

Identification Documents. You will also be required to return the car." There was another slight pause before he continued. "Have you already made the necessary arrangements to leave Pastacula?"

Guido sat up straight on the little bed and drew in a deep breath before answering his colleague. "Yes I am in the process of packing my bag and my few precious belongings now." He looked miserably at his overnight bag. After blowing his nose on the end of his shirt he continued. "But at this moment I am not sure who I will need to report to when I return the car." This was followed by a snuffled bout of nose wiping.

"Actually, there have been a few changes. When you return to Rome you will report back to me at Head Office."

"What you have returned? How can this be? I thought you were still in Monaco. Are you ringing me now from Rome?"

"Yes I was supposed to stay for another week but unfortunately due to these very recent developments I was urgently called back to Head Office," Agent Martinelli hissed back.

"And the job in Monaco; who will be working on it now?"

"I am afraid I cannot divulge such things to you at this moment. Unfortunately as of today you are no longer required for duty and therefore are not allowed to know about any of the operations associated with head office."

"Yes I understand," Guido replied despondently. Casting his eyes around the room one more time he was suddenly distracted by the silent flashing of his other phone.

"Agent Ventosi thank you for your cooperation during this discussion, it has assisted me greatly to consider your past actions. However, at this present moment I think I have heard enough about the current situation. If you like, I would like to meet with you tomorrow morning in head office at 9.00am to discuss your situation further."

"Si …. I mean, yes I understand. You can be sure I will be there." Guido replied. He then bid Agent Martinelli a hurried goodbye and hastily snatched up his phone from the bedside table. He read the text message that was blinking back at him. "Hey babe, I miss you. When are you Comin back to me?"

# 24 HORATIO'S RETURN

After foraging around for a few moments in the cracked flower pot next to the front door Horatio finally found the long antique key, where he always put it when he went away, and placed it in the rusty lock. Pushing gently against the door he was surprised to find it was already ajar and opened quite easily before he had even had the chance to turn the key. 'That's strange,' he thought, frowning down at the lock 'It's not like Algernon to be so irresponsible. Mind you', he chided, 'Algy was getting on in years and it was only to be expected that he would become forgetful from time to time. Truth be told though, it was probably that horrid little upstart Alistair who had been so careless', Horatio shuddered. 'As far as he could make out the Lad was next to useless and a far cry from the wonderful man his father had always been. Oh well no use crying over that now,' he lamented, 'We've all got our crosses to bear haven't we?' He said, as he stepped through the open door.

As he walked with a swift foot along the cool, dark, hallway of the villa, a strange sense of 'Déjà vu' began to descend upon him; it was almost as if time had stood still, everything appeared to be exactly the same as when he had left it. Even Magdalena's old, worn out pair of slippers were still sitting neatly by the kitchen door where she had always kept them. Not only that, as he walked on, he couldn't help feeling; there was something rather off-putting, almost Eerie about the heavy silence that presided in and around the rooms. Normally Sebastion would have at least greeted him with a 'Welcome Home' squawk by now, especially when he knew Horatio had been away for more than a few hours. Usually in this case scenario Horatio would ensure a special treat beyond any Bird's expectations would be forthcoming and it would not only be Belgium Chocolate that was delivered. Horatio always brought back big chunks of the best Blue Vein Cheese for the bird whenever he had been away for a day or two. It was the kind of ritual that Sebastion knew only too well and without a doubt would be expecting today. Horatio had certainly not forgotten about these little treats.

Speaking of which, he placed his neat little suitcase squarely on the bench seat that aligned the ornate wall outside the smoking room and excitedly pinged open the two old locks. Delving diligently in and around the innards of the suit case, for a few seconds, he finally grasped the treasure he had been looking for. Full of glee he withdrew his hand and brought the large chunk of 'Bleu de Gex,' up to his flaring nostrils and gave it a good strong sniff. "Mmmmmm it was still in mint condition,' he marvelled as he glanced towards the smoking room. "Sebastion," he called out. "Look what Daddies bought home for you," he shouted excitedly. He sprung back onto his feet and pushed open the heavy wooden door.

The prized piece of French Cheese hit the ground with a soft thud before breaking up into dozens of crumbly little pieces that glistened and gleaned along the tiny cracks that lay between the dark wooden floorboards.

A deep cry instantly surged its way from the depths of Horatio's saggy belly and up into his wide open mouth before mutating into a loud shrill gasp that whooshed its way past his chattering teeth and out into the still air.

Horatio remained transfixed to the floor like one of those unfortunate bible characters who had been turned into a pillar of salt. The only parts of his body that seemed to be functioning at all were his 'big blue, blinking, eyes' which now appeared to be operating more like a pair of unwilling light-houses. Rapidly blinking, open and shut, open and shut, they managed to covey in just a blink of an eye the cause of Horatio's shattered psyche, which no doubt was connected to the horrified gaze that he had firmly fixed upon the bird cage.

The 'main star' of the brutal, monstrous image, so callously set before him, was none other than his beloved, Sebastion. The poor bird was laying on his back, 'Dead as a Dodo,' both his spindly legs were stuck up in the air and there were neat little clumps of blue and yellow feathers piled high, on either side of him.

"Arrrrrrrrrrghhhhhhhhhh," Horatio squealed in a pitch that was high enough to shatter glass. He rushed over to the deceased bird. Peering intensely into the cage he looked diligently for any clue of what might have gone wrong. Looking even more closely at the remaining carnage he couldn't help noticing the large bullet hole that must have been the cause of the final demise of the tragic bird. Closing his eyes he turned his grief stricken face away and then gasped in horror, when he opened them again and realised he had accidentally stumbled upon the next shocking discovery for the day. Cruelly glaring back at him, via Sebastion's grisly blood speckled mirror was the shattering image of an Open Safe, situated on the wall on the opposite side of the room.

"Noooooooooooo," screamed Horatio. He spun around wildly on his pointy toe heels and raced as fast as he could across the room. Arriving there breathless and shaking, he looked in horror at the 'Easter Bunny' portrait of Alistair, that was now falling off the wall, all mangled and twisted and then back again at the Safe and he knew there was something terribly wrong.

Flinging himself at the Safe, he pulled the door back further and screamed hysterically when he saw a large white envelope sitting there. Frantically picking it up he rummaged around the inside with his other hand only to find it empty. With his hands all a tremble and his heart pounding, he feverishly tore open the envelope, snatched out the neatly folded letter, shook it open and began to read.

# 25 THE LETTER

My Dearest, Horatio,

If you are reading this letter you will have obviously realised I am no longer residing in your house and neither are your Lovely Diamonds. What a wonderful little bonus they turned out to be. I must say, it was a marvellous stroke of luck that the key you had hidden in the little compartment on the back of the frame, fell out, when the painting of the "Epiphany' fell to the floor. Mind you I did think it was rather foolish of you to leave the key in such close proximity to the actual safe. By the way, Old Boy, just for the record I only ever intended to borrow the painting for a while, just until I got back onto my feet. I had no intentions of stealing it, but needless to say that really doesn't matter now, as in this case there is clearly no honour amongst thieves. Even so, finding the key still wouldn't have made that much sense to me, had we not had that very long winded conversation, the night before you left, about 'How one needs to protect one's fortune.'

You see my friend, just as I was about to place the key onto the windowsill for 'Safe Keeping', I suddenly remembered what you said about needing to have something solid behind you. It was as though someone had turned a light bulb on in my head as I found myself gazing at the little keyhole, in the middle of the square that had been cut ever so neatly into the wall. Can you imagine my surprise when I opened the safe and found the tidy packet of diamonds just sitting there, waiting for someone to claim them? My dear friend, I have to say it was at precisely that point, that I had an amazing idea. Still I shouldn't really be bombarding you with these little facts at a time like this, should I? No doubt you will be struggling to keep a level head as you read this final farewell letter and the stark reality of what has become of your much prized fortune, rapidly starts to sink in.

"How COULD you do this to me?" I hear you scream as you pitifully bat those big blue eyes and wring your lily white hands over and over again. But the truth of the matter is Horatio, in order to answer that very important question I would need to ask the same of you.

"Me?" I hear you shriek in that rather churlish voice. "Are, you Mad? What have I ever done to you Algernon to warrant such a blatant act of betrayal?"

Well yes, Jolly good question Old Boy and I think this is where we need to take a little walk down memory lane and perhaps include a bit of Arithmetic along the way.

"Arithmetic!" I hear you exclaim. "What could Arithmetic possibly have to do with the fact that your oldest friend has so callously absconded with your entire Life's Fortune?"

To be perfectly fair Old Chap, I must concede you do have a point and I can well appreciate that you must be feeling so utterly confused and let's not forget you were never the brightest penny in the bank were you? So bearing that in mind, I think it is at precisely this point, that a full and earnest explanation would be most beneficial.

However before I continue dear Chum, I do advise you to sit down as some of the information I am about to divulge to you may unduly affect your heart rate. We certainly wouldn't want you to topple over and die now would we? Not until you have at least had the opportunity to finish reading this letter.

I trust you are comfortably seated by now so I shall commence my explanation. As you already know Old Boy we met each other in Prep school when we were both seven years old therefore it is fair to say we have known each other for sixty three years. 'Take note' this is where the Arithmetic comes into it. Now if we were to take all of those sixty three years and divide them into equal portions of seven. We could discard the Seven at the beginning, before we ever met each other and then discard the last Seven years, where our contact has been quite minimal. Adding these two Units of seven together should now give us a total of Fourteen years.

"What on earth is he rambling on about?" I hear you whine impatiently. And with just cause too, but if you bear with me just a little more, I will reveal All.

So returning back to the Arithmetic, I would now like to demonstrate, how this simple little equation, bears such a heavy weight on your current situation. For example, Sixty three minus fourteen equals Forty nine and Forty nine divided by SEVEN equals SEVEN.

Has the penny dropped yet Dear Chap? Don't worry; just keep reading I am sure it will all become abundantly clear in the very near future.

Now, this is the part where we take a walk down memory lane and our history lesson if you like, comes into play. Do you remember Old Chap when we were both in boarding school and we had to go to chapel each week? Horrible experience but no doubt a valuable one because if my memory serves me correctly Old boy, that was when we learnt about the dangers and snares of the Seven Deadly Sins? Just in case you had forgotten and please don't apologise if you did. Let me kindly refresh your memory. The Seven deadly Sins as far as I recall, Horatio my friend, are 'Lust, Gluttony, Greed, Sloth, Wrath, Envy and Pride.' Once again we have a compilation of numbers adding up to the value of seven.

Surely you must understand where I am going with this by now Old Boy? But if not I shall continue.

Let's go back to those lovely Diamonds shall we? As I mentioned earlier it was a pure stroke of luck that I stumbled upon them in the first place and how delighted I was too when I found all SEVEN of them. And as I held them in the palm of my hand all glittering and sparkly under the single shard of sunlight that had managed to infiltrate that Godforsaken room, I suddenly started to wonder how you as a mere artist had managed to acquire such a wonderful collection of wealth.

Then it hit me like a 'Bolt of Lightning', the only way you could ever have achieved such a lucrative little nest egg in your lifetime, was by doing what you have always done best my Dear Boy and that no doubt would be, 'Lying, Stealing, Cheating and Scheming.' Now please, sit up straight and pay extra attention because this is where the Seven Deadly Sins, the Seven Diamonds and the little 'Trip down Memory Lane' all become a lot more interesting.

"How dare you infer such Preposterous lies and make such unkind judgements about me." I hear you exclaim. "Especially after all the kindness and generosity I have recently bestowed upon you and your family."

To be fair my dear boy you do have a point. But only up to the point that it served you well to invite us to your God forsaken Villa in the first place, who else would have looked after that Hideous Bird? Truth be told it wasn't an act of generosity or kindness at all, more to do with your propensity to act, for as long as I have known you, as an outrageous opportunist at any given moment. Let me explain it to you a little further.

For example, what if I were to take one diamond as my own in exchange for each of the seven deadly sins that I believe you have managed to perfectly emulate throughout your lifetime. Considering I am actually your oldest friend I think I am in a position to make such a judgement.

Perhaps a good place to begin this little analogy would be the years we spent together in boarding school.

Let's begin shall we?

One Diamond in exchange for Sloth *:* To say you were an untidy little blighter would be a gross understatement. How well I remember those days before the weekly room inspection when I had to help you clean off the gooey bits of Toffee Apple and mouldy tart that you had carelessly dropped all over your bedspread. Or how often I had to help you at the eleventh hour to finish your homework in order to prevent you from having to attend yet another school masters' detention.

One Diamond in exchange for Wrath: Oh what a mean streaked temper you had my Dear Boy, I can still remember the time you filled all the sugar containers with salt on the senior boys' table because you were so angry about being made to do the duties of the Fag each and every week. To think I felt such pity for you to the point where I actually picked you up and piggy backed you down the stairs to avoid the Punishment you rightly deserved. Of course you and I both know you would never have survived the harsh reality of life in a boarding school, if it wasn't for me protecting you.

One Diamond in exchange for Gluttony: For a skinny little runt you sure knew how to pack it away didn't you? How often I had to hide my sweets and special treats mother and father used to bring for me every month, for fear you would find them and eat them all. I will never forget the time you managed to steal the entire basket of Easter Eggs that had been set aside for the Form and gorge on them to the point of being sick all over your bed. I still feel ill when I think about how I spent hours helping you clean up your filthy acrid vomit, to prevent you from ever being found out. To this day I have never been able to eat an Easter egg.

"But of course these sorts of childhood behaviours and misdemeanours could be considered trivial compared to more serious offences." I hear you argue.

Rightly so, I do not disagree with you, after all you were a mere child and a much unloved one at that so, it was only to be expected that you would have the tendency to act like a feral cat every now and then. However that does not excuse the lustful, greedy, envious acts of pride that you managed to inflict on all those around you as an adult. Which regrettably brings me to the next and dare I say, barely palatable morsel of truth about you and your indulgences and their connection to the four remaining seven deadly sins? Which regrettably have produced far more serious consequences and in one case caused the 'Death' of somebody, very dear to me.

No doubt this news will come as a bit of a shock to you, particularly because you had no idea that I knew about so many of the underhanded despicable things you had done over the past few decades. However due to a letter I recently received, that had actually been composed forty three years ago by a mutual friend, I was able to piece together the missing pieces, of something that had been a painful mystery to me all my adult life.

"What Mutual friend?" I hear you shriek, as you wipe away your crocodile tears. "And why would it take forty three years for a letter to be received?"

Once again a good question Dear Boy but I must say Fate has a strange way of showing us what we need to know when we least expect it. You see, a few weeks before we arrived in Italy, I received a "Letter" written by somebody we both knew many years ago. Does the name Millicent mean anything to you? Perhaps not, but it may have some more significance if I were to pair it alongside the name "Isabella."

Hmmm, no doubt your memory has been sufficiently jolted now as you read these very words. I would even go as far as to say, that as you scowl down at this very piece of paper, I can be rest assured that a splendid image, no less than the face of an angel, would be ever so delicately floating before you.

"Surely you don't mean, 'That Isabella?' But I haven't heard from her for years, decades in fact, what could she possibly have to do with me now?" I hear you demand selfishly in your belligerent way.

And of course you are right and it grieves me to inform you, that it would have been nigh on impossible to hear from her considering the poor troubled girl passed away in a hospice for nuns back in 1970. You see, she had been tragically banished by her parents, to a convent in the tropics in early 1962, and within a few short years she contracted Tuberculosis, and was eventually sent back to a nursing home to convalesce, before finally departing from this world. However before she passed away she wrote a letter intended for me, begging my forgiveness for what she deemed to be an Inconceivable act of Foolishness.

Sad to say; I may never have known any of this had it not been for Isabella's niece Lucy, the daughter of her sister Millicent. Lucy found the letter amongst her mother's belongings after her mother had passed away. Seemingly Millicent had kept it hidden for all those years as a way of protecting her sister's virtue. However her niece, who had been so greatly inspired by her Aunt's courageous battle to continue on with her faith even in the very face of adversity, felt that after reading the letter that the truth, should finally be told.

I am quite sure by now you will know what I am talking about, but just in case your memory fails you in any way, shape or form, I have made a copy of the letter written to me all those years ago by my beloved Bella and pasted it here for you to read. I trust you will find the other remaining deadly sins of Lust, Envy, Pride and Greed are duly represented by what you are about to read.

***21st of April 1970***

***My Dearest, Algernon***

*How it grieves me to the very bone to have to write this letter to you, but knowing as I do that my remaining time here on earth is so very short I feel compelled to explain to you for once and for all my dear sweet Algy what happened to me and ultimately what happened to us.*

*Looking back now I realised just how much I must have truly broken your heart when I disappeared without a trace. Please, you must believe me when I tell you it wasn't really my doing and if I knew then how much I would desperately pine for you over the years I would never have left your side not even for a moment.*

*My dearest Algy I won't ever expect you to fully understand what happened between us, it was all so long ago and truth be known you may possibly still be very angry with me, but please I beg you, for the sake of what we had and what we cherished so deeply, just give me a moment of your time to tell you my story before I pass away from this world.*

*As you know in the summer of 1961 we became engaged to be married and this was truly the happiest time of my life. I don't believe I had ever understood the meaning of real joy until then. Knowing that a wonderful wedding in Paris had been planned for the following summer made it so much easier to say goodbye when you left England to do your training for the Foreign Service.*

*However my dearest Algy, I want you to understand that during those first few months after you were gone I was so terribly miserable. You see I missed you so much I cried myself to sleep every night and if it wasn't for my sister Millicent I think I may have gone beyond the depths of despair. Realising the pitiful state I was in she kindly organised a ticket for me to attend the University Winter Ball, she also bought a beautiful new Ball Gown for me, so of course I was obliged to go. But had I known Now, what heartache and pain would have resulted from this Ill Fated Evening, then trust me my darling boy, I would Never Ever have gone.*

*It was there on that night that I became reacquainted with your old school friend Horatio. If you recall, I had met him with you on a few occasions during the summer and at that time he appeared to be a pleasant and sensitive young man. Algy, you know I have never been one who enjoys their own company. So after standing alone for half the night with no one to talk to as I watched all the other happy couples dancing by it was a relief to chat with someone I knew and trusted. Horatio also seemed to be very eager to spend time with me and mentioned a few times how it was the least he could do, on your behalf, and in light of your absence.*

*Algernon Dear, please understand when I tell you the next part of this letter is very painful for me to write, but write it I must, hopefully it will provide a way for us to mend the bridges that have fallen down between us over these sad difficult years.*

*Not long after that night at the ball Horatio and I became lovers. Algy, you must believe me when I tell you I can't really explain how this unexpected development came about, except to say I was so very lonely and he was so needy it just seemed to happen. Shortly after that I fell pregnant and had to shamefully confess to my parents what my circumstances were. Horatio at this time was preparing his portfolio to apply for a scholarship to the Montmartre Art School in Paris and so I am sad to say, had very little time or care for my plight.*

*You would have noticed at this time I no longer responded to your many letters or the phone calls you made to my parent's house. Please don't hate me Algy, you must understand I was under strict instructions not to speak to anybody about my situation. I was forbidden to leave the house. Soon after that, a place in a convent in West Africa, where my father's maiden Aunt lived was set aside for me. I left the following week and I never heard from, or saw Horatio again.*

*As soon as I arrived in Africa I fell terribly ill with a tropical virus and sadly as a result of this ongoing illness I lost the poor unborn babe. Perhaps it was a blessing in disguise and a possible respite to the terrible situation I had found myself in. Either way it didn't actually change my circumstances you see, because my father refused to acknowledge me as his daughter and with no means of support of my own I was bound to stay in the convent.*

*I remained there for the next five years working as a volunteer teacher for the children in the village school and only after I contracted Tuberculosis and nothing more could be done for me was I allowed to return to England. Where I am now spending the last few months of my life, in the Saint Francis of Assisi Hospice, only two miles down the road from where we first met.*

*How ironic my dear sweet boy to be so close and yet so far and know that there is nothing either of us can do to change the future or the past. But before I pass away from this terrible world and face my maker on the other side. I would like you to know how much I loved you and how happy you made me and how I have never forgotten the breathtaking painting of the beautiful Tropical Bird you painted for me on my seventeenth birthday. My only regret is that I foolishly showed it to Horatio and after he saw how wonderful it was he begged me to let him take it home and use it as piece to study whilst he practiced and developed his portfolio of art, the tragic thing is I never saw it again. It was only after I returned to England and asked for it to be brought to me that I was told by my sister Millicent that Horatio had taken it and claimed it as one of his own pieces of art. I also learnt that this painting is how he gained entry into the*

*Art school in Paris. The same one he won the scholarship for. My Darling Algy, how I remember how happy we both were the day you gave me that lovely painting. Please believe me when I tell you this because ....*

I trust after you have read this to the bitter end, you would have noticed that the letter was never finished. That's because, according to Isabella's niece Lucy, my dearest angel Bella slipped into a coma whilst she still held this letter in her hand. Sadly, she never woke up again.

So there you have it Horatio, I was not far wrong when I said you were despicable and it enrages me to the point of feeling Murderous that my dear Isabella left my world, via a lifeless letter, merely leaving a trail of misery and destruction. A destruction; so unnecessary and uncalled for that was not only undeserved by me, but least of all by Isabella. A destruction; so sinister that it could only be deemed as a betrayal of our brotherhood and the deep friendship that I had entrusted to you.

But for what purpose? This is what I ask of you Horatio? Why did you willfully destroy my precious flower, my petal? Was it because you were envious of our special love? You of all people knew only too well that you were a lover of men and not women and because of this; nothing permanent could ever come out of this self-gratifying lustful tryst. Except, of course a life of misery for poor Isabella and a marriage of mere convenience for me, which was doomed from the onset to fail.

But you did not stop there, did you Horatio? No you went

on further, and gave me even more pain and suffering and it angers me deeply to know that the scholarship you received for the Montmartre Art School in Paris only came as a result of my talented hands. I now know, from the letter, that it was my painting and my painting alone, that gave you your 'Lucky Break', your acceptance into the most prestigious Art school in Europe, which no doubt shaped your future Ecclesiastical style and ultimately your acceptance as an accomplished artist by the religious art world.

For all these reasons and many more far too numerous to mention I Despise you Horatio and just like your so called Artworks I consider you to be no more than a Fiendish Fake. However I must confess it does give me a slight feeling of satisfaction to know that you know that I know all about your sordid past. Bearing this in mind, there would be absolutely no point trying to prosecute me or hunt me down because as you can see 'Old boy,' you wouldn't have a leg to stand on. The truth of the matter is; 'whether you like it or not', I have well and truly gained the Upper Hand!

And rightly so, don't you agree? May I say 'Justice served Cold rather than in the heat of the moment, is 'Justice Served Well.' Thanks to your own advice and foolish folly, I have been led to your shallow little prize, the hidden stash of your Precious Jewels which will well and truly tide me over until I get back on my feet. Hardly an adequate repayment for such a 'Bitter Ride,' but well worth the taking to see you Squirm and Writhe. Don't you think?

So, my Dear 'Fiend,' make sure you enjoy, whatever is left of your Cucumber Sandwiches and Summer Wine. I dare say, they will be the last remnants of your 'Simple Little Pleasures,' for a 'Long, Long, Time.'

# EPILOGUE

"What do you mean you did it for our own good? As far as I am concerned, this is nothing short of kidnapping," Alistair shouted, as he poked his pointy head between the front and back seats of the car.

"Don't be so ridiculous Alistair; you know full well I have always considered the welfare of your mother and you, to be first and foremost whenever I have made any important decisions for our lives. Speaking of which, would you please keep your voice down? Your mother has finally managed to fall asleep and I don't want your childish outbursts to wake her."

"Childish, Childish! You're the one who is acting childish Father," Alistair snapped. "First of all, you drag us all to one of the most God forsaken places on earth, simply because you ran into a spot of financial bother at the bank. And then you get it into your head, that some International Spies or really Nasty Bad Guys were after you, 'Wooooo', Now that's what I call childish, Father". Leaning in closer he shifted further along the edge of his seat and looked directly at Algernon. "Not to mention, you made us stay with "Horatio the Horrible" a so called friend of yours, just because you thought he would dosh out some of his dough. But at the end of the day, he turns out to be, nothing more than a Bloody old Liar and was simply using us all to mind his rotten stinking bird." Alistair randomly fired saliva droplets into the air as he continued his rant. "NOW, according to you, we are all in some sort of physical danger and need to escape to yet another foreign country. He seethed with rage, his lanky locks shaking and the whites of his eyes bulging. "If I didn't know any better Father, I would say you are starting to display the early signs of dementia," he poked his pointy finger into Algernon's face.

Alistair kept looking hard at his father for a couple of seconds, obviously expecting a response, but when he realised Algernon was not going to bite he continued, "And THEN you have the nerve to call ME childish, simply because I protest about being forced to jump in a car and go where the four winds happen to take your fancy. Purely on the basis of another one of your 'Mad Hatter' stories" he complained. "Arrrrghhhh this family will be the death of me." He flopped back into his seat, laid his head back and closed his tired eyes. 'A Hostage, that is what I am a Bloody Hostage,' he lamented.

Algernon squirmed around in his seat for a few seconds more, obviously waiting for the lad to cool down. When he was finally convinced, that the coast was clear, he decided to stand his ground. "Believe me Alistair, I can fully appreciate your level of frustration and I sincerely sympathise with you, but without wanting to alarm you anymore, I am asking you for your own sake, to simply trust me a little bit longer. I am sure in due course everything will be resolved and our lives can return back to normal." He shot one of his famous furry frowns into the rear view mirror.

"Trust you, Ha ha ha, what a joke Father." Alistair shot up quickly and poked his head through the opening again. "I would say, after all the shenanigans of the past week, it's bleeding obvious to all of us that you wouldn't even know the meaning of the word Trust," he sneered. "That would be like putting a newborn baby into a nest of vipers and expecting it to come out completely unscathed. Trust You? Ha, ha, ha give me one good reason why I should trust YOU? And as far as normal goes Hah! When has this family ever been normal?" Alistair laughed bitterly and flopped back down onto his seat.

"What in God's name are you arguing about now, Alistair?" Cornelia asked. She sat up and rubbed her eyes so hard they almost squeaked. "Can't this family ever have just five minutes peace?" She turned her head away and gazed longingly through the window, out across the meadows and onto the rolling hills. She sighed deeply as she watched the first golden rays of the morning sun gently pour themselves over the top of the mountains, shimmering in the distance.

"Oh, I am very sorry dear; we didn't mean to wake you. Alistair and I were just having a little debate about where we should be going but I think we have said all that needs to be said for the time being haven't we Ali?" He shot one of his 'Looks' into the rear view mirror. "Why don't you just go back to sleep? We will try very hard to keep the noise levels down," he patted her lightly on the shoulder.

Cornelia, reluctantly turned back to face him and said in a very matter of fact tone, "Thank you for your undying concern Algernon but I think I have had quite enough sleep for the moment. Actually, if the truth were told, I tend to agree with Alistair on this one. I don't think it is unreasonable at all to ask where we might be going, especially under the circumstances we currently find ourselves in."

"Errrr ooo errrrm," Algernon cleared his throat loudly. "Yes and quite right too Dear, of course I fully understand, everybody wants to know their future and what possibly lies in store for them. But the sad reality is we don't always get what we want, do we?" He looked wistfully through the windscreen.

"Yes, but I don't think Mother actually means that in the literal sense Father. I think what she wanted to know is 'Where' the bloody hell are you taking us now?" Alistair demanded.

"Yes, for once in your life you might just happen to be right, Algernon. I whole heartedly agree, you don't always get what you want," Cornelia commented. She looked him firmly in the eye and said, "Believe it or not, I really did want to stay in Pastacula. For some strange reason I cannot explain, the 'Beastly' little town had grown on me and what's more, I even found myself looking forward to helping those two young men with their English.

However, instead I find myself as an unwilling accomplice gallivanting across the countryside on some sort of wild goose chase, with absolutely no idea where we are going?"

"Well yes," Algernon leant forward and checked the Tom Tom before continuing. "I can see how that could be both upsetting and unsettling my Dear. Never mind though, I am sure there will other opportunities to help those less fortunate than yourself, once we get settled somewhere."

"Hah, join the club Mumsy. I know exactly how you feel and as I said earlier, I really think Father has completely lost his marbles this time. I for one can't wait for this wretched car to stop. So I can get the hell out of here and run away as far as I can and start getting on with my 'Own' life," he warned.

"Well you won't have to wait too much longer Alistair my boy. I think we could all do with a bit of a 'Pit stop.' The lads in the back will most definitely need a break very soon, they haven't been out all night and their bladders aren't what they used to be. Why don't I turn into the little village, just up the road from here? I see by the Tom Tom they have a rather nice Guest House. I don't know about you two, but I could certainly do with a good strong cup of tea and a nice bit of crumpet," he declared raising his two mammoth eyebrows as high as they could go, as he looked through the mirror again.

"Hmmm yes, perhaps we could ask if they have a couple of spare rooms. God only Knows I could do with a long hot bath and a good clean bed," Cornelia groaned as she arched her back and stretched her long thin neck.

"Well yes dear, that is definitely a possibility," Algernon nodded his head sagely in her direction.

"Hang on a minute Father, correct me if I am wrong. But I thought you said we were down to our last Penny. How can we afford to just waste money at 'the drop of a hat.' I mean who is going to pay for it all?"

"Yes well, there's no need to worry about that anymore my boy, everything has been taken care of in that department," Algernon replied casually.

"What do you mean Father?" Alistair blurted, he suddenly jumped to attention. "I thought we were broke!" He leant forward again and glared at his father. "When did this all change? Why didn't you say something earlier Father?"

"Well we haven't really had the chance to sit down and chat now, have we? What, with all the running around, and Winston not being well, it just sort of slipped my mind."

They had finally reached the fork in the road that Algernon had seen earlier on the Tom Tom. "So shall I turn into the next village then?" He asked. His hand was poised over the indicator.

"Well, I must say, that certainly sheds a whole new light on the situation now doesn't it? Yes, Father why not

Turn?" Alistair instructed. "Just like the old saying goes 'One good turn deserves another', doesn't it? To be honest Father, I have a feeling this could be the start of a whole new Venture."

As soon as Alistair finished speaking, the dogs in the back started up a fearful bout of barking. This was followed by a heavy BIG bump and a series of "Crank, Crank Cranking" noises that coincided with a loud CRACKKKK and a sudden jolting motion that sent them slip sliding across the road. Algernon puffed in and out heavily, as he pulled up hard on the hand brake and carefully maneuvered the steering back towards the middle of the road.

For the next few seconds the startled little group sat there in a stultified stunned silence as they stared numbly at the big crack in the windscreen. They were more than likely counting their blessings as they quietly considered how lucky they had been to escape from this very recent danger. Alas, this golden reprieve of silence was only ever short lived and was soon shattered by an extremely loud 'Honk Honking' noise that came from the fuel belching tractor behind them.

Which no doubt, was responsible for drowning out their unanimous 'GASP of Horror,' when they saw the caravan, with Winston and Churchill still sitting in the back, merrily sail past their car and down the hill, on their way to the quaint little village.

THE END

| GLOSSARY | | | |
|---|---|---|---|
| **ITALIAN** | **ENGLISH** | **ITALIAN** | **ENGLISH** |
| Arrivederci | Goodbye | Mamma Mia | Exclamation |
| Bagno | Toilet | Nonna | Grandma |
| Bella | Beautiful | Pallazza Communale | The Town hall |
| Bravo | Well Done M | Paella | Spanish Rice Dish |
| Brava | Well Done F | Parrucchiere | Hairdresser |
| Buona | Good | Pastacula | A town |
| Buon- giorno | Good Day | Pensione | Small Hotel |
| Buonasera | Good Night | Piazza | The Town Square |
| Buongiorno | Good Day | Polenta | A Maize Porridge |
| Capo di Tutti | The Boss Mafia | Pronto | Hello |
| Casa | House | Prosciutto | Ham |
| Centro Storico | Historical Central | Prosecco | Sparkling Wine |
| Di | Of | Roma | Rome |
| Dimmi | Tell Me | Si | Yes |
| Donna | Woman | Scusa | Excuse me |
| Empanada | Popular Spanish Dish | Scusa non capisco | Sorry I don't Understand |
| Entrata | Entry | Signora | Woman |
| Fromage | Cheese | Signore | Man |
| Fiesta | Fiesta | Una Momento | One Moment |
| Fuoco Del Vigili | The Fire Brigade | Viale | Tree Lined Promenade |
| Grazie | Thank You | Vigili Del Fuoco | The Fire Brigade |
| Non Capisco | I don't Understand | Villa | Italian House |
| Eetaly Italia | Italy | Vino | Wine |
| Limoncello | A Lemon Liquor | Vino Della Casa | House Wine |

| INCORRECT ENGLISH WORDS | | | |
|---|---|---|---|
| Burna | Burn | Ouse | House |
| Canna | Can | Oopabyta | Uberbite |
| Cheeck | Check | Pickka | Pick |
| Cos | Because | Sheeits | Sheets |
| Clotheses | Clothes | Sheeeits | Sheets |
| Dontcha | Don't You | Theenk | Think |
| Eef | If | Theesa | These |
| Feelin | Feeling | Theeese | These |
| Gonna | Going To | Thisssa | This |
| Cos | Because | Sheeits | Sheets |
| Havva | Have | Ungry | Hungry |
| Handzome | Handsome | Uppa | Up |
| Hinglish | English | Verry | Very |
| Hizza | His | Wanna | Want |
| Horeatzio | Horatio | Wantta | Want |
| Kinda | Kind | Watcha | Watch |
| Leetle | Little | Weel | Will |
| Maestro | Conductor | Whatta | What |
| Meanna | Mean | Whenna | When |
| Needa | Need | Wotta | What |
| Notta | Not | Ya | You |
| Mumma | Mother | Yourra | Your |

Printed in Great Britain
by Amazon.co.uk, Ltd.,
Marston Gate.